Desert Virgin

Based on a true story.

A narrative of a sex hungry sixteen year old girl in the rugged outback of the Yuha Desert.

by

Ralph W. Harrington

Order this book online at www.trafford.com
or email orders@trafford.com

Most Trafford titles are also available at major online book retailers.

Note for Librarians: A cataloguing record for this book is available from Library and Archives Canada at www.collectionscanada.ca/amicus/index-e.html

Printed in Victoria, BC, Canada.

ISBN: 978-1-4251-8324-0 (sc)
ISBN: 978-1-4269-0400-4 (hc)
ISBN: 978-1-4269-0740-1 (eBook)

Our mission is to efficiently provide the world's finest, most comprehensive book publishing service, enabling every author to experience success. To find out how to publish your book, your way, and have it available worldwide, visit us online at www.trafford.com

Trafford rev. 07/06/2010

 www.trafford.com

North America & international
toll-free: 1 888 232 4444 (USA & Canada)
phone: 250 383 6864 ♦ fax: 812 355 4082

Dedication

Dedicated to all my friends in the desert southwest, with particular thanks to Jay von Werlhof, famous archaeologist who taught me so much about the history of Imperial County, California, and who inadvertently gave me ideas for this story.

With generous thanks to my sisters, whose masculine sobriquets include Mickey, Billie and Steve, and Russell Daugherty, who through the years furnished me with lively debate; to Angie Sienko, who was constant companion and buddy on hazardous excursions into the wild outback of the Yuha Desert.

I thank them all.

Ralph W. Harrington
Grants Pass, Oregon
January 2008

Preface

The deserts of the world are usually thought of as harsh, barren, and treeless, tracts of land, insufferably hot, inhospitable to life, and characterized by a prospector and his donkey.

Much of this is true, of course, but not entirely. There are some differences between a high desert and a low one. The North American Desert includes 500,000 square miles of arid land in the western United States and northwestern Mexico, with four divisions: the Great Basin, Mojave, Sonoran and Chihuahuan.

The following story takes place at the junction of the Great Basin and the Sonoran Deserts, in Imperial County, California at a place called the Yuha Desert, which is roughly a tract between Calexico, California, Plaster city and Ocotillo. This is where General George Patton trained for desert warfare during World War 2. During the days when the author lived in Ocotillo, he did have a Dodge 4WD Power Wagon as portrayed in the story, and he did belong to an archaeological group headed by Jay von Werlhof.

The Yuha Desert, like all of Imperial County, is below sea level, and is rife with intaglios, Indian pictographs or hieroglyphs, but is just as rich in legends of buried treasures, lost cities, abandoned gold mines and other lore.

This area and it's environs is a haven for snowbirds now, and it's winter's visitors still enjoy hiking and exploring the vast outback: Shell Canyon – with it's petrified oyster shells left when the ancient sea dried up; the Anza-Borrego Desert State Park with it's strange mud caves and elephant trees; Davies Valley with it's palm tree studded oasis; and Agua Caliente Hot Springs.

Although this story is fiction, as are the cast of characters and love scenes, the names of places are real; most of the things that happened, are based on fact: the water war, the illegal aliens, the flood, and some of the field trips.

Enjoy.

CHAPTER ONE

Rocking back and forth slowly on the front porch in the late afternoon coolness, he gazed out across the desert where vultures soared on thermals above the ubiquitous creosote bush and ocotillo covered sand. It had cooled down to 90 degrees on this April day and white cirrus clouds were moving north from Mexico, a few miles to the south.

In reverie, he tapped his cigarette over the ash tray on the small table beside the rocking chair, thinking back nostalgically and hardly noticing the roadrunner that was drinking from a small puddle of water under a dripping faucet at the well just thirty feet from where he sat.

An old wives tale had said that roadrunners got their moisture from their prey, but Frank had seen something like this before. They will drink, sometimes, if water is available, especially during very hot weather.

A lot had happened in the five years since he had returned from Vietnam, where he was a Green Beret in 1972, and where he learned to love guns and the great outdoors. Coming home to San Diego, he married a woman he met in a bar – Margie Rashid – but she could drink him under the table anytime, a fact that he was to regret after they had been married only a year.

Not only did they argue frequently about her drinking, but she was a city girl, an urbanite, while he was a natural-born outdoorsman. Although he liked his beer, he was averse to formality and decorum. His mode of dress was simple Levis and western shirts, no more, no less, topped by a red and white baseball cap.

With growing disdain for city life and the burgeoning population of San Diego, he often sojourned to the desert in Imperial County, one hundred miles to the east, where he would strap on his 44 magnum and explore the outback in his 4WD Dodge pickup. Always alone, because Marge wanted no part of it, he dreamed of finding lost treasure, especially the famous Peg-Leg-Pete black nuggets.

One night after supper, as he scanned the want ads, he spied a house for sale at a place called Coyote Wells, which he recognized as near the hamlet of Ocotillo, where he often went to a café – The Roadrunner Restaurant – while exploring in the Jacumba Mountains.

"Look, Marge," he had said. "There's a place for sale in the desert. They're only asking $2500 or best offer. WE could buy it and move out there. The cost of living would be less in a small town and I could pursue my love of prospecting. I might even strike it rich. You never know."

Sullenly, Marge put her hands on her hips and glared at him. "For god's sake, Frank," she had fairly screamed in disgust, "You are as naïve as a 10 year-old child. Strike it rich, indeed. You have been reading too many stories about old prospectors. Well, I've got news for you! I'm not about to leave civilization for your pipe dream and move to some desert where rattlesnakes and scorpions crawl in bed with you. No way!"

At first, Frank tried to rationalize with Marge. "You make it sound almost dirty. For your information, they've got TV, telephones, and everything else we have here except malls and wall-to-wall people. I think it would be great to live out in the desert."

"Frank, people are moving to San Diego because it's one of the best places in the world to live. I will not give up all this for you and your silly dream. If you want to move out there, you just go ahead, but I will not go with you. If it means divorce, so be it."

In the days that followed, Frank was angry and confused. He had driven out to Coyote Wells one day to look at the property, an old rundown house sand blasted by high winds and close to the old highway 80. The owners had showed him inside and he found it to be quite homey. He pictured himself in it, but he got a shock when the old couple accepted his offer of $2000 and explained why they were selling.

"We're both in our seventies," the man said. "We are moving to San Diego to be closer to our doctors. Emma may have to go on dialysis and I'm having problems too. We just can't continue to drive so far every week for tests. It's just one thing after another when you get our age."

Frank had bought the place without Marge's knowledge, but when he told her, she hit the roof. They had argued bitterly and she had filed for divorce, but he didn't care. Marge was right in one sense, though. For most people, the big cities have more to offer, yet he was undaunted. Living out here was a challenge and an adventure. He was closer to nature first and foremost, but the lure of the outback with its mysteries was compelling.

As he sat quietly reminiscing, he saw a car coming down the old highway. He stopped rocking and lit another cigarette. The only people who used this road were occasional desert rats, the Border Patrol, and sometimes a lost soul who had gotten on the wrong road by mistake. There were times, of course, when he could see wetbacks walking north from the nearby Mexican border, headed towards Indio or Los Angeles. Though he often felt compassion for these illegal intruders, he resented their presence and disliked them sneaking up to his property under cover of darkness to steal water or any other thing they could use.

But the smugglers, known as Coyotes, and the drug runners, were another story. The Coyotes, who loaded vans with illegals, and charged them $500 to $1000 per head, could be dangerous if intercepted. The huge profits from drugs and human smuggling across the Calexico corridor made it one of the hottest areas outside of San Ysidro, and potentially, one of the most dangerous. That was why Frank had a virtual arsenal in his house and why he carried a gun on his hip.

He watched as the car came closer and slowed to a crawl. He could see steam pouring from the radiator as it came to a stop directly in front of his house. He leaned forward, watching a woman get out and raise the hood. As steam billowed up, another female got out and they both stood looking into the engine compartment.

Frank cursed. He knew the women were in trouble, and he knew that they would be coming up to his place to ask for help, and this wrankled him. Now the women got back in the car and were trying to start it. He could hear the starter grinding on and on.

"Damn fools," he thought to himself. "It's boiled dry and they think it'll start."

Minutes later, the women got out of the car and looked toward his house, but when they started to walk, he shifted uneasily. "The only thing I don't like about this property is that it's too close to a road," he thought as they came closer. He could see that one woman was taller than the other, and both wore jeans and men's shirts tucked under their belts.

Blondes, they appeared to be mother and daughter, and cute as hell. Soberly, somewhat distraught, the tall woman called out. "Hi. Have you got any water?"

Frank jerked his head toward the well, "Help yourself."

"We're having a little trouble. Car's overheated."

"So I see." He and she were face to face, now, as she came up to the porch, which was three feet above the ground. She was a pretty woman, though she appeared to be tired, and the smaller woman looked like a carbon copy. "You'll find a bucket over there," he said. But as he watched them walk away, his eyes were on their backsides. They looked like they had been poured into their jeans.

With each step, their shapely butt cheeks undulated hypnotically. He hadn't seen anything this good since he had left San Diego where he had ogled young girls at Balboa Park or at the beach. The sight before his hungry eyes engendered erotic thoughts of young love. He recalled the young virgin he had slept with in Saigon, in 1968, whose favors he had purchased for a pack of American cigarettes.

He and Lisa had developed a fondness for each other, and he had slept with her many times after the first time, for she was a very beautiful 15 year old who dreamed of marrying an American and someday moving to the United States. But now, as he watched the two women struggling with the heavy bucket, he silently dreamed of bedding one of them, or better yet, both.

"I'll bet I could ring their bells if I had a chance," he thought. "I may be 40, but I'm as good as I was at 20 when I slept with Lisa."

Frank suddenly realized that his thoughts were unrealistic, since these women would soon be gone, but he had been without sex for five years since his divorce from Marge, and there was little hope of finding romance in the tiny village of Ocotillo where the basic population of retirees consisted of elderly women who were either homely or fat, often both.

"You bring that bucket back after you get done with it," he yelled after the girls, as he stood up and walked into the house to get a beer. But his curiosity was growing. When he returned to the porch, he wanted to witness their next blunder, and he didn't have to wait long.

As they both lifted the bucket and started to pour cold water into the radiator, a great cloud of steam arose, and they both jumped back in surprise, spilling the rest of the water. He heard the older woman cry out in pain.

Now, they were hurrying back with a sense of urgency, the smaller woman carrying the bucket, and both were soaking wet from the waist, down. Frank set his beer on the small table as they came up to the porch. He knew something was wrong when the older woman looked down at her outstretched left hand.

"Hurt yourself?" he asked with growing concern.

"When we started to pour water in the radiator, it spilled on the engine," the woman explained, shaking her hand in pain. "It seemed to explode in our faces. Ow. Oh. It hurts."

"Hold on," Frank said as he hurried towards the door. "I'll get some cold water." He was feeling genuine compassion, now, as he went inside.

When he returned, he told the woman to hold her hand in the pan. The cold water would ease the pain. Face to face, he asked her, "Is this your daughter?" The girl appeared to be in her teens, about 15, he guessed.

"Yes. Her name is Cindy. Mine's Kathy. I'm sorry we caused you so much trouble."

"Do you have a last name?" Frank wondered aloud.

"Winters," Kathy said. "Kathy Winters."

"Mine's Frank. Frank Kelly. And you aren't any trouble at all." He had her come up on the porch where she could sit in his rocker and rest her hand in the pan on the small table.

He picked up his beer and took a swig, then lit a smoke as they fell into conversation. "How's your hand? Does the cold water help?"

Kathy nodded, "It does, but I am worried about my car. I'm supposed to be in San Diego tonight."

"Oh?" Frank wondered, "Do you have family there?"

"No, but it's a long story."

Frank sat on the edge of the porch with his legs dangling. "Well, you aren't going anywhere tonight. You aren't going anywhere until you get your car running."

Kathy became alarmed, "Can you fix it?"

Shaking his head, he retorted in no uncertain terms, "No way can I fix it. I'm not a mechanic. I'm not sure I would fix it even if I was." He took a drag on his cigarette, twisting around to face her. "See. I have a problem with people, especially with motorists who run out of gas or break down. I have an average of one every two weeks or so. That old gas pump out in front leads people to think this is a gas station, but it hasn't been used for years, according to the man I bought this place from."

"I had a woman stop and ask me if I had seen her lost dog. And some city dude in a red Cadillac asked me to change a flat tire for him. The point is that I moved out here to get away from people and their problems. I just can't get involved because it interferes with my plans."

Kathy apologized. "I'm sorry I broke down here, but I surely didn't plan it. The car just overheated or something." She raised her hand and looked at it.

"We'll leave as quickly as we can, but it's getting dark and I don't know what to do."

Cindy leaned over her mother and whispered. "I've got to go to the bathroom."

Frank, so close, heard her. He told her to go in the house and walk straight ahead. "The bathroom is on the right." Kathy got up, saying she'd go with Cindy.

The setting sun cast an orange glow over the jagged Jacumba Mountains to the west, turning the peaks into black silhouettes. By now, it had cooled down to 80 degrees, but a hot breeze still wafted over the desert. Frank tipped his beer to his lips, draining the can and tossing it away thoughtlessly and gazed down toward the road where Kathy's car sat, thinking of her predicament.

When the girls came back out, Frank told Kathy he was willing to take a look at her car, but they would have to tow it up by the porch where he could rig an extension cord. He said he would pull it with his pickup, but she would have to steer it. She agreed.

Twenty minutes later, when they had her Pontiac close to the porch, Frank was holding the light over the engine compartment, peering intently at the wet, still warm motor.

"You might have a cracked head," he advised her. "When you poured cold water on it, it...oh, wait a minute. It looks wet right there," he pointed as he leaned in to look. "It's more likely that the head gasket is leaking."

"Is that serious?" she asked, hoping it wasn't.

"Yeah, I'm afraid so," he said. "You've probably been leaking water for a long time. That would explain why the engine overheated in the first place. If that's what it is, you'll need a mechanic to remove the head and replace the gasket. That could run you anywhere from a hundred to two hundred bucks, I would guess."

"Oh God!" Kathy wailed. "I've only got about fifty dollars, just enough to get to San Diego and rent a motel room. Maybe enough for breakfast."

Frank snapped off the light and shrugged. "Sorry, but you are not going anywhere tonight. You're stuck here but good and there's nothing you or I can do about it." He started to gather the extension cord, walking back to the porch.

Cindy looked downcast. "Mr. Kelly," she began, "I'm hungry. If you could make me a sandwich, I'll pay you for it. I've got three dollars mad money I've been saving for an emergency."

As they went inside, Frank stopped to look Cindy in the eyes. "Little girl, you don't have to pay me anything. I'm hungry too. I'll fix us all something. It won't be anything fancy, but it'll fill you up." He layed the cord and light down and moved towards the kitchen where he snapped on the light. "And you guys don't have to call me Mr. Kelly. I've always said I don't care what you call me, as long as you call me for dinner. But seriously, I don't like the mister bit. Just call me Frank and we'll get along good."

Both women were grinning now as he went to the refrigerator. He looked over his shoulder and asked if one of them would turn on the light in the living room. When Cindy complied, he said "turn on the television too, I like to watch the evening news."

Kathy, standing near the table in the kitchen, glanced around the room. She had peeked into this bedroom when they went to the bathroom, and she had seen his gun rack, full of long guns. And now she saw a rifle behind the front door. She was mulling over her and Cindy's predicament. Frank seemed like a nice enough man, but he could rape and kill them both if he wanted to, and no one would ever miss them, because no one knew where they were.

While Frank was busy opening cans and frying wienies, he glanced over and told her to have a seat. Cindy was watching something on the TV. She pulled out a chair from the table and sat down. "You are being very kind," she said, "but I've been thinking. Since we are stuck here, would you mind if we slept in the car tonight? We've been sleeping in it all the way from Omaha."

Frank called out to Cindy. "Come on, little girl. Stuff's just about ready." He told Kathy to pull up her chair. "No, I don't mind. You can sleep out there if you want to, but I've got an extra bedroom and you are welcome to use it. It's got a double bed all ready to sleep in. You can use the shower if you like. You must be awful sweaty and tired after all you've been through. What do you think?"

Cindy brightened. "Let's do it, mom. I'd like to freshen up before we start out again." But Kathy had serious reservations. In her mind, bed and shower meant undressing, and the thought of nakedness in a remote house with a gun-crazy man seemed like inviting rape or worse.

"No," she said, "I don't think so. I'm just worried about my car."

Frank was spooning pork and beans onto the plates. "It could be dangerous out there. Illegals coming over the border like to snoop around cars, looking for something they can swipe. And if they found two women sleeping, they could rape or kill you if they didn't find something more valuable." He sat the pan back on the stove. "And furthermore, if you got out of the car, you'd likely step on a sidewinder."

Cindy grimaced. "Yuck. I don't want to sleep out there." But Kathy, her mind in turmoil, was weighing her options. She realized she had little choice. She could choose between rape and murder by illegals outside, or by this friendly guy, inside. As she watched Frank scoop two weenies onto each plate, her curiosity got the best of her.

"You don't have a wife?"

"No. I was married for awhile, but we divorced."

"Significant other?"

"No. I've lived out here for five years and never met the right woman."

Kathy picked up her fork and shook her head. "I can't imagine anyone living way out here, alone. Don't you get lonesome?"

As they started to eat, Frank began explaining. "Ain't got time to get lonesome. I guess you could say I'm a loner. Anyway, I hate to admit this, but I had a dream. I've read a lot of stories about the desert – Peg-Leg-Pete, the Lost Dutchman Mine, things like that and I wanted to come out here and look for lost treasures. In fact, I am going up the mountain tomorrow morning to explore a cave I found the other day. I didn't have a flashlight with me then, so I didn't go in. Might be cougars holed up in there."

Cindy was eating as if she were starved. "I wouldn't want to go in there," she said. "You must be very brave."

Frank chuckled, "Not really. I always carry a gun in the outback, though. I was in the Army for a couple of years. Vietnam. I've been in some dangerous places."

Kathy was intrigued by his stories. "I find it interesting that you are living your dream. My dad used to read stories of lost gold mines. Stuff like that. I remember in particular that he had a book about the Lost Dutchman Mine. I saw it in the bookcase. Did you ever read Louis L'Amour's books? My dad read them all. But he is getting old, now, and never lived his dream like you are doing."

"Yeah, small world," Frank said with a mouth full. "I've got all of Louis L'Amour's books. Read them all too. I take the Desert Magazine, now. It's got some of the best stories I've ever read. I've got a ton of books over there," he nodded toward the bookshelves in the living room.

Kathy turned sideways to look. There was a lounge chair facing the television set, a closed door behind it, presumably the bedroom he mentioned, the bookshelves against the far wall, and a stack of magazines on the floor in disarray. She noticed two well-worn overstuffed chairs flanking the lounge chair, which seemed out of place, but the TV, barely audible, caught her attention momentarily. They were discussing a rape in El Centro. Lingering a minute, she heard the reporter say that two men were being held on suspicion of raping a 38 year old waitress.

Turning back to the table, Kathy said, "Before I forget it, I'd like to look in your telephone directory. I want to have some numbers ready so I can call people tomorrow."

Frank shook his head. "Sorry, but I don't have a phone."

Wearing a look of disbelief, Kathy muttered, "Oh my God."

They had finished eating now and Cindy asked for a glass of water. After she drank it, Kathy told her to go watch television, and asked Frank if she could change the station. Once Cindy had gone into the living room, Frank looked at Kathy. "Tell me something about yourself," he said demurely, "You said earlier that you were on your way to San Diego, and you don't have family there, so are you on vacation or what? It's none of my business, of course, but I'm just curious. You also said you were down to fifty bucks and had been sleeping in your car. So what gives? Are you one of those homeless people?"

Kathy hedged. First, she pushed her plate away and asked for a glass of water. She squirmed, brushed her hair back, then glanced toward Cindy. "Well...I told you it's a long story. I...I'll try to make it short."

Frank nodded. "That's okay."

"Actually, I'm on the lam. Running away from my boyfriend." She looked at her hand. "We always got along well until quite recently when things changed. He worked in construction and I was a waitress. We never had any real problems until last year when he started staying out late and coming home drunk. I accused him of being unfaithful and we argued."

"It went along like this for a long time. I finally told him I wasn't going to put up with this any longer and he slapped me. From then on, things got worse. About two weeks ago, we got into another argument when he came home in the wee hours with lipstick on his face. When I told him I was going to leave him, he went ballistic. He pinned me down on the bed and held a gun to my head. He told me if I left, he would hunt me down and kill me."

Frank was listening emphatically, as he had heard similar stories before. He lit a cigarette, nodding as Kathy continued. She glanced towards Cindy. "When I told Pattie, a waitress I worked with, she advised me to get out quick. She said not to lose a minute, that I should leave town and not tell anyone where I was going."

"I had heard that jobs were plentiful in California, where I had always dreamed of living, and chose San Diego for its climate. I wanted to escape the cold winters of Nebraska. I decided to leave while Eric was at work, so packed a couple suitcases and hit the road."

"So you're going to San Diego to look for work and hide out from your boyfriend at the same time," Frank said in a cloud of smoke.

Kathy nodded, "And start a new life."

Frank got up from the table and glanced at the clock. He suggested that the girls might want to examine their bedroom, open a window to air it out, and perhaps take a shower while he cleaned up the kitchen. He said he had a few other things to do in preparation for tomorrow.

"In the morning, when I go up to explore the cave, you can ride in with me. It's only a few miles. Not much to see, but to me, it's God's country. Lots of flowers in bloom now, but you've got to get out and walk to see them."

He said he would stop at the post office in Ocotillo to pick up his mail, then drive to Cliff Brown's place. "Cliff likes to tinker with cars and he often makes repairs for some of the old widows in town. Maybe he'll take a look at your Pontiac."

An hour later, they all sat quietly in front of the television. Kathy and Cindy had brought in their luggage, then showered and put on their nightgowns under their robes. Lacking a hair dryer, their tresses hung lifelessly around their shoulders, but Frank was stealing glimpses of Cindy's legs where her robe had ridden up past her knees.

As the program ended, the news was coming up next. It was eleven o'clock. Kathy jumped up and told Cindy to come to bed. She said she was so tired from all the problems of her car breaking down, that she couldn't keep her eyes open any longer. Frank agreed it was late.

"I'm going to watch the news for awhile," he said, "If there's anything you need, just holler."

CHAPTER TWO

Kathy Winters awoke to the smell of coffee. Crawling out of bed wide-awake, she slipped into her bathrobe and tiptoed to the bathroom, seeing Frank in the kitchen when she emerged. When he didn't look up, she didn't speak. She would wake Cindy, get dressed, then go out and talk, since she was excited that they were going to drive to Ocotillo to see Cliff Brown, who might fix her car.

When the girls finally came out, they were wearing the same clothes as yesterday, but they had combed their hair and appeared freshened by a good nights sleep. Frank greeted them with a smile and offered coffee, but Cindy asked for a glass of water.

"Have a seat," Frank gestured toward the table. "I hope you like toast and peanut butter," he said. "That's all I've got." Kathy sat down, saying that was fine. As he poured her coffee, she noticed his keen blue eyes, the bluest she had ever seen. His face, sun-tanned, wore yesterday's stubble, but he had put on a clean Western shirt which intensified the color. When he leaned over the table, she became aware of his macho belt buckle, a two by three inch silver rectangle overlaid with his name in gold, with gold trimming.

"How did you guys sleep last night?" Frank wondered as he moved to the counter where the toaster sat. "Did you hear the coyotes howling?"

Kathy shook her head. "No, I konked out. I didn't hear a thing until I heard you in the kitchen. It's so quiet here."

"I did." Cindy chortled. "They sounded like they were real close."

Frank glanced at her. "They were. They come right up to the house at night. In fact, this place is known as Coyote Wells, and it got its name from them." He turned back to the counter but started to explain. "In the old days, say a hundred years ago, the pioneers crossing the desert on their way to Los Angeles, had to have water, and they had regular stops from Yuma on west."

"This house sits near a wash, where flash floods are common, and a lot of that water sinks in the ground. Sometimes you can find water by digging down a foot or so, and the coyotes knew that instinctively, but the wagon trains also knew it.

Once, long ago, a party was camped here, low on water, and the men noticed where coyotes had been digging. They dug down at the same place and found a good supply. In those days, camps were known by makeshift names, whatever came to mind, so the party called this Coyote Wells."

Frank brought toast to the table and told the girls to help themselves. The plates, butter and peanut butter with knives was already set out. He continued talking about water.

"In later years, U.S. Gypsum Company dug wells out here, and they found the water was of exceptionally good quality." He looked at Kathy. "You went through an industrial complex about ten miles before you broke down. Right?"

She nodded. "Yes, I remember that. At first, I thought it was a small town."

"Well, that was U.S. Gypsum. We call it Plaster city because they manufacture dry wall, sheetrock. Anyway, they needed good clean water, so this area was an ideal place to set up a factory."

"Today, you can see their wells around Ocotillo. The water is piped to the factory. I have my own well, as you know, and Ocotillo has its own, but the water is so good that it's in big demand. Everyone wants it. In fact, we've got a water war going on now. A San Diego attorney owns a well on the main drag, and he's selling water to the Mexicans. The people in Ocotillo don't like it. They're afraid he will pump the aquifer dry, then their homes would be worthless."

He stopped to sip his coffee, looking over at the girls who sat at rapt attention. "Because it would affect my well too, I have joined them in fighting this shyster. We're fighting him in court. There's a steady stream of tanker trucks coming into Ocotillo from Mexicali, and they're all pulling trailers, so – I've heard – each double tanker is carrying 5000 gallons per trip, and that's a lot of water."

Frank stopped talking abruptly. He saw that Kathy's cup was dry. "Oh I guess that subject is pretty boring." He got up to pour her more coffee. "How's your hand this morning?"

Kathy looked down at her hand. "It's okay. It doesn't hurt anymore."

Breakfast over, Cindy got up and stood by her chair. Frank noticed that her jeans were low-slung, since she had tucked her shirt under her belt, but the belt itself was star-studded in brass. When she said she was going outside to look around, Frank and Kathy sat alone at the table.

"You've got a cute kid," he said. "How old is she?"

Kathy was picking up her cup. "Oh she's 15, almost 16. She's boy-crazy, you know. I have to watch her like a hawk. I don't want her to get in trouble. When I get settled in San Diego, I've got to get her back in school."

Cindy burst into the house excitedly, "Your dog went under the back porch. I called him but he wouldn't come out. What's his name?"

Frank, puzzled, wore a look of disbelief. "I ain't got no dog," he said. "What did it look like?" Cindy said it was a German Shephard.

Frank got up. "Show me where he went." He started for the front door with Cindy leading the way.

As they went down the steps, Cindy explained, "I was standing by our car and he came out of those bushes over there and went under the house."

When Cindy showed Frank, he realized that the dog was a coyote, and it had gone through an access hole under the back side of the porch. But he had never spent much time looking around the place and was surprised that a coyote had resided there. When he explained to Cindy that it was a coyote, she was incredulous. She hadn't known that a coyote looked like a police dog.

Kathy had stayed in the house and had gone to the bathroom while they were outside and she told Frank she had been looking at his books. "I noticed that you have a book on cancer," she said. "Are you interested in that too?"

Frank pursed his lips sardonically. "Oh, yeah. I got this Hodgkin's disease, a form of cancer. Got it from Agent Orange in Nam. I bought that book hoping for some answers, but it doesn't help me much. There is so much written about the Big C, but no one seems to have any real answers. But I get along pretty well by taking medicines."

Kathy nodded. "It seems like everyone gets cancer. My dad has been battling prostate cancer for a long time and my mother died of breast cancer when she was only 38 years old. It seems to run in my family, so naturally, I worry because I'm already 34."

Frank shook his head hopelessly, glancing at his watch. "Yeah. Well we gotta get going. I pick up my mail every morning before I go out exploring and I can't wait to get into that cave." He picked up his flashlight and pistol, and they went out of the door.

Shoving his holstered 44 mag under the seat, he told Cindy to sit in the middle, with her mother on the far outside. Kathy looked at her car as they drove off, thinking aloud. "I sure hope that guy can fix it today. If we leave tomorrow morning, we should be in San Diego by tomorrow night. Right?"

Frank couldn't believe his ears. How naïve could anyone be? "Wrong," he said with a quick glance past

Cindy. "If Cliff will fix it, which is doubtful, there's no way in hell he could have it running by tomorrow night. Not unless it was something extremely simple. If it needs a head-gasket…well, I'm not going to explain it. I told you. You are stuck here for a couple of days at the least and a week at the most."

"Oh my god," she moaned, "what are we going to do?"

"You aren't going to do anything," he grinned to himself. "You're stuck here, baby."

When they parked at the post office, Frank left the girls in the pickup with the engine running, and dashed in to get his mail, but as he came out, he ran into Cliff, who was just going in. "Oh Hi, Cliff," he said. "You're just the man I'm looking for."

Cliff was puzzled. "Why? What's up, Frank?" They were only a few feet in front of Frank's vehicle as they moved away from the door. The girls could see Frank explaining Kathy's breakdown and Cliff shaking his head.

When frank got in beside Cindy, he laid his mail on the dash and cut the engine. "Cliff can't look at your car for a couple of days," he said. "He's taking his wife into El Centro this morning to see her doctor." Frank was reaching for a cigarette. "I'm going up the mountain from here, so what do you want to do? You can either stay here or come with me, but I want to warn you, it's a rough walk back to the cave. You guys are wearing tennis shoes and that's not good. There's cholla cactus all over and if you step on the spines, they'll go right in your foot."

Cindy grimaced. "Yuck!"

Kathy pouted. She was near tears. "I can't believe what is happening to us," she complained bitterly, "I just can't believe this nightmare. We can't stay here, for god's sake, and I don't' want to go up to some god-for-saken cave. I want to get my car fixed so I can get to San Diego."

Frank lit his cigarette and leaned forward to look past Cindy. "So?" He watched the smoke billow toward the windshield. "Do you want to stay here?"

Kathy was at her wits end. "Well, it seems I have two choices, and I don't like either one," she said sarcastically. "I wish I'd never come to California."

"Mom," Cindy piped up, "We better go with Frank. We better not get separated. He's all we've got right now."

Kathy softened and admitted that truth. "Cindy's right, Frank," she began, "You're all we've got. And I do appreciate your hospitality. I don't know what we would have done last night if it hadn't been for you. It's just so nerve wracking...I..."

Frank started the engine. "That's okay," he said. "I can sympathize with your predicament. It's hell to break down in a strange place." He backed to turn toward the highway, when he saw a Mexican water tanker coming down Imperial Avenue, and another, loaded, heading out. "Look," he pointed through the windshield, "there's those water trucks I was telling you about. See Cindy?" He took one last puff and threw his cigarette out of the window. "The guy that owns the well gets ten cents a gallon, and the Mexicans sell it to the peons for thirty cents. He's making a fortune, believe me."

Driving up Imperial Avenue a few blocks, Frank got on the Interstate Highway and headed up the grade toward Mountain Springs. While the engine of the Dodge Power Wagon hummed up the 6% incline, the huge rugged tires made their own music. The girls sat quietly, looking out at the rock formations of which the Jacumba Mountains are composed, lulled hypnotically by the sound of the tires.

At the 2500-foot elevation, Frank pulled off the highway and parked as far back as he could, and got out. "Okay," he said, "We walk in from here." The girls got out and stared at the landscape confronting them, a moonscape of jagged boulders and cacti.

"I don't know about this," Kathy told Cindy as they gazed afar.

"Frank said it would be a tough walk. And it's not so hot. Do you think we should go in with him or wait here?" Brimming with youthful energy, Cindy welcomed the opportunity of a good hike. They had sat in the car for days, and last night at Frank's place, they had just stood around. "I want to go in," Cindy said. But Kathy wasn't so sure. "Oh, mom," Cindy punched Kathy playfully, "You're not that old. Besides, you need the exercise as much as I do."

Frank came around the pickup, now, carrying a 3-cell flashlight. He had strapped on his holstered Smith & Wesson, and had hooked a canteen on the same belt, opposite side. Cindy looked at the pistol and wondered aloud if there was any danger ahead.

"Well, there are mountain rattlers up here," he explained, "but I always carry a gun when I'm in the outback. Just in case." He looked at Kathy. "You ready for this?"

She shrugged. "As ready as I'll ever be."

The Jacumba Mountains, at the east end, just before they slope into Imperial Valley, are a hodgepodge of rocky terrain, interspersed with patches of alpine meadows, where only cactus-like plants grow. Most abundant are the wicked cholla cactus and the ocotillo, with some hedgehog and beaver tail. The cholla have spines that when imbedded in flesh, almost always require pliers to remove, and Frank had warned the girls that they were at risk wearing tennis shoes, for often, segments of this plant became dislodged, fall to the ground and are not easily seen among the detritus, dried organic material and animal droppings.

They were well on their way up the slope with Kathy complaining about the heat and wanting Frank to slow down when he spotted an agave. He would stop for a few minutes to let her rest and maybe tell a story. Waiting for them to catch up, he stood by the cactus and pointed.

"This is agave," he began. "You don't find many at this elevation. Most are on lower flood plains, but these are interesting plants. The Indians, years ago, made tequila from them. Well, they still do down in Mexico, but they also ate them and made needle and thread from the sharp spine you see here." He poked the spine with the flashlight. "See how sharp that is? They used it as a needle."

The girls were watching him closely, and their curiosity made them forget the travails of the hike. Cindy piped up. "Okay, but where's the thread?"

Grinning now, Frank enjoyed having and audience. He laid the flashlight down and pulled out his pocketknife. He said he would show them some magic.

Holding one of the fleshy segments with his left hand, he sliced under the spine, careful not to cut completely through, then pulled it sideways, thus tearing the outer edge from the leaf and leaving a long stringy, fibrous thread still attached to the spine.

First, he held it up for them to see, then handed it to Cindy. "Clever," she grinned, "those Indians were pretty smart."

Kathy wore a faint smile and was nodding, "Yeah, pretty smart." But Frank kept talking as he picked up the flashlight and they started out again. And when Cindy asked him where he had learned that trick, he was happy to explain.

"Well, I've learned an awful lot in the few years I've lived down here, some of it from various people I know, and a lot from studying books and maps. But I've probably learned more through archaeology than anywhere else." He stopped to light a cigarette. "See, when I came down here to live, my sole interest was looking for lost treasure, but I really didn't know the desert nor how and where to look for buried treasure."

"There's an old guy, a professor from El Centro, who comes out to Ocotillo –he's a famous archaeologist – and he holds classes for the snowbirds, or anyone who's interested, once a week. He gets paid by the college and the more students he signs up, the more he makes."

"When I heard about him, I signed up and have been going out with the group ever since." He blew a cloud of smoke. "You may wonder why I would be interested in archaeology, but I figured going out like they do, I would learn the lay of the land and get some ideas of names and places."

Kathy broke in, "Frank, could we stop again? I'm all out of breath."

Then Cindy spoke up. "Where do you go to the bathroom out here?" Frank said, you yell 'bush' and you go behind one, but Cindy could see there was nothing big enough to hide behind, so Frank told her to go behind those rocks over there, since they were now nearing the cave and this area was a mass of rock and boulders, some in great piles and others scattered randomly.

"Watch where you step!" He yelled after her. But when she returned, Frank offered the girls a drink from his canteen, which they refused, but when they had gone farther, they came upon a huge promontory that overlooked the valley below. A man standing up there could see across the entire Imperial County, which appeared bowl-like, since it was entirely below sea level. Frank had been here once before, the day he discovered the cave.

According to legend, this depression was an inland sea a million years ago, and the fossilized oyster shells found in abundance there attested to the veracity of the legend. But when the sea dried up, it eventually filled with fresh water and was known for centuries as Lake Cahuilla.

Frank pointed out the promontory, a jumble of rocks and boulders. "The cave is in there," he said. "The entrance is down in the rocks. You girls better wait up here while I go in." He started to walk toward the rock face, his mind filled with trepidation and doubt. There could be mountain lions holed up in the cave. It would be a natural place to hide and to keep cool.

After climbing up to the opening, he fingered his pistol and checked his flashlight. He lifted his cap, scratched his hair briefly and replaced it snuggly. Sweat was running down his face. As he lowered himself into the three-foot hole, a musty smell assailed his nostrils.

Advancing cautiously, shining the light on the walls and floor, he noticed that the cave sloped downward and the narrow opening gave way to widening walls and six-foot ceilings, all composed of hard packed clay mixed with small pieces of granite and some mica. The entire passage appeared to be well worn, as if used by hundreds of people.

Kathy was complaining bitterly. There was no place to hide from the sun, and no respite from the heat. She wished now, that they hadn't come up here. Perspiring profusely, the girls milled about, hoping Frank would hurry and come out. Cindy decided to sit down on a rock.

As Frank went deeper, he was to get the shock of his life. While his flashlight shone ahead, the cave widened into a large chamber, and the beam playing on the walls revealed a sight that made him shudder. All along one wall was a shelf-like projection on which a row of bone-white human skulls with red eye sockets sat, glaring back at him.

Heart racing, he stood motionless, transfixed by the macabre sight. Had this been an Indian burial cave? Or a trophy room? Maybe it had had a religious purpose. He knew that some native cultures like the Aztecs sacrificed humans to the Gods. Was it possible that the Mayans or Toltecs had lived this far north?

When he thought about that, he realized that this cave and the area around Ocotillo was actually close to Mexico; not over a mile or two, and a thousand years ago, or a million, natives knew no boundaries.

Frank was keenly aware that he had discovered something of importance, since his experiences with the archaeology group proved that much was unknown about ancient civilization. But now, he was so excited he couldn't wait to tell Jay. Maybe there was more skulls further on, but they could wait until Jay could arrange a field trip. Without a doubt, Jay would want to explore this cave.

Frank exited the cave with exuberance. "You won't believe what I found in there," he smiled with excitement. "It's a good thing you didn't go in with me, cause you'd have been scared out of your pants."

Cindy got to her feet. "What did you find? Gold nuggets?"

Kathy too, wondered. "A cougar?"

Frank shook his head. "Human skulls!"

Cindy looked aghast. "Yuck. You gotta be kidding."

"No," Frank said, "I think it was an old Indian burial site or something. I've got to tell Jay about it."

"Jay?" Kathy didn't understand.

"He's the archaeologist I was telling you about," Frank explained. "He comes out to Ocotillo once a week to teach the snow birds, and I signed up with him. His name is Jay Bradford. Nice guy."

The long walk back to the pickup – all downhill – was easier than the trip in, yet the girls complained incessantly. They were sweaty, they were thirsty, they were hungry. But when Cindy stepped on a cactus thorn, she turned angry. "Fricken son of a..." she spat irascibly as she looked down at her foot, but Frank was more amused than concerned.

This girl, almost 16, seemingly a nice girl, had surprised him with her vulgar language, and he wondered if she was still a virgin. Probably not, he assumed. Not many girls still have their hymen at that age.

"I told you to watch your step," Frank said as he reached in his pocket for a pair of miniature pliers he always carried. "Come here lil girl. It's no big deal."

But Cindy disagreed. "No, it's never a big deal when it happens to someone else."

Frank chuckled, "That's why I wear these heavy boots. They protect me from thorns, sharp rocks and snake bites."

The cholla thorns are shaped like a fishhook, making them painful to remove, but Cindy didn't complain much when Frank yanked the barb out. It had gone through the canvas shoe just above the rubber sole.

When they reached the pickup, Frank removed his pistol and hid it under the seat. His canteen and flashlight went into a box in the cargo bed. "Well, I could go for a cold beer right now," he said as they got in and started heading back to Ocotillo. "I guess you guys are as thirsty as I am."

"Thirsty?" Kathy joked, "I'm so thirsty I could drink pee."

Surprised at her vulgarity as he was with Cindy's, he demurred. "Hey, you may be kidding, but a lot of people dying of thirst in the desert have drunk their own pee. It may sound gross, but when you are facing death, you'll do a lot of things you wouldn't ordinarily do."

"Well, I'd never do that," Cindy retorted, but Frank told her.

"Never say never." He was reaching for a cigarette. "There's a restaurant just south of Ocotillo off the Interstate. It's in a big truck stop. It's air-conditioned and they've got the best hamburgers you'll ever sink your teeth into. That's where I'm heading. How does that grab you guys?"

"It's the best news I've heard in days," Kathy said. "If it's a truck stop, they will have a mechanic. Why didn't you tell me yesterday?"

Frank lit his smoke. "Because the truck stop is closed. Not enough business. It's only about 30 miles to El Centro, so most truckers do their business there." He blew smoke out of the open window. "When I moved out here, the place was open. A lot of motorists bought gas there and ate at the café, but the facilities were inadequate for the big rigs, and other reasons, so he went broke. But another guy came along and leased the restaurant and gas pumps. In the last couple years, the café has become quite popular. It now attracts tourists, locals and Border Patrol customers. It's gotten to be a hangout for desert rats, too. We get a lot of RV'ers down here on weekends and holidays, so it all adds up to a lot of hungry people."

They were now in sight of the café. Frank pointed to the big sign on the hill behind the establishment. It read: ROADRUNNER CAFÉ. "I know the guy who runs it. Real friendly guy. His name is Brian. I eat here so much I know him a lot of the waitresses by name."

The café was a white stucco building of Spanish design sitting on the hillside, with the failed garage behind it. With acres of parking space around it, and highly visible from I-8, it looked down on the village of Ocotillo. But because it was far from other towns, there was a constant turnover in waitresses. Only one woman, Rita, a little Mexican with big brow eyes, was a long time employee. She had been with Brian for two years.

When Frank and the girls entered the café, there were people sitting at the tables near the big plate glass windows, two Border Patrolmen at the counter and several at the tables closest to the counter. The only place to sit was near the Border Patrol officers. As Frank's party moved towards the seats, Kathy was surveying the interior décor. There were old time pictures of the desert lining the walls, many of cactus and one of a stagecoach. One depicted a gold mine and another of a roadrunner.

As they sat down beside the patrolmen, Kathy looked over at a picture of an ocotillo cactus in full bloom. She asked Frank what it was, as she had noticed a lot of the tall, vase shaped plants along the roads and highways. When he explained that it was an ocotillo, she was confused. He had spoken of the town as Ocotillo, and now he was saying this plant was an ocotillo.

"They named the town after the plant," he said. "It's a Spanish name."

A waitress emerged from the kitchen, carrying a tray of food. A minute later, Rita passed in front of them, hurrying toward the kitchen. She glanced sideways, "Oh hi, Frank. I'll be with you in a sec." But Cindy was turned sideways on the stool, looking toward a teen-aged Mexican boy.

Frank, sitting next to the Border Patrolmen, noticed that they were finished with their meal and were ready to leave when Rita came back to take his order. "Hamburger and a Corona for me," he said, "and put their orders on my check." He gestured toward Kathy and Cindy.

But Kathy protested. "No, put ours on a separate tag."

After they had ordered hamburgers and Pepsi, Kathy told Frank, "I'm paying for our meal. I'm not having you support us. You've done enough for us already."

Frank shrugged. "Whatever." He was glancing sideways as the Patrolmen got up and left, and watched as a young looking man took a seat in their place.

"Well, at least it's cool in here," Kathy observed as they waited for their orders. "It was so hot in our bedroom last night. I opened the window but it was still too warm. You don't have air conditioning do you?"

Frank shook his head. "Can't afford it. You get used to the heat when you don't have it."

They sat talking even after Rita had brought their orders. Cindy wolfed down her hamburger, drank her Pepsi and ordered another. Frank downed his beer and did the same.

Now, Kathy began to worry. "Did you say that Cliff couldn't look at my car for a couple of days?"

Nodding, Frank agreed. "Something like that. Cliff is retired and works on cars for some of the old widows in town. If your car has a serious problem, I doubt that he could fix it. He might be able to install a new head gasket, but it's possible you've got a cracked head. Anyway, Cliff works when he wants to and only for people he knows."

The young man sitting beside Frank spoke up. "I couldn't help hearing what you said, but if you've got car trouble, maybe I can help you."

Frank looked at the skinny kid with contempt. "Just how in hell could you help us? We need a mechanic."

"That's what I figured," the man said. "I'm a certified GM mechanic. I'm a Mr. Goodwrench."

Frank exploded derisively. "Ha! And I'm the President of the United States!"

Kathy had got up and stood behind the men. "Wait, Frank." Then she addressed the youth. "Are you really a mechanic?"

The boy answered politely. "Yes mam. I'm certified to work on General Motors cars."

But Frank was doubtful. "You don't look old enough to be a mechanic."

The young man appeared to be of German descent, with tousled dirty blond hair, a sober mien, and his slight build made him appear younger than he was, as he explained that he was 26 years old.

"What's your name?" Kathy asked as she stood face to face with him.

"Don Shuger," he said. "Ain't that a sweet name? And I can fix anything but a broken heart."

Frank smiled now. "I'll bet! Well, at least you've got a sense of humor."

Don explained that he had been working for Graves Chevrolet in Los Angeles and was laid off when the company downsized, and he pulled out a ballpoint pen with their name on it, to back up his statement. He went on to say that he was heading for Arizona to look for work and would appreciate a chance to make a little cash. He said that his charge would be far less than a garage, since he didn't have any overhead.

"I've got my own tools and my car's outside," he said as he vacated his seat. "What do you say?" Frank and Kathy looked at each other questioningly. Frank pushed his empty bottle away and nodded. Kathy glanced at Don, saying that he could do the work, but she didn't have a lot of money. Don put her at ease. "Whatever you can afford," he said.

Frank scooped up his and Kathy's guest check, then on second thought, picked up Don's. They had decided that Don would follow them out to his place, but as they moved away, both Kathy and Don noticed that Frank had picked up their tabs and protested meekly. As the group neared the cash register, Frank shoved the checks onto the counter just as Brian came out from the kitchen.

As Brian rang up the sale, he asked Frank how everything was going, then he informed him that Rita was quitting. She was getting married. "Did she tell you?"

Frank shook his head. "She was too busy. We didn't have time for chit-chat today."

"Yeah," Brian said, "she's moving to Pine Valley. Too far to commute. None of them stay here very long. Rita is one of the best I've ever had."

Frank was nodding. "Yeah, she's been here a long time." Kathy, of course, heard everything; Brian's parting words especially. "If you run into anyone interested in working here, send them over."

On the way to Coyote Wells, with Don following closely, Kathy was in good spirits. "I can't believe it," she enthused. "All this time I'm looking for a mechanic, and one comes to me when I least expect it."

CHAPTER THREE

While Frank and Don Shuger bent over the Pontiac engine, assessing the damage from overheating, Don determined that they would need a new head gasket and a radiator hose. Frank suggested that Don start work and that he would drive into town to pick up the needed parts, since he wanted to get groceries anyway, as he was out of almost everything.

Kathy could go with Frank to pay for the parts, and Cindy would stay home watching television, because this would be a quick trip and she would only be in the way. But as Frank as Kathy drove into El Centro, she made an offer Frank couldn't refuse. In appreciation for getting her car fixed, she would pay for some pork chops and she would cook a nice meal. Frank saw the merit of her plan quickly, because he would not only have a home cooked dinner, but the girls would be leaving, once their car was running again. In the few hours before darkness, Don should have the car operating, and it would be time to eat. Kathy would either leave then, or she might wait to leave in the morning. In any event, he would be rid of the girls and could get back to his normal routine. Everything was working out perfectly, he thought, but he hadn't reckoned with fate.

When he and Kathy returned home and drove into the yard, they saw Cindy standing near Don, laughing, but what angered Kathy the most was Cindy's attire. She had put on a pink T-shirt that accentuated her ample bosom, and with her low-slung jeans and bare mid-riff, she appeared as a sex goddess. She had combed her golden hair so it framed her cheeks and, by contrast, intensified the blue of her eyes. It was obvious she had freshened up so she could flirt with the cute mechanic.

"Cindy!" Kathy shouted as she and Frank exited the pickup, "you get over here and help us get these groceries in the house." But once this was done, she ordered her to help in the kitchen, as she was going to prepare a nice meal. It would be her way of thanking Frank for his hospitality and a way of rewarding Don for his assistance.

After Frank showed Kathy where everything was in the kitchen, he went out to his vehicle to retrieve the parts and hand them to Don who stood leaning against the Pontiac. He had removed the head, cleaned it up and taken off the old radiator hose. Dirty and disheveled, hair in disarray, Don was wiping his hands on a red shop towel. His blue trousers, as blue as his eyes, were smudged with grease. He nodded gently as he inspected the gasket. "Now I gotta put this bad boy on the block," he said, "but all this garbage takes time." He gestured towards the fan belts, water pump, alternator and air cleaner.

Frank was lighting a cigarette and nodding, "Yeah, big job. They broke down out here and came up to my place asking for help. What do you think of Cindy?"

Don brightened. "Oh, she's okay. She's cool."

But in the house, Kathy had Cindy peeling potatoes and was chastising her for flirting with Don. "I've got enough trouble without you getting mixed up with boys," she said, "and you didn't have to put on that loud T-shirt."

"Oh mom," Cindy reasoned, "all the girls wear this kind of stuff. It's not like I was making out with him."

As the hours passed, Don had the engine put back together, and Frank stood by ready to jump the battery. They were ready to fire up the Pontiac. By now, Kathy had the spuds cooking and supper was almost ready. She and Cindy had come outside to see how the work was progressing, and they stood watching as Don coaxed the engine to life. When it coughed and sputtered, with white smoke bellowing from the exhaust pipe, he gunned it and soon had it running smoothly.

Wide-eyed with wonder, Kathy broke into a grin and Cindy's jaw dropped in disbelief. Frank looked at Don, nodding and smiling, when Kathy's exuberance exploded in a happy outburst of joy. "Hooray!" She gushed with uninhibited abandon. "I've got wheels again." She grabbed Cindy and kissed her out of sheer excitement. "Honey, we've got our car back!"

With darkness approaching and everyone calmed down, Kathy announced that supper was almost ready and they should all come inside. "Yeah," Frank said to Don. "Come on in and get cleaned up."

Don nodded. "Okay, I'll gather my tools first. You didn't think I could fix it, did you?"

Frank admitted his error. "My mistake," he said. "I apologize. When we met at the café, I just thought you might be a con man. You look pretty young to be a certified GM mechanic."

At the dinner table, Cindy and Don kept looking at each other. Cindy would steal glances at Don and he would look at her as young boys do when they are interested in a girl. But Frank, too, was stealing glances at Cindy. The pink T-shirt hugging her bosom was like a red flag in front of a bull.

Frank would glance at Don occasionally, wondering what he was thinking. Don had cleaned up and combed his hair, and Frank could imagine that Cindy would think he was cute. As they passed food around the table, Kathy was like a mother hen caring for her chicks. If she wasn't urging Don to have another pork chop, she was asking him about his parents.

When dinner was over and they had pushed their chairs away from the table, Don said it was time for him to hit the road. It was also time for Kathy to pay Don as she had promised. Now, as she handed him $35, she apologized for not having more, but she explained that she had paid for the car parts and bought the groceries, and this was all she had left.

"That's okay," Don said, "this is fine. I hope to pick up a few more little jobs along the way. Or better yet, get another steady job." He said he was glad to be of help. When he headed for the door, the others followed. They wanted to see him off. But when he was about to enter his car, Cindy said, "I hope we'll meet again."

As Frank and the girls watched him drive away, Kathy turned sour. She suddenly realized she was broke and still a long way from San Diego. When she started to complain, Frank didn't want to hear it. He needed a break from all these people and all the excitement, but he also needed a beer. When Kathy started yapping about her predicament, the same old garbage, he put her off and went to fetch a cold one.

Kathy shrugged and told Cindy they would have to go inside to do the dishes. "Yuck," Cindy scowled as they passed Frank coming out the door with his beer. But Kathy continued to complain to Cindy as they faced a mountain of dirty dishes, pots and pans.

"We're broke, honey," she said disparagingly. "I gave Don the last of our money. I don't know what we're going to do now."

"I know, mom," Cindy said. "I've still got $3 dollars mad money. We'll find a way. Maybe Frank will loan us twenty bucks. At least we could ask him."

By now, Frank was sitting in his rocker, looking out into the darkness. He could see the lights of El Centro reflecting off the clouds thirty miles to the east and he could hear the 18-wheelers speeding west on the Interstate. Falling into reverie, he sighed. It was so peaceful to be alone with his thoughts.

Tomorrow was Wednesday, the day the archaeology class always met, and he couldn't wait to tell Jay Bradford, their teacher, about the cave he had discovered. The human skulls intrigued him. What was the story behind them?

Jay would probably know, since he often narrated stories of the native Indians – the Cahuillas and the

Yumans – who were hunters and gatherers centuries ago when life flourished around this former inland sea. Frank remembered the day they went on a field trip and Jay was explaining the stone circles they found on the desert, with Jay calling them "sleeping circles." He said that the Indians, when traveling long distances, would gather stones, lay them out in perfect circular fashion, within which they would sleep.

Frank had questioned Jay. In the first place, the diameter of the circle couldn't accommodate a five or six foot man, and furthermore, why go to all the trouble of arranging stones to sleep in? But one of the students argued that rattlesnakes won't cross over rocks, and therefore, the sleeper would be protected from snakebites.

There were many contentious subjects that were questioned on these field trips, but that was understandable when you were investigating aboriginal people. Nevertheless, most of what Jay taught was based on fact, some, like the inland sea being there at one time, was obviated by the oyster shell fossils found in Shell Canyon even today.

When Frank no longer heard the rattle of dishes, he took his nearly empty can of beer with him into the house, where he found the girls sitting at the table with their Pepsi's, taking a break. Kathy's back was hurting from bending over cooking and now washing dishes, and she began lamenting her plight as he took a seat next to her.

"Frank," she said matter-of-factly. "I've got a problem."

"Yeah," he replied, "you seem to have nothing but problems. What's the matter now?"

"I'm broke," she whined. "I gave Don all the money I had."

Nodding, Frank retorted, "Well what did you expect?"

She glanced at Cindy and back at him. "Frank," she said emphatically, "I am dead broke. I got 85 cents in my purse. What am I going to do?"

"Well," he said with a hint of derision, "you said you were going to leave the minute you got your car fixed. You said you were in a hurry to get to San Diego."

"Yes," she admitted, "but I didn't know this would happen. I wasn't thinking."

"Okay, now. Back up a little," he began, "You are asking me what you should do and I will tell you, even if you don't like it." He reached for a cigarette. "In the first place, your rush to get to San Diego doesn't make sense. If you're hiding out from your boyfriend, this little burg is about as good a place as you can get. And if you are looking for work so you can support yourself, just remember, things are cheaper here than in the city..."

Kathy broke in, speaking sardonically. "I know what you are saying, but you don't know my circumstances. Where could I get a job in this dump? Where could I live? What could I do with Cindy while I'm away at work, and where could she go to school next fall?"

"Whoa, there, Kathy," he cautioned, "one thing at a time." He blew a cloud of smoke toward Cindy who was listening intently. "You heard Brian, the guy who runs the café. He said Rita is quitting and he is looking for a waitress. You told me you were working as a waitress in Omaha, didn't you?"

"Yeah, but Eric was making good money. Here, I couldn't make enough on minimum wages to rent a house, buy groceries, school clothes and all the other things I need."

"No," Frank admitted, "but the tips are great. You smile at the Border Patrol guys and they leave a big tip. The bigger you smile, the bigger your tip."

Cindy grinned from ear to ear. "Yeah mom, put your mouth where the money is." Frank gazed at Cindy a long moment. Such a pretty girl. He knew where he'd like to put his mouth if he had the chance.

Kathy took a negative stand no matter what Frank suggested. To hear her talk, San Diego was like the Holy Grail; if she could reach it, her quest would end. Her goal would be accomplished.

"What I'm saying, Kathy, is that you're chasing rainbows. All your problems would be solved just by taking that waitress job. If you want to start a new life, start now. You and Cindy can stay here in exchange for house work until you save enough to be on your own."

"Hmm," Kathy said, glancing toward Cindy. "Well, let me give it some thought."

Cindy laid her hand on Kathy's arm. "Let's do it, mom," she said pleadingly. "If we lived here with Frank, maybe I could go out treasure hunting with him sometime. Maybe we'd find a lot of gold nuggets. Then we'd be rich."

Kathy broke into a big smile. "Okay," she said. "We'll do it. We'll give it a try. I could sure use a few gold nuggets right now."

"Let me tell you something, Kathy," Frank said as he stood up to fetch a beer, "There is a story about gold nuggets being found here in this valley. Actually, it's a legend." He sat down again. "It seems there was an old prospector, called Peg-Leg-Pete, who roamed this desert a hundred years ago, and he became famous for his alleged discovery of the black nuggets." Frank popped his beer and tipped the can to his lips.

"You see, black nuggets are unusual," Frank continued. "When stones are exposed to sunlight for long periods of time, they get something like a patina, called desert varnish on them, which makes them look black. According to legend, this old prospector found a cache of them somewhere around here. They could have been gathered and piled up where he found them. Maybe the Indians gathered them. No one knows."

Cindy was on the edge of her seat. "Well, what did he do with them?"

"Yeah," Kathy chimed in, "What happened then?"

Frank was lighting a cigarette and reaching for the ashtray. Grinning, he said that here was where the story got interesting. "Old Peg-Leg-Pete couldn't take the nuggets that day...them things big as golf balls are heavy...so he marked the area figuring to come back with his mule later on, but he could never find the place again." He was still grinning and watching the girl's expressions. "And that means that they are still there!"

"And you figure on finding them?"

"Sure do! Out here, the sand blows and forms drifts, just like snowdrifts. Some things are covered and some are uncovered. Someday, if I'm lucky, I hope to find them, because I've got a feeling they're buried under the sand."

Cindy couldn't wait to speak. "Mom," she said, "if we stay here with Frank, can I go out looking for gold with him while you're at work?"

Kathy shrugged, "Well, I don't know, I haven't even got the job yet."

Frank made a suggestion. "It would be good for her, Kathy. A good way to spend summer vacation. Better than hanging out in town and getting on drugs and alcohol."

Kathy glanced at her watch, "Yeah," she managed, but her mind was on Cindy and Frank. The idea of them spending so much time together was unsettling. With Cindy at the age where she was boy crazy, and Frank being a single man, the chance of something happening was great. Kathy knew that from her own experiences when she lived with Jim, Cindy's father, long before she moved in with Eric.

Ever since Cindy was old enough to use cosmetics, she'd go in the bedroom and sneak Kathy's lipstick and come out looking like a precocious prostitute and strutting around in Kathy's high heels, but she was a natural-born actress, a show-off, and as cute as they come.

When she was only six years old, Cindy walked in on Kathy and Eric when they were making love, and thinking they were playing a game, she slipped off her panties and gleefully shouted, "My turn next!" But by age 12, she was having her period and starting to be interested in boys. Then one day, Kathy caught her masturbating and realized that now, as she turned 16, she would be most vulnerable. To leave her with Frank could be dangerous indeed.

When Frank saw Kathy look at her watch, he was reminded that it was getting late and he would be taking the girls to the archaeology class in the morning. It was understood that Kathy would take the job and stay on for a while if Brian would hire her.

"Yeah," he said, "We'll hit the sack and drive over to Ocotillo in the morning. Jay comes out every Wednesday. I think you guys will enjoy taking the class with me and all the old folks. Sometimes we hold class in the Community Hall and sometimes we go on field trips." He smiled now, glancing at Cindy. "Sometimes Jay brings fresh donuts out."

As Cindy's face lit up, Frank said that the girls could use the bathroom first, as he would like to catch some of the night news. "I want to see if there's anything on about the water war and I can't wait to tell Jay about the cave tomorrow."

CHAPTER FOUR

A battered, old red Jeep pulled up in front of the Community Hall and a grey-haired man jumped out, flinging his cigarette to the ground and grabbing a handful of papers from the front seat before walking toward the front door of the building.

"That's Jay Bradford, the archaeology instructor and curator of the Imperial Valley College Museum in El Centro," Frank explained to Kathy and Cindy as they pulled up to park near the student's cars to the right of the building. "He's a good ol guy, a professor at the college."

"He doesn't look like a professor, the way he's dressed," Kathy said disparagingly, "And that Jeep. Can't he afford anything better than that old pile of junk?"

Jay's Jeep was an old World War II model, faded, full of nicks and scratches, but the topless gutless wonder was still reliable, and it was an ideal vehicle for traversing the rough terrain of the desert. True to its vintage, it carried the traditional five-gallon cans on the back, for gasoline and water.

"How do you expect him to dress?" Frank frowned. "And the Jeep belongs to the county. They're as broke as you are. Imperial County is one of the poorest counties in California." He opened his door. "Okay, let's go in."

Weekly, on Wednesdays, Jay would drive the battered Jeep the twenty-five miles to Ocotillo, where he had made arrangements to use the "hall," and where his students would assemble to hear him talk about the desert, its legends and the ancient hunters and gatherers. The students were mostly elderly retirees, some of which lived in Ocotillo only during the winter and others who lived there permanently. Most of them had signed up for archaeology as a means of entertainment, or in Frank's case, to learn about the desert.

There were usually about ten couples and a few singles comprising Jay's classes, and he lured many of them with his charm and mild manner, since he was paid for his services by the college. Had he not signed enough students, he'd not receive his grant.

When Frank and the girls walked in, most of the seats were taken, as the locals had arrived early and came to sit in the air-conditioned room where they could discuss the news of the day with their neighbors. Jay, leaning against one of the tables, was arranging his lecture, dressed in blue Levis and faded blue shirt, which bulged with pens on one side and his cigarettes in the other, for he was a chain-smoker seldom seen without a fag in his lips. Around his neck, he wore a red kerchief.

His wild uncombed grey hair might have lead the casual observer to believe he was some downtrodden hippie, but Jay was a highly educated and very intelligent archaeologist who could tell you more than you cared to know about the Cahuilla Indians who inhabited the area in times past, and the intaglios which dotted the desert from Yuma to the Jacumba Mountains. He could – and often did – expound on the reasons for the Indians demise, and theorized on the ancient lake that once covered this valley, eons ago.

From Red Bluff, where he grew up, to the San Francisco area, to Inyo County and south to the Mexican border, now, he had studied and mapped archaeological sites and noted major geoglyphs, most of which were visible only from the air.

The voices of the class droned on as Frank and the girls found three empty seats in the back, but the chatter of voices stopped abruptly as Jay spoke. "Well, I guess we're all here," he said in his usual laid-back manner. "As you know, I had planned on going up to Davies Valley this morning. There's some Indian pictographs up near Palm Grove and I wanted to map their location." He reached for a cigarette. "But something has come up that's more important."

"The BLM has notified me that the area to the south of Nomirage will be off-limits after the first of the month, so I want to comb the area for artifacts today. My plan is for us to spread out and walk the area to make sure there's nothing of archaeological importance out there. It's our last chance to investigate that section." He lit his cigarette. "How many of you remembered to bring your lunch and water?"

Everyone except Frank raised their hands, but he whispered to Kathy that they would eat at the Roadrunner Café tonight, when she could talk to Brian about a job. By now, everyone was expecting to leave, when Jay spoke up again. "Before we leave," he said in a cloud of smoke, "I wonder how many of you saw on television last night where a man using a metal detector found a gold hoard worth $15 million just a foot or so under the surface of ground?"

Many hands went up, but 74 year-old Pierre Miles, looking over his bifocals, said, "I saw it. I think I'll buy me one of them metal detectors. There must be a lot of buried gold around these parts. Don't you think so?"

Jay nodded. "Yes, according to legend, this valley is full of lost and buried treasures. In the old days, banks transferred gold bullion, currency and notes via stagecoach. We are on the stagecoach route, here. In those days, bandits would seize the strongboxes which were very heavy...too heavy to carry on horseback... too cumbersome, so they'd bury them, hoping to come back later when the heat was off, to reclaim the loot. But as far as we know, may outlaws were killed and never came back while others returned but were unable to locate the boxes due to shifting sand."

Slim, blond Susan Rider, widowed last year when her husband was killed in a mine cave-in, took up the discussion. "My husband used to say that there was more gold buried around here than any other place in this country. He always dreamed of finding the Peg-Leg-Pete black nuggets. But of course, he never did."

Geoff Weisse, a thirty-eight year old widower, smiled sardonically. "I don't believe all this crap. Take the story of the Lost City of the Yumans for example. Ever since I've lived here, I've heard wild tales of this city of gold. It's supposed to be somewhere in the Jacumba Mountains. I don't know how these stories get started, but as far as I'm concerned, they're all B.S.

If they had any basis in fact, how come no one has ever found any evidence of them?"

Frank was highly amused by the conversation. When Susan Rider said that her late husband always used to dream of finding the Peg-Leg-Pete black nuggets, it strongly fortified his resolve to find them; the more determined he was to search the outback.

Jay glanced at his watch. "Well...are there any more questions before we leave?"

"Jay," Frank's voice rang out unexpectedly, "I've got something I think the class would be interested in." Everyone swiveled their heads around to look at him. "I found a cave full of human skulls!"

Jay's jaw dropped. "What?" Everyone groaned.

"Yup," Frank continued, "I was exploring up by Mountain Springs when I saw a hole back in the rocks. I jumped down in it and found that it was the opening to a tunnel. I went back there yesterday with a flashlight and got the surprise of my life. About ten feet in, the tunnel widened into a cave. When I shone my light ahead, I saw human skulls lined up on a ledge."

"Are you serious, Frank?" Jay couldn't believe what he had heard. "Not in the Anza-Borrego?"

Frank shook his head. "No. No, this one's just up the mountain. You can drive up there in 20 minutes."

But Jay was shaking his head doubtfully. "Frank, he said, "the only cave up that way is the Smuggler's Cave, and that's up in In-Ko-Pah."

Susan Rider, sitting near Geoff, spoke up again. "Frank, there are no caves in the Jacumba Mountains as Jay says, except Smuggler's, and we've been all over that area."

Frank was adamant. "It's well concealed. It would be hard to spot by the average hiker. I just happened to climb a rock face, and saw it. I almost literally fell into it, but yesterday I went in and saw those skulls, it made my skin crawl. I got out of there fast, but afterwards, I just couldn't wait to tell the class about it."

"Well hell," Jay said with amusement, "You've got my curiosity. I think we should go up and take a look."

"Yeah," Frank nodded, "there seemed to be something sinister in there. I got a creepy feeling."

"Well, just offhand, I'd say you've found an Indian burial site," Jay theorized, "but I don't know of any tribes that buried their dead or collected their skulls. If this was further south, I'd suspect human sacrifice. Something on that order. The Mayans and the Aztecs killed thousands of their own – usually young virgins – to appease their gods."

Geoff was getting excited. "This I gotta see," he said. "Let's make a quick trip up there, Jay."

Susan was nodding. "Yeah. It sounds more interesting than walking that area south of Nomirage."

Jay agreed whole-heartedly. "It's a done deal," he said. "I'm just as curious as the rest of you. Let's move out."

Kathy and Cindy hadn't said a word the entire time they had been inside, feeling out of place among strangers and not being familiar with the names and places mentioned. But upon leaving the air-conditioned hall, they were assailed by 90-degree heat and both complained bitterly.

It was customary for the class to all pile in the 4WD vehicles available when going on field trips, but Frank explained that there was no need for rugged transportation since they would be driving up I-8, yet some couples did double up, to save gas, as usual, while Kathy and Cindy rode with Frank, as they always had.

"You'll get used to the heat," he said as they pulled out of the parking lot. "I want you to become familiar with the people and places around Ocotillo, because you, Kathy, will be seeing a lot of these retirees at the café if you get hired. Cindy, if you go with me exploring the outback while your mom is working, you'll have to get toughened in and wear practical clothes. Your tennis shoes are okay if you watch your step."

Kathy was thinking aloud. "Assuming I get hired, I'll be working inside where it's cool, and assuming we'll be living with you until I get on my feet, I think we should set some ground rules."

"Like what?" Frank glanced at Kathy.

"Well, if we do housework and make meals," Kathy reasoned, "will I have to pay rent too? If I'm on my feet all day, I'll be dead tired when I come home. Slinging hash all day and possibly getting a lunch break, making meals for you and Cindy would be awful hard to do."

"You worry too much," Frank tried to put her fears to rest. "I see where you're coming from, Kathy, but I wouldn't expect you to make meals for us since I've always fixed something simple or eaten at the Roadrunner. And depending on your hours, Cindy and I might drop in for a burger or something. And as far as you paying rent, no! When we talked about that before, I said you could live at my place rent free, so you could save money and support yourself. Does that answer your questions?"

"Yes and no," Kathy replied. "There' something else about your expectations."

"My expectations? Do you mean my intentions? Just what do you mean? I thought we had everything settled. My offer had no strings attached. I felt sorry for you."

"Yes, and I appreciate all you've done to help us, but..."

"But what?"

"You and Cindy will be together a lot."

Frank reached for a cigarette. "Oh, I see. Well, we'll talk about that later."

Cindy, who was looking straight ahead through the windshield as the small caravan sped up the grade, finally spoke up. "Mom. If Frank and I find Peg-Leg-Pete's black nuggets, we'll all be rich. Then you won't have to work anymore."

"Atta girl," Frank grinned at her remark. He knew that Kathy was worried about him and Cindy making out if they were alone together so much, but now as she sat beside him, their bodies touching, his thoughts took wing and he imagined a scenario that sent shivers to his groin. He visualized her in bed, naked, and he was kissing her youthful lips passionately while her tongue darted in and out of his mouth and her left hand was feeling its way down his abdomen. So real was his illusion that he almost climaxed, he let out a little war whoop that seemed out of place. But when Cindy asked him what that was for, he lied and said he was so excited anticipating her remark that they would all be rich when they found the black nuggets that he couldn't contain himself.

Now, as they pulled off the highway, he put out his cigarette in the ashtray and glanced at the rear view mirror. Jay and Geoff were right behind him in the red Jeep; Pierre was with Susan in her Datsun; Billie and Russ Dalton were close behind in their yellow 1974 Chevy pickup, and Al and Juanita Hyer brought up the rear.

When they stopped off-road in a cloud of dust, Frank jumped out and went back to the Jeep. "Where's the rest of the class?" He asked Jay, but Jay said he guessed some of them had not wanted to go out because of the heat. Now, as everyone exited their vehicles and were congregating around Jay and Frank, Jay announced that they would make it back to the cave only to confirm Frank's discovery, and if it panned out, they would plan a major exploration at a later date, as he wanted to search for artifacts south of Nomirage today.

Kathy and Cindy were standing by Frank's pickup, debating whether or not to hike in with the group. "I don't feel like it," Kathy said.

"We've already been up there, and it's so darn hot." Cindy agreed. "We can sit in the truck. At least we'll be out of the sun."

"How far back is the cave, Frank?" Jay asked so everyone could hear him, and when Frank said it was about a mile, many of the group decided not to take their lunches. But when they started the short trek, they were all carrying canteens and several had their trusty binoculars slung around their necks. Juanita Hyer wore a big floppy hat, while mostly they were hatless.

Within fifteen minutes the group had reached the promontory where the cave lay hidden above them. When Frank stopped and told Jay where the entrance was located, and pointing up in the rocks, Jay understood why this cave had lain undiscovered all those years. "Who'd ever climb up there to investigate?" He wondered aloud. "The whole hillside looks like a huge pile of rocks."

"Yeah," Frank said as the others gathered around him and Jay. "We gotta climb over a lot of them and it ain't going to be easy."

Juanita Hyer was the first to voice her disdain. "I'll just wait down here," she scoffed. "Thanks, but no thanks."

All of the women except Susan Rider refused to climb the rock face, but all the men except Pierre Miles, were eager to make the climb. Susan took a swig from her canteen, then laid it on the ground, as she wanted to make herself as unencumbered as possible. Seeing her, the men climbers did likewise. Frank had not brought his .44 Mag with him today, and only Jay had a flashlight.

On the way up through the maze of boulders, Susan narrowly escaped being bit by a rattler, but she spotted it before she put her foot down. "Snake over here!" She called out to warn the others.

When at last the party had reached the summit, with Frank leading the way, he stopped and pointed at the entrance to the cave. As the others gathered around to look, Jay exclaimed with awe, "I'll be damned! You weren't kidding, Frank."

Russ Dalton peered down at the hole silently, but Geoff Weisse moved closer to gawk. "Hey Frank," he said. "This is where the skulls are?"

Frank would lead the way with Jay close behind. The others would follow. Jay handed the flashlight to Frank who dropped into the hole and moved laterally into the tunnel. As Frank had told them initially, the tunnel widened the deeper they went. About 10 feet inside, the light fell on the walls of a larger room, and when Frank waved the flashlight, it lit up the skulls.

At first, there were cries of surprise, then nervous laughter. "Oh no!" Susan wailed.

"God damn!" Said Russ.

Geoff sounded off with a snort of surprise. "Holy Cow! This must be the Devil's Den."

Frank and Jay stood transfixed, looking ahead at the macabre sight. "What do you think of it, Jay?" Frank finally asked.

But Jay was at a loss for words. "I don't know...I..."

Susan's voice cut him off abruptly. "Let's get out of here. This is too spooky."

Everyone turned to exit the catacomb amidst excited chatter, but as they emerged into daylight, they were bombarded with questions from those who were waiting outside. "Did you see any skulls? How far did you go in?" Everyone was asking questions or answering them.

Frank was the last to climb down through the rocks. He handed the flashlight back to Jay, grinning. "You didn't believe there could be another cave up here, did you?"

Jay shook his head. "No, but we learn something new every day. I'm at a loss to explain those skulls. I noticed that the air in there was not too dank. It seemed to be moving slightly. You know what I think? There must be another opening lower down. Air tends to rise, as in a chimney. This cave must extend down the mountain, and the opening we went in is where the air comes out."

Frank was nodding. "That makes sense. I have a gut feeling that as you say, there's a chimney effect. That tunnel could go down a mile." He reached for a cigarette.

Susan, who was picking up her stuff, saw Frank lighting up and smiled. "I'm dying for a smoke." Frank grinned at her, barely nodding.

"Frank." Jay said demurely, "I just thought of something. I noticed when you shone the light on those skulls that there was a red glow emanating from the eye sockets. There's an old garnet mine up by the Smuggler's cave where the Indians could have gotten plenty of it, and I would guess that what we saw was garnets imbedded and arranged somehow in the sockets. What do you think?"

Frank blew a cloud of smoke, glancing over at Susan, who was now lighting up as she talked to Geoff. "I didn't know about the garnet mine, but what you say make sense. Anything is possible."

Jay was reaching for a cigarette as he looked up at the rock face. He had another theory. "There isn't much doubt that the skull thing is the work of

Indians," he said, "but as far as I know, none of the tribes around here collected and displayed skulls. Not the Cahuillas, the Yumans nor the San Dieguitans. However, if any tribe is suspect, it would be the San Dieguitans. They ranged from here to the coast, all at higher elevations."

"San Dieguitans?" Frank frowned. "Was San Diego named after them?"

Jay was lighting his cigarette. "I think so, but I'm not sure."

Of the entire group, only three smoked: Susan Rider, Jay Bradford and Frank Kelly, but many of the others were former smokers who had quit. Those who had quit were now intolerant of smokers. Russ Dalton wasn't too bad, although he liked to make anti-smoking jokes, but Al Hyer was a real radical. He had smoked for many years and then quit, and to hear him talk, smoking was even worse than blasphemy. He was extremely egotistical and thought he was God's gift to women, and he often endured Jay's smoke to get close to him, since he believed that Jay's fame as an archaeologist would rub off on him. Now as the group had descended from the rock face and stood talking, he sidled up to Jay with his thoughts on the tip of his tongue.

"You know what I think?" He began, "I believe that those skulls have some significance beyond the obvious. They may have been placed there to scare off anyone entering the cave, meaning that there is something of great value lying beyond, or they may be the work of some Devil worship culture. But in all probability, they had something priceless they wanted to protect."

Jay was nodding in assent. "Good possibility, Al. What I think we should do is to organize a search party. Go in well equipped and see what's down there." He glanced at his watch. "Right now, I'd like to go down and map out the area I told you about earlier."

Billie and Russ Dalton were already sauntering towards the cars where Kathy and Cindy waited, and Juanita was waiting for Al to stop talking, while Susan puffed away as she talked to Geoff.

"Okay," Jay announced finally. "We confirmed that there was a cave, as Frank said, and that there were skulls. Sometime in the near future, we'll come back to explore it thoroughly. We'll go back to our vehicles and eat lunch, then go down by Nomirage."

On the way down, Frank and Jay led the group, talking about the cave, with the others straggling behind. But when they arrived back at the cars, Kathy and Cindy were sweating it out in the pickup. They were hungry and thirsty. When Frank told them that the others were going to eat here and then go down to Nomirage, they were averse to the idea. They had had enough of the heat for one day and didn't feel like walking out in the hot sun.

"Why can't we go to the café?" Kathy said. "I'd like to see if Brian will hire me."

"Yeah," Cindy chimed, "I want to get a hamburger and a Pepsi. Mom, I've got three dollars yet. I'll pay for yours if I have enough."

Frank had already planned on eating at the café since they hadn't brought lunches from home. He smiled at Cindy as he got in beside her. "Hey, lil girl," he quipped. "Don't you worry about paying for it."

When he started the engine and turned the pickup around, he yelled at Jay as he headed out. He told Jay to honk as the group drove past the café, then he would meet them at the site down Highway 98. Ten minutes later, they arrived at the Roadrunner.

"I've got butterflies in my stomach," Kathy said as they went inside. "I'm getting nervous." But Rita greeted Frank at the counter, asking if he knew she was quitting. "Yeah. Brian told me last time we were in." Rita had plenty of time to talk, as the noon crowd had left and there were few people in the restaurant.

"I hear you're getting married," Frank said to make small talk. "Who's the lucky guy?" Brian came out of the kitchen just then, carrying a tray of clean dishes. Sliding the tray under the counter, he saw Frank and interrupted Rita's conversation.

"Hey, Frank. How they goin?" Brian glanced at Kathy.

Frank shrugged. "So-so. Can't complain much." He looked sideways at Kathy and back. "I think I've got a new waitress for you." He jerked his thumb towards Kathy. "Friend of mine. Kathy Winters."

"Great!" Brian smiled, looking at Kathy now. "Experienced?"

Kathy nodded. "Six years."

"Can you work odd hours if necessary?"

"No problem."

"Could you start tomorrow morning at five? I'd like some time to break you in."

"Yes."

"Okay. I'll give you a form to fill out before you leave. You can bring it back in the morning."

When Brian left, Kathy turned to Frank. "That was easy. I feel better now." She looked sideways at Cindy. "We got a job, hon." Rita came back to take their orders, returned again to talk to Frank and Kathy, but when it came time to leave, neither Kathy or Cindy wanted to go back with the group and walk in the hot sun. Frank agreed to take them back to his place, whereupon he would drive back alone, to join the class.

That evening, however, after Cindy had gone to bed, Kathy and Frank sat watching the news when Kathy broached the subject of Cindy being alone with Frank while she would be working. "I didn't want to talk about it this morning in front of Cindy," Kathy reminded Frank, "but there are several issues I'd like to get cleared up if we're going to be living with you temporarily."

"Well of course," he said, "The ground rules."

"Yes. The boundaries and expectations."

Frank jumped up to turn the television off. "Expectations? You mentioned that this morning. What do you mean?"

"Well, okay. I don't have to pay rent? I don't have to make meals or do housework? I don't have to go out in the boondocks with you?"

Frank nodded. "Right. You don't have to do any of them. I don't expect you to."

"Okay. But living together...living so close in the same house...you expect me to...to pay in some other way?"

Frank stopped to think about what she meant. He reached for a cigarette. "I'm not sure what you mean," he said," but if you mean what I think you mean, the answer is no. I don't expect that."

"I just don't want anyone to own me," she said, "I just don't want to be obligated to anyone. My boyfriend, Eric, thought he owned me, and I don't want that to ever happen again."

Frank now understood more about Kathy than he had anticipated. He realized that she didn't want him to feel he would be master over her, or that he could expect sex as payment for his hospitality. She didn't rule out sex, per se, but that it didn't come with the territory.

"I understand where you're coming from," he said as he lit his cigarette, "so everything is settled. Right?"

"One more thing," she thought aloud. "Cindy. I worry about her because she is so boy-crazy now. With you and her being alone together all day, something could happen, and I have enough problems to worry about already."

"Oh that!" Frank said in a cloud of smoke, "You don't have to worry about us. I'll keep her so busy she won't have time to think of boys, but if you worry about me doing something, forget it. My God, Kathy, I'm 40 years old and she's just a child. What kind of a guy do you think I am?"

"But she comes on to guys," Kathy reminded him. "She's the aggressor. I think I can trust you, but I don't trust her. She's a little devil when it comes to boys. Remember when we came back from El Centro and she was flirting with Don Shuger?"

"Yeah. She had prettied up for him. She looked very nice, very mature."

"Well, the question is, what would you do if she came out of the shower in the morning, wearing a towel, and she came on to you?"

"Well, I'd..." Frank could picture this scenario in his mind, and it bothered him. It would be something he could only dream about, a situation he would die for. What <u>would</u> he do? What would he <u>really</u> do if it happened and they were alone in the house?

"What would you do, Frank? I have to know."

Frank was nervous. He knew what she wanted to hear. "Well, ah, I, ah...ah...I would tell her to go get dressed. And if she persisted. I'd slap her silly. I'd tell her that I wouldn't tolerate her behavior. No, you don't have to worry about me. Kathy. I'll keep her so busy she won't have time to think of flirting."

Kathy smiled and got up from her chair. "I feel better about it now," she said. "Our staying here is a gift. You're doing it out of the goodness of your heart."

"That's right. When you first came up to get water, I didn't like it. I hated to have people asking for help. But you and Cindy were so...so pathetic. I felt sorry for you. I empathized with you. It was kinda a there-but-for-the-grace-of-God-go-I thing. I helped you as I would want to be helped if I found myself in a similar situation. And you can stay here with no strings attached, until you can support yourself."

Kathy took one-step towards her bedroom, then stopped to look at Frank. "You're a nice guy and I'm getting to like you," she said. "I'll do what I can to help out here, but I just wanted to set things straight."

"You got it," he smiled. "Kinda a business deal. Serious but no hanky panky. Right?"

"Well..." Her voice was warm and friendly. "Good night, Frank."

Frank got up and shoved his hand toward her. "Business deal. Shake on it." Kathy extended her hand and grasped his. This was the first time he had ever touched her, and he felt something. He felt like he wanted to kiss her.

"Good night, Kathy."

CHAPTER FIVE

Dawn was breaking over the desert and the crescent moon was low over the Jacumba mountains to the west. The only sounds were the occasional creaking of the house and the far off yelping of the coyotes. Kathy had left for work in the dark and Cindy lay half-asleep in her shorty nightgown. Frank was sound asleep, lying naked on his bed, with open window and door ajar.

Because of the stifling heat and lack of air-conditioning, it was common practice to sleep in the nude with open doors and windows, to obtain maximum air circulations. When Kathy got ready for work, she had tried to be as quiet as possible, lest she wake up Frank, but sleeping in the same bed as Cindy; it was inevitable that Cindy would awaken.

Drifting in and out of consciousness, she lay listening to the coyotes and thinking about Kathy's new job. Today would be the first day she would be alone with Frank, and he had promised to take her along when he explored the outback, looking for Peg-Leg-Pete's black nuggets.

In the faint predawn light, she opened her eyes and looked up at the window, where she could see the pale moon in the brightening sky. An hour later, she was wide-awake and restless. She could see that the sky was bright, now, with the rising sun. Deciding to get up, her first stop was the bathroom, but when she came out, she peeked into Frank's bedroom where she saw him lying nude, sound asleep.

Shocked at first, her curiosity was overwhelming. Transfixed, she stood motionless, staring. With a quickening heartbeat, she watched his eyes; afraid he might waken and see her. Trembling in fascination, imagination running wild, she visualized herself stealthily going over and touching his thing. What would it feel like? Would it get bigger and hard?

With only a rudimentary knowledge of male genitalia, things she had heard from other girls at school, and from things she saw when her mom and Eric were living together, she had a fairly good idea of how things worked, but she longed for hands-on experience.

Frank suddenly moved, shifting his position. Thinking he was going to get up, she ducked back in the hallway and walked toward the front door. She would go out on the porch and feel the cool morning air under her flimsy nightgown.

Standing on the wooden floor barefoot, she looked out over the sandy landscape and saw cars speeding along the main highway in the distance. Inhaling the cool air, she spread her arms wide and brought her shoulders back squarely. Reveling in the stillness and remoteness, she considered removing her nightgown and prancing around naked, as she often did when she was alone, but she didn't want to take the chance that Frank might get up and see her through the kitchen window.

Inhaling deeply and exhaling, she brushed a strand of hair back and sauntered over by Frank's rocking chair to gaze out over his well and east toward El Centro, when a movement in the bushes caught her attention. Galvanized, she sunk slowly onto the seat, her eyes riveted on the bushes. Minutes passed. She sat motionless, wondering what was out there.

As time passed, she was almost ready to give up when the bushes moved again. Now, her eyes focused intently on the creosote shrubs. First, she saw grey fur, then she saw two baby coyotes emerge into view. They were on their way to their den under the house, playing with each other along the way.

She smiled in amusement. They were so cute. Remaining seated on the edge of the rocker, she sat motionless, but when they disappeared from her sight, she got up to go back in the house.

Once inside, she marched straight down the hall. She would take a much-needed shower before Frank got up, but when she pushed the bathroom door open, she was met with a roar. "Hey!" He bellowed. He was drying off with a towel and hadn't heard her coming. "What the hell are you doing?" He said angrily. "Are you in a habit of walking in on people when they're in the bathroom?"

"I didn't know you were in there," she admitted truthfully. "I thought you were still sleeping."

Frank had quickly covered himself with the towel, but the sudden unexpected intrusion was provocative. Cindy said she had already seen what he was trying to hide, and she observed that Frank was "bigger" than Eric, Kathy's significant other. This infuriated Frank.

"Get the hell outta here," he thundered, "Or I'll put you out."

She didn't move. "I don't know why you're so mad. Eric used to say that the human body was beautiful. he and mom were naked around the house a lot and sometimes I was too."

"Look, kid, I'm not used to people talking back to me, and when I tell someone to do something, by God, they better do it or I'll…" His voice hung on the air.

"You'll do what?" She fairly smirked, staring him down.

Frank's eyes shot daggers at Cindy. Letting it all hang out, he dropped the towel and jabbed his finger at her face. "On the count of three, if you don't leave, I'll put you out forcibly. One…two…three…" When she didn't move, he quickly grabbed her by the shoulders and started pushing her out.

"Stop it, you're hurting me," she pled in fear. "Stop it, Frank. Ow. Ow. Stop it or I'll kick you where it hurts."

As they wrestled, his hands were all over her torso as she squirmed and flung her hands up around her chest. "You do and you won't live to tell about it," he threatened, "now move or I'll pick you up and carry you out."

"Stop it Frank," she raised her voice. "Stop it or I'll tell mom you tried to rape me."

Her words struck him like a bullet. Glimpsing himself in the large wall mirror, he saw this naked man hurting a little girl. This was him? The word "rape" struck terror in his heart. He had heard many stories about men forcing themselves on unwilling girls, and society viewed this as one of the most despicable things men could do. If she told Kathy, there would be no doubt. This was exactly what he and Kathy had talked about last night, and to make matters worse, he had even used the words, "I'd slap her silly."

Frank was in deep trouble. Cindy now had bruises to prove her case. As all these things flashed through his mind, he was suddenly filled with remorse and sorrow. The fear he felt exceeded any he had experienced in Viet Nam when he faced death in the jungles. Cindy had a weapon, now, that was more devastating than a 30.06. She could bring him down in a minute.

Trembling, Frank released her and offered an apology. "God, Cindy, I don't know what came over me," he said sorrowfully. "You didn't do anything wrong. When you came in, I wasn't expecting you. It startled me, I guess. You were right about the body being beautiful. I've always believed that. I know that everyone is touchy about nudity, but it's really no big deal. I think the best way to handle this is to kiss and make up, as it were."

A grin crept over Cindy's mouth. "Okay." She put her hands on his shoulders and puckered up expectantly. He pecked her on the cheek. "No-no," she said. "On the lips."

Kissing her was fulfilling his dream and satisfying a teen's lust for romance, yet it went against his promise to Kathy that he would try and stifle any and all advances on her part, and it was contrary to society's rules against adults taking advantage of children. Frank realized he shouldn't have used the term, kiss-and-make-up, even though he meant it figuratively, for it allowed her to take it literally. And he did kiss her on the lips only to pacify her.

At the moment, he would do anything to make amends, since she had the power to destroy him. she could bring shame and even prison time upon him, just by saying a few words. That was now, but the threat could be used over and over if she decided to use it. The entire ugly incident, though inadvertent, made Cindy his master for as long as she lived with him.

"Okay, hon," he said cajolingly. "I want to get dressed. You go ahead and shower or whatever. I've got some ideas…some things we can do today." He reached to retrieve his shorts and moved towards the doorway. "Your mom and I had a good talk last night after you went to bed. She was worried about leaving you alone with me while she was at work."

Cindy's hair was in disarray from the struggle, and she brushed it back with her hand. "She doesn't trust me, I'll bet. She's always yelling at me. She's afraid I might get pregnant."

"Well, we'll talk about it later," Frank said as he headed for his bedroom. But as he dressed, his thoughts concerned both girls. From the moment they had arrived at his place, he had dreamed of bedding one or both of them, but he knew the odds were against him. Last night as he talked to Kathy, she had warmed up to him and today, the explosive confrontation with Cindy had led to physical contact with her.

He had not only touched her, but kissed her, and that kiss lingered on his lips. He believed that this boy-crazy girl would be an easy conquest, yet the consequences could cost him everything he had; his way of life, his freedom and his reputation.

"My God," he thought to himself. "She and I went form virtual strangers to extreme intimacy in ten short minutes. She saw me naked, we talked about nudity, we touched and kissed, and we both learned a lot about each other." Frank, in retrospect, had enjoyed the ordeal, but he worried about Kathy. If she found out about them in the bathroom, she would hit the roof, probably kill him.

A few minutes later, Frank was in the kitchen, making toast and waiting for Cindy to come out. A glance at the clock told him it was 8:00 am. Looking out through the open window, his gaze swept over the front yard, from the gas pump to his pickup. Kathy's Pontiac was gone, of course, and he wondered how she was doing.

When his thoughts were interrupted by Cindy's presence, he turned to extract two pieces of toast. "Oh, you're dressed," he smiled. "Did you ever shoot a gun?"

She was wearing white shorts and a green top. Her hair was combed back but still damp and she looked fresh as early morning dew. "I shot a small pistol one time," she explained as she sat down by the table. "Eric used to take his gun with us when we went to the dump, and he let me shoot it once. Why do you ask?"

Frank was buttering the toast, "I just thought it would be fun. Did you see that little .22 rifle behind the front door? We could do some plinking. I've got a lot of tin cans and beer bottles."

He shoved the plate of toast in front of her and reached for two more slices of bread. "Another thing we could do today would be to hike up toward Coyote mountain. There's a gold claim I could show you."

"A gold claim? Are there any gold nuggets lying around?"

Frank smiled. "There's an old guy, name's Clanahan, he's staked out several claims around here, mostly around Shell Canyon. I ran into one of them about two weeks ago. Wanna see it?"

After they had eaten, Frank gathered the rifle and cartridges, and they went outside. Setting bottles and cans as targets, he showed Cindy how to hold and shoot the gun, but she couldn't hold it high enough with her left arm.

"You're shooting low," he said. "Hold it straight out. Don't let it sag." Finally, after three tries, he stood behind her to the left and cuddled up against her back, with one hand on her shoulder and the other supporting her left arm. "Get the sights lined up and then pull the trigger," he said soothingly. "Squeeze the trigger slowly and firmly. Don't jerk."

Cindy finally got the hang of it and could send the tin cans sailing. She was enjoying her newfound entertainment very much when Frank set up two beer bottles at 30 yards. When she hit them, they exploded, and she'd cry out in excitement.

After an hour of shooting, however, both of them were tiring of it. The sun was climbing higher and it was getting warmer there behind the house. He suggested that they put the rifle away and hike up to Clanahan's gold claim, Cindy wanted to see.

"It's only two or three miles," Frank said, "And we can be back before it gets too hot, because you are not used to this extreme heat."

Before they left, Frank strapped on his .44 Mag Smith & Wesson, filled his canteen with fresh water and stuffed a plastic grocery bag into his back pocket. Cindy looked out of place in her white shorts and green top. Bare headed, she looked like the city girl she was, and when Frank offered her one of his caps, she refused.

As they trudged through the creosote bush covered sand toward Coyote mountain, vultures soared above, and heat waves, like a mirage, shimmered in the distance. But when they neared the base of the mountain, they could see the opening to a mine among the rocks.

"See that?" He pointed. "That's one of Clanahan's gold claims."

When they got close to the mineshaft, Cindy peered inside, while Frank studied the footprints in the sand. Someone had been here quite recently, he thought. Probably wetbacks. He told Cindy that illegals often hid out in abandoned mines where they could get out of the sun, and he showed her the claim registry in a tin can on a post.

Cindy was kicking idly at stones near the entrance, and she bent down to pick one up. "Could this be one of Peg-Leg-Pete's black nuggets?" She wondered aloud. It was heavy, golf-ball size and was black. Yet it appeared to be ordinary limestone.

"Could be," he agreed. "You never know."

"Well, I'm going to take it home," she enthused, picking up several more. Frank pulled the plastic bag from his pocket and told her to put the stones in it, but he took one and scratched it with his pocketknife. He saw yellow.

Could this really be what he had searched for in the months since he had lived in the desert? There was always the chance of a fluke, an accidental discovery. "Hmmm," he mused aloud. "Wouldn't it be something if this really was a nugget?"

"Frank. It's getting awful hot," Cindy piped up. "Can we head back? I'm getting hungry and thirsty." Frank offered his canteen but she refused it. He took a swig and replaced it on his belt. With her carrying the bag, they started back, but took a different route. They were now headed toward a cluster of trees and thick underbrush, a short distance from the houses of Ocotillo.

"I want to show you something, hon," he said pointing. "See that little house among those trees? That's one of Plaster City's wells. They pump the water out there and pipe it to their drywall factory on the old highway you and your mom came through just before you had car trouble."

The pump house, a fair-size building of corrugated metal, had an 8-inch discharge pipe protruding from the east side, from which they would flush the well at certain intervals. Over the years, this water formed a pond of crystal-clear water surrounded by lush vegetation whose roots took advantage of the unlikely source of moisture. It was a place where hikers would seek, or sometimes boys and girls would come to carve their initials on the big yellow palo-verde.

When Cindy saw this little oasis, she looked around in wonderment. The pond had natural sandy beaches, was three feet deep at the most, and sparkled invitingly. She bent down to test the water's temperature. "This is cool," she said, not referring to the water. "It reminds me of the Garden of Eden. "You know what I'm thinking, Frank?"

Frank grinned. "I hope it's not what I think you're thinking."

Cindy nodded. "It is! Why not? I'm so hot and sweaty. The water is warm, Frank. I feel like jumping in.'

He chuckled. "Well, you go right ahead, kiddo."

"No, I mean like skinny dipping," she protested. "Why can't we?"

"Because. Just because!" He spoke with determination. "Cindy, I'm supposed to protect you. I don't want any more temptation. If you really want to have a swim, go right ahead, but leave your under-things on."

"No, I can't," she answered, "I'm not wearing anything underneath. It's too hot."

"Well, dammit, I'll turn my back while you undress and go in."

Frank knew that things were moving too fast. He and this 16 year old had had enough intimacy this morning to last a while, and if Kathy ever learned about their shenanigans, she would blow up. He could still hear her plea last night: What would do if Cindy came on to you? What would you really do? But he knew in his heart that there was a breaking point, that given enough temptation, he might succumb.

"Okay, Frank, I'm in." She called out. "The water feels so good."

He turned to see her nakedness outlined imperfectly under the clear water as she flailed her arms in reckless abandon. With her large boobs fairly floating under her, he was surprised at their size for such a young woman, yet it engendered thoughts of holding her close and pressing his chest against her voluptuous bosom.

The water looked so inviting that Frank wished he could strip down and join her. They could rub their bodies together, their arms encircling each other and maybe they could kiss under the water. But despite the thought, he waited patiently while she played like a child, splashing and thrashing with glee.

After watching her having fun for a long time, he glanced at his watch to see that it was noon already. The thought that truth was stranger than fiction was not lost on him, as he pondered the irony of their relationship. When she and her mother had arrived at his place and asked for help, he was taken aback with their erotic beauty. He had watched their hips swivel as they walked to his well, and he had dreamed of the possibility of bedding one or both of them.

With today's experiences, Cindy's attitude about nudity and a host of other things, he believed that he could fornicate with her if he tried. But the irony was that if he could, he couldn't. Because of his promise to Kathy and because of societies constraints.

"Okay, Cindy," he said to get her attention. "Let's go. You're hungry and so am I. Let's go back to the house and get my pickup. Let's go and see how your mom is doing and have a burger. How does that grab you?"

"That's cool."

"I'll start walking and you can get dressed," he said. "You can catch up with me."

When they got back to Frank's place, Cindy's hair was a mess from submerging in the pond. She threw the bag of rocks onto the porch and went to the bathroom to freshen up and comb her hair, while Frank removed his pistol and canteen, but before they left, he threw the bag into the truck bed with the other junk.

On the way to the restaurant, Cindy said that she had enjoyed her swim and would like to go back sometimes to do it again. But then she came up with a devilish joke she would like to pull on Kathy. If her mom asked what they had been doing all morning, she would tell her that they had found the black nuggets, and would soon be rich.

Frank chuckled. "Good idea. Maybe we can get a few laughs out of it."

The Roadrunner Restaurant was full of people when they arrived and went in. There were locals sitting at tables, Border Patrolmen at the counter, a couple of truckers and tourists. Kathy and Rita were frantically trying to serve everyone, and Brian was manning the cash register. Frank looked in vain for two seats, when he noticed a couple picking up their guest check.

Moving towards the table, which was directly behind those men at the counter, he was quick to claim the spot and sat down even before the dirty dishes were removed. There would obviously be a long wait for service.

As the minutes passed, Kathy finally spotted Cindy and she gave her a quick smile and a brief wave of acknowledgement. Frank lit a cigarette and relaxed patiently, but his idle gaze fell on the man sitting close by at the counter. Wasn't that Clanahan?

Frank didn't know Clanahan. He had seen him at the Eagle Talon Saloon down the road a few times, but he had heard many stories of his adventures and exploits. Everyone in town knew him as a crazy old prospector who owned claims around the valley, but few wanted to engage him in conversation because his long-winded narratives were boring. To hear him talk, he had been prospecting around these parts for twenty years and had made fabulous discoveries, but the guy drove an old run down Chevy van, dressed like a bum and was overbearing.

Seeing a man from behind, Frank couldn't be sure, but the more he looked, the more certain he became. It was Clanahan, all right. Now, as his gaze wandered, he spotted Ralph Smith, deputy sheriff of Imperial County, sitting at the counter far to the right. Everyone in the valley loved Ralph Smith. He was a handsome, congenial and helpful sheriff, and he would drive around town at night, looking for illegal aliens. Always cooperating with the Border Patrol, always stopping to talk to the elderly citizens, he was the most liked and most popular sheriff ever assigned to the Ocotillo sector.

Frank blew a cloud of smoke and told Cindy, "I'm starving. I wish they'd hurry up."

Cindy agreed. "Me too. It looks like some of the people are leaving now. I hope mom waits on us."

A young Mexican dishwasher was pushing a wheeled cart among the tables, collecting dirty dishes and wiping the tables clean, and when he came to Frank's table, he took the ashtray and left a clean one. Rita came over to take their orders and remarked that she had never seen it so busy as it was today. Then she said that Kathy was doing very well and that Brian was pleased with her.

Ralph Smith had got up to leave and spoke to Frank as he passed. "Hi, Frank. Have you found anything interesting, lately?"

Frank smiled. "Sure. We just found Peg-Leg-Pete's black nuggets this morning" Ralph broke into a grin, chuckling at the joke.

"Yeah, sure. Who's this little doll?" He nodded towards Cindy. "Your girlfriend?"

"I could be so lucky," Frank joked. "Cindy, this is our sheriff. His name is Ralph. if you ever rob a bank, he'll come after you."

They all laughed, when Frank turned serious. "No, she's the new waitress's daughter. They are staying out at my place and my job is to take care of her while Kathy is working. You met Kathy this morning, didn't you?"

"Yeah, Rita introduced us." He moved towards the register. Making a lecherous grin, he told Frank, "Any time you want to trade jobs with me, just say the word. I'll take real good care of her."

Frank muttered under his breath, "Yeah, I'll bet!"

People were leaving now as Frank and Cindy sat eating, and as the crowd thinned, Kathy finally came to their table. Her first words were apologetic. She was so busy she couldn't get over here any sooner and she hoped that they wouldn't be so busy again.

"Whew! My feet are killing me." She pulled up a chair beside Cindy.

Cindy asked about the tips. "Are they good?"

Kathy smiled. "Oh, they're fabulous. Most of the people left two bucks and the sheriff left a fiver. The only thing hard for me is getting up so early. I wish I could get on a later shift."

Frank was grinning. Happy that she liked her job, he said, "I told you the tips were good, didn't I?"

Cindy cut in. "You must have put your mouth where the money is."

Kathy laid her hand on Cindy's arm. "You bet I did. I gave everyone a nice big smile and complimented as many as I could. When Rita introduced me to the sheriff, I told him that men in uniform were my weakness, and he hit on me."

Frank frowned. "What do you mean, hit on you?"

"Oh, it was nothing really. He just said his weakness was blonds. He asked if I was married and I told him, no, but then he said he came in often and he hoped he'd see more of me."

Frank felt a pang of jealousy, although he had no reason to be jealous. He didn't own Kathy, but he knew that Ralph was single and had the reputation of being a ladies man. It kind of rankled him.

Cindy was becoming impatient. She wanted to play a joke on her mother. "Mom," she blurted out, "We went out this morning and we saw a gold mine. We didn't go in, but we found Peg-Leg-Pete's black nuggets."

Kathy smiled in amusement. "That's wonderful. Now I can quit work. Right?"

Cindy hedged. "Well, I wouldn't say that. We have to sell them first. Frank said we'd have to have an expert look at them to see how much they're worth."

Clanahan was sitting quietly, smoking and dawdling over his coffee, but he swiveled around to face them now, obviously listening to their conversation. When Frank told Kathy that Cindy had picked up the stones and he had seen gold in them, Clanahan butted in rudely.

"Ain't you the fella I talked to down at the bar one night?"

Frank nodded. "Yeah, I remember talking to you."

Clanahan, speaking in his gruff voice said, "If'n you got a nugget, I kin tell ya in a minute if it's gold. They ain't nobody round these parts knows gold bettern me. I bin minin since I was knee-high to a grasshopper and I got claims all over this valley."

Looking at Clanahan face to face, Frank suddenly realized that this was the man who owned the claim where Cindy had picked up the rocks. If Cindy's stones contained gold-bearing quartz, they would legally belong to Clanahan. The situation could be embarrassing.

He told Cindy to go out and fetch the stones, and Kathy got up, saying she had to get back to work. While

Cindy went out to the pickup, Clanahan asked Frank, "Where'd you find em?" But Frank didn't answer, stalling by lighting a cigarette.

When Cindy returned, she sat the bag on the table in front of Frank, but Clanahan stood up, came over and grabbed the bag. When he peered inside, he pulled out one of the stones and looked at it. "Looks like some of the stuff I mined up at Coyote mountain," he sneered. "Ain't worth a tinker's damn." He reached in his pocket for his jackknife and scratched the stone, revealing a sparkling yellow color. He shoved it in front of Frank's face. "Iron pyrite," he said. "Lots of it around these parts."

Frank frowned in puzzlement. "Sure as hell looks like gold to me."

Clanahan nodded. "It is gold! Fool's gold. Fools just about everybody. That's why I wanted you to get a good look at it." He turned to leave. "Sorry, boy," he said as he walked away.

Cindy sat down and looked at Frank. "Our little joke fell flat, didn't it?"

Frank shrugged. "I guess."

Cindy smiled. "We'll find the real nuggets someday, won't we?"

He nodded and got up from the table. "Let's go home."

While Frank paid Brian, Cindy went over to Kathy and told her about the little joke they had planned, when Kathy asked what Clanahan had said about the rocks. "He said they were worthless, mom. We're going home now. I need a nap. We had a long hike this morning and I'm pooped. See ya later."

CHAPTER SIX

In the weeks that followed, Kathy was making good money at the café, and Ralph Smith came in often, since his designated beat was the Ocotillo area. That she liked him was no secret, but she also had a growing fondness for Frank, who treated her kindly, yet never romantically.

Frank and Cindy, spending a lot of time together in the outback, explored Painted George, Shell Canyon and Dos Cabezas Spring. They would take along lunch and water, of course, and Frank was always armed, but he also carried a shovel, pick and assorted items in his pickup, so they would be available if needed.

One day, as they climbed around the rocky outcropping of Shell Canyon, Cindy, poking around overhanging cliffs and crevices, found a suspicious looking package, which she showed to Frank, who suspected a drug cache. He decided to leave it untouched, but to notify the sheriff as soon as possible.

Driving through town, looking for Ralph Smith's Blazer, he drove on up to the café where he saw the Sheriff's vehicle. When he and Cindy went inside where the noon rush was over, they saw Kathy learning over the counter, laughing at Ralph's jokes, only a couple of feet from his face. They seemed to be very friendly, which again rankled Frank, as he approached them.

"Hi guys," he said to make them aware. "What's so funny?"

"Oh," Kathy said, still grinning. "He just told the cutest joke."

"Yeah?" Frank wore a quizzical expression. "Like what?"

"Hickory, dickory, dock. Two mice ran up her sock. The first one stopped at her garter, the second one was smarter. Hickory, dickory, dock." Kathy repeated the joke, still chuckling mirthfully. "Don't you think that's cute, Frank?"

Two things flashed through Frank's mind. Kathy and Ralph seemed to be a bit more friendly than one might expect between a waitress and her customer, and the subject's connotation seemed unusually intimate.

"Ah…I guess so." He looked at Ralph. "The reason we came in, Ralph, we were hiking up in Shell Canyon this morning, and Cindy stumbled onto a suspicious-looking package hidden down in the rocks. I told her not to touch it, because I thought it might be a drug stash. I thought you might want to investigate it."

"You bet!" Ralph was adamant. He stood up beside Frank, while Cindy sat on a nearby stool to rest. "The smugglers are using a new ruse now, Frank. The Calexico port of entry is getting too hot for them, and now they're bringing the stuff up on foot in small amounts and stashing them at collecting points. The runners pick up shipments in vans, and have clear sailing up S-2 to Riverside. No one stops them from there to L.A."

Frank reached for a cigarette. "They walk the stuff through the port of entry?" Ralph shook his head. "No, they come across down by Nomirage, around Highway 98. We think some of the stuff is coming across the border in the Mexican water trucks too. You know, they have freewheeling from Mexicali to the well. No one ever stops them, not even the Highway Patrol."

"I'll be damned." Frank said with a sad shake of his head. "Well, do you want to go up and have a look?"

Ralph suggested that they go up in the Blazer, with Frank leaving his pickup at the restaurant. When they went out the front door, they both went into the restroom, and Cindy was following close behind to the women's room opposite.

As they stood side by side at the urinals, Ralph posed a question. "Are ya bangin Kathy?"

Frank shook his head. "Nope."

"Why not?" Ralph smiled. "If she was living with me, I'd sure as hell be getting a lil. Does she pay you rent?"

Frank again shook his head. "Nope."

Ralph persisted. "How about the kid?"

Frank couldn't get angry at Ralph's questioning because this was the way men talked when they were alone. Not only that, but the questions reflected Frank's inner thoughts.

"Too young. Jail bait."

Ralph smirked. "It'd be worth the risk. I'll bet she'd go for it."

"Maybe. But if I knocked her up, I'd be in big trouble."

"Get yourself some condoms, Frank."

Before boarding the sheriff's Blazer, Frank got his pistol from his pickup and strapped it on his belt, but when Cindy tried to enter the vehicle, Ralph didn't think she should go along. There was no place for her to sit.

Cindy protested. "Maybe there's more packages hidden around there. We could spread out and search the area." Frank agreed, and Ralph told her she'd have to sit in the back.

The sheriff's vehicle was equipped with a short-wave radio, two-bucket seats flanking a locked-in shotgun, a spotlight, and emergency equipment. Cindy crawled back and tried to get comfortable. Silent at first, Ralph drove past the Stouffer well, and headed up Highway S-2, when he suddenly had an idea...

"Y'know Frank," he began, "this could be dangerous. If that package is part of a drug stash, there could be a shootout."

Frank agreed. "Yeah, them druggies play hardball. I thought of that. If they see this vehicle, they could panic."

As they climbed the grade in the sheriff's car, the 4WD Blazer groaned in second gear when they entered the canyon where steep walls rose high above them, but once through, the vista opened up to rocky crags, scattered boulders interspersed with brittle-bush and skinny ocotillos.

"This is the area we were in," Frank advised Ralph. "Park here."

When they got out, Frank checked his weapon while Cindy came alongside the sheriff. Pointing, she looked up through the side-canyon, which rose high above them. "We hafta climb up there," she told Ralph.

"Jeez," he said. "You picked a hell of a spot to find something."

The climb was slow and laborious. As they inched up through the boulders, they stopped to rest. "Yeah, the way I figure," Frank said, "If they spotted your vehicle and then see you up here wearing that uniform, there's gonna be some shooting."

"I realize that," Ralph nodded. "But it's a chance I have to take."

A few minutes later, they were near a small overhanging cliff and valleys, a dense stand of brittlebushes obscured the alpine meadow.

Cindy pointed. "Over there," she told the sheriff. "See those rocks. It's near them."

"I'll stand guard," Frank said. "You guys go on over and I'll cover you."

As they came to the spot where the package was hidden, Frank scanned the area for signs of men, but all he saw were a bunch of crows flying over. As Cindy revealed the spot, the sheriff looked around, then got down on his hands and knees to pull the package out. He hefted it and stared for a short time, feeling the texture.

"What are you looking at?" Cindy wondered, glancing at the three-foot long package.

But Ralph wore a look of puzzlement, calling Frank over. "I was looking for a booby trap, but this don't look like a drug stash. I'm going to open it."

The package was bulky, the wrapping seemed to be canvas, and when Ralph cut the string, the contents fell out. They all gasped in surprise. There was a cheap compass, an army surplus frying pan, salt and peppershakers, waterproof match container and a coil of nylon rope, all wrapped in canvas. But when they spread the canvas out, they saw it was a cheap pup tent.

"For Christ sake," Ralph said in amazement, "What the hell do you make of it, Frank?"

Frank began to chuckle. "Looks like somebody's camping gear."

Ralph nodded. "Obviously! But why would they stash this stuff here like this?"

"Kids," Cindy piped up. "I'll bet its young people from town. They probably got tired of lugging the stuff back and forth, so they hid it for future use."

Ralph nodded. "Makes sense." Frank was shaking his head. "Oh, boy. What a drug bust this turned out to be. Lucky we didn't call the DEA in on this. We'd be the laughing stock of the town."

While they put the camping gear back together and stuffed the package back in its hiding place, they began to think of the event as rather humorous. All grinning, they made light of the incident. They had approached the situation with suspicion and dark thoughts, but it had turned out to be much ado about nothing.

Returning to town, they passed the Stouffer well again, where Mexican water trucks were loading under the 6-inch overhead pipe. Several were sitting back in the salt cedar trees, waiting their turn to fill. As the sheriff's vehicle came even with the well, one of the loaded trucks pulled out in front of Ralph, water slogging from the fill hole on top.

"Look at that s.o.b." Ralph cursed. "Them guys think they own the road. Look at the water they're wasting. They fill them tanks so full that when they start or stop, the water sloshes out the fill hole."

"Yeah, it's a pain in the ass," Frank gasped. "We're doing everything we can stop them. Matter of fact, we've got a hearing with the Board of Supervisors in El Centro next month. We're trying to get a restraining order, but that damn Stouffer has a lot of clout. I think he's bribing the supes."

As they followed the truck down Imperial Avenue toward the café, Ralph told Frank something he hadn't known. The Sheriff's Department, working with the DEA, suspected that the Mexican Mafia might be using the water trucks to smuggle illegals and drugs into the United States. It would be the most clever ploy ever devised, because there was no inspection anywhere between Mexicali and Ocotillo. Once the cargo – humans or drugs – reached the well, they would have clear sailing up S-2, to Los Angeles.

"We suspect them, but so far, we don't have evidence," Ralph said. "But figure it out for yourself. The trucks are empty coming in. There's room for 25 or more people in one tanker. The open fill hole would provide enough air, especially when the vehicle is in motion. Of if they hauled drugs, they'd be able to carry tons at a time."

Frank was nodding thoughtfully. "For Christ sake. I never thought about that. Rather than risk a peon hauling fifty pounds of marijuana through the Calexico port of entry, they could circumvent our entire inspection program."

"You better believe it," Ralph stated as fact. "We've got a mole in Mexicali. If he sees actual loading, he will notify us. He will give us the truck number and license. We'll make the bust here at the well."

Now as they arrived at the café, Ralph got a call and had to leave, but Frank and Cindy exited the sheriff's car and were walking toward the entrance when Frank asked Cindy what she thought of the sheriff.

She said she kinda liked him. "He's a nice man. I think mom likes him too."

"Well I kinda like him too," Frank agreed. "But your mom has to be nice to everyone. That's part of her job and it helps with the tips." But Frank knew that Ralph was a ladies man and he knew that everyone around town liked him. He always had a ready smile, was never aloof like most law enforcement officers, and always congenial. At 48, he was the youngest sheriff on the force, and with his big brown eyes and dark hair over a white shirt, he was rumored to be popular with the younger women who frequented the Eagle Talon Saloon down the avenue.

"And I like him because he let me ride in the sheriff's car." Cindy enthused. But despite what Frank knew, he felt a pang of jealousy at the thought of Kathy and him. Yet, why he felt that way, he didn't know.

As they entered the Café, Frank got a big surprise. Sitting a table, Jay Bradford and his wife Sherilee looked up and smiled. Frank asked Jay what he was doing here, and he didn't see Jay's red Jeep outside. Jay said they were returning from San Diego where he visited the Museum of Man, seeking information on the skulls in the cave.

"I was looking for some historical evidence of Indian rituals and religious practices that might shed some light on the subject, but so far, I don't know any more than I did before."

Sherliee spoke up. "We don't drive around in that pile of junk."

"No," Jay nodded. "We drove over in our car."

Cindy was walking towards Kathy. She wanted a Pepsi. Frank yelled after her. He wanted a beer. Jay lit a cigarette, and Sherilee followed. It was obvious that they had just finished their meal. Frank pulled up a chair, glancing at Sherilee. Dressed nicely, she wore a gold pendant on a chain around her neck, just above her ample bosom, and it was inscribed with the S-word.

That word, in plain view, had always been a topic of wonder by everyone in Ocotillo. Jay and Sherilee were prominent citizens in El Centro and around the college campus, and since Jay was a rather famous archaeologist, anyone who saw her pendant was, at first sight, shocked. No one could understand why she wore it, except a few who believed it was a carry-over from her hippie days.

"Frank," Jay said, "We have made some changes in our Wednesday class. Word got out about the skulls in your cave and it hit the press. People are intrigued by the story, In fact, today in San Diego, Peter Williams, curator of the Museum of Man and an Egyptologist was so curious that he suggested we form an expeditionary party to explore the depths...the lower regions of the catacomb."

Kathy interrupted Jay when she brought Frank's beer and left a guest check for Jay. Frank thanked Kathy and asked Jay what he meant by an 'expeditionary party'. "Sounds big, like climbing Mount Everest with Sherpa guides."

"Look," Jay said as he flipped the ashes from his cigarette. "Peter and I Talked about it. When I described the cave and told him there was a movement of air, indicating a possible entrance further down, he warned me that this was no job for amateurs. You can get lost in a labyrinth. You can be trapped in the darkness if your light fails. Peter said that we might be underground for as much as two days; more if we have trouble."

Frank lit a cigarette and took a swig of beer, thinking. "I see," he said. "It makes sense...but...but won't that cost money?"

Jay nodded. "There's a lot of people interested in this thing. Because of the skulls and the unusual nature of the cave, the Museum is willing to foot the bill. But they want it to be professional. Peter will plan a head the expedition. Anyway, while we work on details, we'll have our class Wednesday as usual. Right now, we've got to get back to town." He and Sherilee moved to get up. While Jay went to the cash register, Frank remained at the table, sipping his beer and finishing his smoke.

Cindy, carrying her Pepsi, and Kathy, wearing her blue apron, came over and sat with Frank. Kathy wanted to know more about the package they had found earlier, and Cindy wanted to hear what Jay had said. But later, when Frank drove home, he and Cindy got a shock as they pulled into the yard. Over on the east side of the house laid the coyotes.

Cindy jumped out of the pickup and ran over to investigate. The mother coyote lay dead and one of the pups laid motionless a short distance away from her. The other pup was trying to crawl under the house.

"Oh no," she wailed. "Frank! Somebody killed our coyotes." She ran over to the live one and picked it up. "Oh you poor thing." The pup was barely alive and offered no resistance as she cuddled it in her arms. Frank told her the pup would probably die too. He said that the BLM had put out poison because there had been a rabies epidemic, and the El Centro police were shooting dogs that came over the border form Mexico.

Cindy was on the verge of tears and wanted to nurse the little coyote back to health, although Frank doubted that possibility. Nevertheless, Cindy wanted to get a cardboard box for the pup to sleep in, and she would give it milk. Maybe she could save it. Maybe she could make it a pet.

CHAPTER SEVEN

Wednesday dawned bright and clear. The sky was robin-egg blue, save for a few cirrus clouds moving in from Mexico at high altitude. It promised to be another scorching hot day.

Kathy had gone to work as usual, and Cindy was riding into Ocotillo with Frank, but when they arrived at the Community Hall, Jay's red Jeep was already there and cars crowded the parking area. Entering the Hall, they saw Jay standing by the long table in front of the class, and Frank, glancing over the room, saw many of the regulars – Susan Rider, Geoff Weisse, Al and Juanita Hyer and Pierre Miles – but there were some new faces here today.

Since the class was composed of elderly retirees, snowbirds and lonely singles, the makeup of the amateur archaeologists varied with the whims of the individuals. There were regulars and there were some that came sporadically. The new faces today belonged to Tom Goode and his wife, Janet, Bonnie Goldman, a widow, and Stevie Jensen with her second husband, Alvin.

"Well, I guess we're all here," Jay intoned with a glance at his watch. "You all know that I've been wanting to make a field trip up to Davies Valley, for some time now, but Frank's discovery of that cave has upset my plans. So today, we'll go up there and map out the Indian pictographs." He reached for a cigarette. "Now, ah…before I forget it, how many of you saw in the paper about the discovery of a horse head in the Anza-Borego?"

Most of the class raised their hands. "How about you, Frank?"

Frank shook his head, "I don't take the paper."

Jay lit his cigarette. "Well, my colleague, George Miller, uncovered a full sized horse head. It was well preserved, well fossilized, so there's no question as to what it is. But you know what? This discovery is going to change history."

"We've been taught that horses were brought over to this country by the Spaniards, but they were actually indigenous here as were the camel. It's true that the Spaniards brought horses, but it doesn't mean that they were not native hundreds of years ago."

Pierre Miles, looking over his bifocals, raised his hand, then spoke. "But from all this, it looks like horses became extinct here, and the Spaniards actually revived them. I think the horses we have running wild in Nevada are descendants of those the Spaniards brought."

"That's what I think," Susan Rider blurted out. "So, if all this is true, it still won't change history. Or at least not much."

Geoff Weisse waved his hand. "Who cares?"

Frank punched Cindy, chuckling audibly. Geoff's remark seemed quite fitting at the moment, but the way he said it brought smiles to many faces.

Jay blew a cloud of smoke, looking out over the class. "All right," he began. But seeing the smiles, he broke into a broad grin. "Well, so much for that. You made a good point, Geoff, but I always invite comments and criticism. Our interest, my interest, is in the past, in what lived here hundreds and thousands of years ago, how the ancients lived, and how this area has changed from eons ago."

Juanita Hyer raised her hand. "Jay. How far is Davies Valley from here?"

Jay looked down, frowning. "Oh golly," he said. "It's about...ah...well, I'd say it's about ten miles from here, maybe fifteen. We'll go down Highway 98, past Nomirage where we were last time, and head for Pinto Wash."

He advised the class to double up in the 4WD vehicles as the road into Davies Valley was almost impossible once they got up on the mountain. "Geoff will ride with me in the lead," he explained, "and the others can follow, but Frank, I wonder if you could bring up the rear?"

It was sometime later they were headed for Pinto Wash, on the lee side of the Jacumba mountains, a stones throw from the Mexican Border, and once across, the caravan swung up a secondary road, toward Skull Valley. Crude weather-beaten signs were visible in some places and Frank was quick to notice the latter sign. He wondered why they had named it Skull Valley. Was there some legend about skulls here?

Next, the caravan snaked around through rock studded steep inclines and took a left fork toward Davies Valley, but they were headed for a formidable crossing where a jagged monolithic granite promontory blocked their descent. It was impossible for an ordinary vehicle to cross-here, and just barely possible for a 4WD.

Jay and Geoff in the lead, were the first to cross the barrier. The little Jeep did well, but got hung up once, and Geoff and Russ Dalton got out to guide Jay and to push. As each vehicle encountered this hazard, the able-bodied men swarmed around it, guiding, pushing, sweating and swearing. Frank and Cindy were the last to cross, of course, Frank's big Dodge Power Wagon with its huge tires made it across the easiest of all the rest, because it had the biggest clearance of any of the others.

From here, Davies Valley could be seen with a bird's-eye view. Frank pointed through the windshield, telling Cindy how impressed he was by the expansive beauty that lay below them. As he followed the others, he told Cindy that he had always thought of Viet Nam as the most beautiful place in the world, but now, viewing this mile-wide rough slashed through the side of the mountain, he realized that it equaled Nam but in a different way. The jungles of Viet Nam were a maze of lush vegetation, with rivers and tiny streams and hot steamy ambience, while this desert's beauty lay in its wide-open vistas, dry heat and obtuse shapes.

As the caravan wound down into the valley, the rocky terrain gave way to a green alpine meadow where a tiny creek flowed silently.

When Jay parked in a flat area near the one-foot wide stream, the others parked nearby and got out. Some inspected their tires for rock damage, while others lugged out their backpacks, cameras and lunches. Juanita donned her floppy hat, Geoff adjusted his sunglasses, and Frank lit a smoke.

Frank and Cindy had brought brown-bag lunches like the others, and had a cooler in the back of his pickup, where Cindy was reaching for a Pepsi. Dressed in white shorts and a tank top, she was wearing sunglasses and tennis shoes.

Jay moved closer to the group. "It's about a mile hike up to Palm Grove," he said. "And as you can see, it's all uphill. Geoff is going to help me catalog the pictographs halfway up there and you can fan out and look for stuff in the rocks. There's some metates on the bigger rocks."

When they started uphill, following the creek, some wore backpacks and others had slung their cameras around their necks, but many just carried their lunches and thermos's in their hands. Cindy carried her and Frank's lunches in a plastic grocery bag along with a cold Pepsi, while Frank had his canteen on his belt.

Along the way, Susan Rider was just ahead of Frank and Cindy, and as the group would stop to admire a tiny flower, Susan would identify it, and it became obvious that she was well versed in the desert plant names.

At the halfway point up the grade, Jay and Geoff swung off to the right into the rocky field where the Indians had scratched pictographs on the rock faces hundreds of years ago, and the others followed. While Jay took compass readings and Geoff entered them in the logbook, the class meandered amongst the waist-high granite boulders seeking their own hieroglyphics.

Susan stopped beside a huge rock, glancing at Frank and pointing. "Look at that," she said in amazement. "Some Indian woman sat here grinding seeds into flour hundreds of years ago." She was looking at a metate, a mortar ground into the stone where a pestle was used to do the grinding. "They made flour out of all kinds of seeds and fashioned it into tortillas."

Cindy, up close and looking into a bowl-like depression, didn't understand what Susan was talking about. How could a woman grind seeds in this hole in the rock? Susan tried to explain it to her while Frank gazed off into the distance.

"This must have been a summer camp for the Indians," Susan said later. "Most seeds are produced in late summer or early fall. And the men had a lot of leisure time, obviously. Like people today, they scratched graffiti on these rocks just for the heck of it."

"Well, the Indians didn't have it too bad, then," Frank assumed aloud. "Living here in this beautiful valley, they didn't have to punch a clock like we do now. They had water year around, food from the plants and complete freedom, something we don't have today."

Bonnie Goldman was snapping a picture of Pierre Miles nearby, and Juanita was looking down at some flowers. Cindy saw a little lizard, then she spotted a roadrunner some distance away. This was the first roadrunner she had seen since her arrival in the desert.

When it came time to move on, the students started up the grade again, following the little stream of water. At one point, Jay stopped to point out an ant lion.

While everyone closed in to get a look at it, Cindy watched in fascination as an ant walked into the trap. As it tried to escape, the sand gave away under its feet and it fell lower into the 3½" wide and deep conical hole with each struggle. The lion then grabbed it.

Palm Grove, an oasis, overlooked the valley below. A spring-fed pool of crystal-clear water supported a community of wildlife whose existence depended on it for survival. Ringed by Washingtonian Palm trees, the potable water sparkled where the sun's rays shone through the huge fan-shaped fronds. In the wild, these palms do not shed their fronds, but they fold down around the trunk, where in time, they form a rather tight skirt under which many animals live. Bats make their home here and birds nest in the upper stories.

Entering this pristine enclave after their exhausting climb in the hot sun brought sighs of relief and cries of pleasure. Bonnie Goldman dropped her baggage to the ground, her eyes taking in the shady surroundings and shouted to the sky. "God, I love this place."

Susan Rider told Jay. "This is really something."

Juanita and Al, looking for a place to sit, bumped into Pierre Miles, who said, "I could stay here forever."

As the group took places on the soft sand, Frank plopped down with his back against a tree trunk, with Cindy sitting close by. Now as everyone squirmed to get comfortable, they dug into their lunches. Billie Dalton craned her neck, looking up into the dense foliage above.

"Hear the birds singing?" She said as Russ pulled out a sandwich. "I wonder what kind of bird that is?"

Jay, leaning against a tree, held a sandwich in midair near his mouth when he revealed his thoughts of the moment. "These palm groves are found all over in the mountains of Southern California. Lot of them up by Mountain Springs, up S-2, and Palm Springs. Wherever there is water."

Bonnie Goldman piped up. "Do they produce dates?"

Jay shook his head. "Oh no. It takes a certain type of palm to bear edible dates. The date palm is tall and has a different type of frond. They are grown up around Indio."

Susan Rider spoke up. "The date palm is Phoenix Dactylifera. That's the botanical name."

"Well, anyway," Jay continued, "these desert plants have evolved over the centuries to where they can survive the hostile climate like we have here. Our annual rainfall is 2 to 2 1/2 inches, and we don't always get that. Imperial Valley is called the salad bowl of America, because we grow vegetables throughout the winter, but the farmers don't depend on rainfall. No. Everything here is irrigated by water from the Colorado River. Imperial County is all below sea level, excepting the outer fringes like where we are, so our irrigation is all gravity fed. But this has nothing to do with the native desert plants. They are at the mercy of natural precipitation."

While Jay was speaking, the class was busy eating. Cindy, the only person wearing shorts, had hastily consumed half a sandwich and was sucking on her Pepsi. But as she sat on the sand, ants began to crawl on her bare legs. She got up suddenly, brushing them off and announcing her disdain.

"Fricken ants," she said irascibly, "Fricken nuisance."

Many of the group smiled or chuckled at her antics, as she walked over to the pond, still swiping at the ants. While Jay was eating, Billie was still trying to locate the bird whose songs filled the air. Frank was lighting a smoke and Geoff was pouring coffee from his thermos. Cindy now stood with her drink in one hand, looking down into the crystal-clear pool, where water bugs skated on the surface and brightly colored stones and pebbles shimmered iridescently below.

She wasn't particularly interested in what Jay had to say, and being a teenager amongst all these old people wasn't her idea of fun, although she did enjoy the great outdoors, the hiking and the new vistas. As she gazed down into the pool, her thoughts took wing, and she recalled the day when she swam in the large pond by Plaster City's well. If she were alone here, she would shed her clothes and jump into this tiny pond. At least, she could get wet and cool off a bit.

While the main group wrapped up their lunch mess, they relaxed against the tree trunks, as Jay began to talk about the desert again. "The Indians loved this area because of the water here," he said as he lit a smoke. "They ground their flour here, chipped arrow heads; prepared gourds for carrying water... this was their home...they lived out here in the open. They utilized everything, the sticks and stones, the plants, seeds, animals, plant fibers, animal skins and just about everything."

Frank and Susan had both lit up their smokes, and they listened to Jay with interest. The group hung on his every word. Pierre's eyes, over his bifocals were glued on Jay. Bonnie was nodding. Juanita's face was stern as she listened, while Billie and Russ were nonchalant. Billie's gaze wandered up into the trees as Jay continued his narrative.

"This isn't the only area I want to catalog," he said. "There are several geoglyphs I want to map out. Most of them are visible only from the air, like those you may have heard of in South America. Down there, one mammoth figure in the Atacama Desert of northern Chile is the world's largest representation of a human being. At 405 feet, the towering Atacama Giant is over twice the height of the Statue of Liberty."

"There's one figure known as the "candelabra" carved in the Nazca desert of Peru that is 840 feet long; then there's massive snake figures at Samaipata in Bolivia. It is believed that the ancients were more intelligent than modern man, and that they may have possessed some ungodly power derived from Megagods. To add credence to those theories, we only have to look at the pyramids down in Mexico and compare them with those in Egypt."

"The Mayans invented smoking, they understood mathematics and the use of zero, and their calendar was superior to the one in use in Europe at the time. As most of you know by now, our regular Wednesday classes will be suspended indefinitely because of the great interest in the cave. I hope to get back to our local geoglyphs in the future."

"For those of you who don't know, I talked with Peter Williams, curator of the Museum of Man in San Diego. He's an Egyptologist. He's an expert on antiquities both here and abroad. He suspects a connection between the Mayan cultures and the Aztecs, the Egyptians and possibly the Cahuilla and Yumans who lived here a thousand years ago."

"Anyway, he is organizing a party to explore our cave, so I expect them out here any day soon."

Billie spoke up. "Jay, I've heard so many stories about Imperial Valley being an inland sea. The oyster shells prove that. But I've also heard that the whole area was a fresh water lake. How do you explain that?"

Jay snuffed his cigarette out and glanced over at Cindy, still standing by the pond. "Easy," he said. "We're talking about two Geological periods. Most archaeologists believe that this area was part of the Gulf of California during the Pliocene epoch, 12 million years ago, and that the Colorado River's silt formed a delta and finally cut this area off, as it is today. Being cut off, the salt water evaporated, making it a desert."

He reached for another smoke. "We think that the Colorado then opened up the peninsula so the fresh water poured into this valley to form Lake Cahuilla, about two million years ago. The Indians enjoyed the good life around the lake for perhaps ten thousand years or more. We can't pin down the time accurately. They fished, swam, built boats, and came up here in summer, because it's a few degrees cooler up here. So anyway, this was both a sea and a fresh water lake at different geological times."

He was lighting his cigarette. "By the way, Billie, the Cahuillas were also known as the Yumans. That's how Yuma got its name." He glanced at his watch. "Peter is also interested in the legend about the lost city of the Yumans. This legend passed down from elders of the tribes from one generation to the other."

"Yeah," Geoff countered. "It's a legend. Just like the story of Peg-Leg-Pete. Or the tale about Bigfoot. People like to believe stories like that because they're mysteries, and people love mysteries."

"I agree with you, Geoff," Jay replied. "I think many of the stories we hear are just pure bunk, like the Lochness monster, but here in the Valley, there is a good probability that great treasures or lost cities could be buried under tons of sand. Look at Egypt. For the last hundred years, archaeologists have been finding artifacts buried under the sand, there."

"Here, we find mostly pot shards, arrow heads and scrapers, but these are from the more recent tribes. If you go back far enough, say 20 thousand years, the people who inhabited this area then may have enjoyed a more advanced civilization like the Mayans. In fact the Mayan cultures might have even lived this far north at one time. The drying up of Lake Cahuilla or the ancient sea could have driven them further south. Who knows?"

Susan, lying back on the sand, rose up. "Well, who knows why I'm getting tired or why my leg is going to sleep?" Frank stretched and got to his feet. Cindy came back to the main group, looking impatiently toward Frank, while Jay acknowledged that it was time to head back to their vehicles.

When Frank and Cindy got home, Frank headed for his lounge chair. He was tired and soon fell asleep. Cindy, on the other hand, went straight to the baby coyote's box, where she had made a bed for him in a cardboard box and was nursing him back to health.

She picked him up tenderly and petted him, whispering softly. "Poor little baby. I feel so sorry for you. Do you want some milk?" The little coyote opened his eyes and lay limp in her arms, a good sign that he might survive.

Frank had boarded up the access hole under the house at her request, and she had placed the box on the porch near the rocking chair where she could watch over it while seated, and she sat silently now, rocking the little guy back and forth as if it were a human.

When Kathy came home, Cindy was still sitting there, still rocking. "You're wasting your time, honey," she said as she came onto the porch. "That little coyote isn't going to make it." But Cindy wasn't so sure. She told Kathy that he had opened his eyes, and she could feel his heart beating.

"I'm going to make him a pet, mom," she answered. "I'm not going to let him die."

"We'll see," Kathy said thoughtfully. "We'll see."

Cindy changed the subject abruptly. "We had fun today, mom. We went on a field trip."

"Oh?" Kathy was curious. "Where did you go?"

Cindy then told her all about their trip to Davies Valley, but finally, Kathy had heard enough and turned to go into the house.

Frank heard her come in, and he opened his eyes and yawned. Kathy, heading for the kitchen, said, "I've got some news for you."

Frank got to his feet and stretched as she took a Pepsi from the refrigerator. He asked if she would fetch him a beer while she was at it, and they sat down at the table to talk.

"News? What's going on that I haven't already heard about?" He wondered aloud.

"Well," Kathy began, "people are getting fed up with the Mexican water trucks. I hear my customers bitch about them every day. Some say the courts are not doing enough. They say maybe we should do something more drastic."

"Yeah," Frank agreed. "Like shooting the tires out as they climb the grade up to Highway 98."

Kathy sipped her Pepsi. "Ralph was in for lunch today and he said the DEA was planning a raid on the well. Do you think that will stop them?"

"Oh, I don't know," Frank said as he popped his beer. "Ralph and I had a big discussion about that. The DEA and the INS think they are bringing illegals and drugs into Ocotillo in the empty tankers, then taking loads of water back. Pretty clever. Those trucks come and go across the border, and they aren't ever inspected. Not even the Highway Patrol can cite them. They don't have California drivers licenses, California plates or even insurance. But even if the raid is successful, it won't shut the well down because Stouffer is a lawyer and he can buy off the El Centro supervisors. They may bust the Mexicans they catch, but that wouldn't involve Stouffer, unless they could prove his collusion in the Mexican Mafia."

"Well, okay." Kathy nodded. "That's the news. I didn't know that you knew." She sighed. She was tired from being on her feet all day. "Now about Cindy. Do you think her little coyote will live?"

Frank shrugged and reached for a smoke. "I don't know," he said. "The way I got it figured is that he didn't get a lethal does of poison. Maybe he got a small amount in his mother's milk. The fact that he is still alive is encouraging."

Kathy shifted on her seat and brushed a strand of hair away from her eyes. "She tells me everything. She really enjoyed the trip up to Davies Valley. She told me she saw a roadrunner and an ant lion. She told me about the Indian petroglyphs on the rocks, and she said you guys had a nice hike up to those palm trees. But she was surprised to see a pond of crystal-clear water up there. It was so hot that she wished she could jump in the pond. You know Frank, she's a water baby. She loves to swim. She takes long showers or baths. When we were living with Eric, she would lay in the bathtub for an hour at a time."

Frank smiled as the smoke curled up toward the ceiling. He wondered if Cindy had told her about the time she had swam nude in front of him at the Plaster City well, or about her walking in the bathroom while he was taking a shower. Apparently not, and he suspected that she didn't want Kathy to know.

"She thinks a lot of you, Frank." Kathy tipped her Pepsi to her lips. "From what I've heard, she looks up to you as a father-figure. You have taken her out on hikes, shown her things in the desert, taught her things..."

Frank chuckled. "Yeah. And I like her too. She also likes Ralph."

"Well, so do I," Kathy enthused. "He's a real nice guy. But you know, Frank, she's at the age where she likes older men. That's why I was worried about leaving her with you. I was afraid something would happen."

Frank, half-smiling, reached over to touch Kathy's arm. "Kathy," he said, "You don't have to worry about me and her. I made you a promise, remember? Even if she came onto me, I'd put her off. I'd never take advantage of a child, or break my promise to you."

They talked for well over an hour when Kathy said she'd like to lie down. Her back ached and her feet were tired from her long shift, a fact that Frank could readily understand. "Well, you go ahead," he said. "I'm going down to the bar for a while; talk to the boys and see if there's anything new going on."

The Eagle Talon Saloon was a popular watering hole. The bald eagle was its icon, its logo. Besides a picture of an eagle sitting atop a saguaro cactus on one wall, there was a mounted specimen suspended from the ceiling with wires, depicting the raptor with a mouse in its beak, swooping down toward its nest.

A long bar and half a dozen small tables, surrounded by desert scenes and beer posters on the walls provided a macho ambience in the dimly lit room, a hangout for desert rats, single men and often, Mexican girls from Jacumba, who came hoping to meet men. But the air-conditioning atmosphere and ice-cold beer was the big draw in the 120 degree desert heat.

When Frank walked in, looking for a seat, his gaze swept along the bar stools where he spotted Susan Rider talking to a man, and a short distance away, Ralph was joking and laughing with a cute seniorita. Spotting an empty stool at the far end of the bar, he took the seat only to learn that the old desert rat, Clanahan, was sitting next to him.

Clanahan glanced sideways at Frank. "Find any more gold, boy? Heh-heh," he said leeringly sarcastic. Frank shook his head, looking away. "It's out there, boy." Clanahan continued. "You just gotta find it."

Frank looked impatiently towards the bar tender. "I've been too busy." It was true. He had been so involved with Kathy and Cindy the past few weeks, plus the growing interest in his cave discovery and archaeology that treasure hunting was all but forgotten.

When the bar tender, Tony, saw Frank, he brought him his usual Bud Lite, smiling. "Whatcha been up to, Frank? Haven't seen you for a while."

Frank shook his head. "Oh Jese! I've been so damn busy. I'm taking care of Cindy, that new waitress's daughter up at the café, and we've been going out on field trips..." He was reaching for his drink. "Then on top of it all, we've been going to the Supervisor's meetings in El Centro. We're trying to get a restraining order against the Stouffer well. But the wheels turn slow. That guy, Stouffer, is pretty clever. He uses every trick in the book to get around the law."

Clanahan interjected with a nudge of his elbow. "Listen, boy," he cut in, "If'n we're gonna get rid of Mexican water trucks, we gotta get around the law too. Ain't no way to stop em legally. Ain't no problem that a lil dynamite can't fix."

Frank took a swig from his bottle, glancing at Clanahan. "You talk big, man," he said brazenly, "You haven't got the guts to blow the well. Even if you did, the sheriff knows you're the only guy around this neck of the woods that's got dynamite. He'd have your fat ass in a minute."

Clanahan grimaced angrily. "We'll see!" He stood up, leering down at Frank. "We'll see!" He left in a huff while Tony turned to wait on customers, laughing.

"You hit him where it hurts, Frank," he said grinning.

Grinning, Frank looked up at Tony. "He had it coming. He's always bragging about something. He's the only guy around here that knows anything about gold, he's the oldest prospector in the valley, and the way I see it, he's the biggest braggart in the county."

As Tony turned away, the man sitting on the other side of Frank spoke up. He had been listening to the conversation all along and he now offered his opinion. "The guy's got the right idea, though," he said. "Someone oughta blow the well. That's for sure."

Frank was lighting a cigarette. "Yeah. You got that right." As he nursed his drink, Frank was thinking about what Clanahan had suggested, and he knew that the man was an expert at demolition. He had blasted out several mine sites around Ocotillo, although he had never struck it rich, but it was common knowledge that he kept a supply of dynamite at his place on the north side of town.

Frank felt someone behind him. Someone was taking the seat Clanahan had left. Glancing sideways, he saw it was Susan Rider, and she was carrying her beer. "Frank," she said as she slid onto the seat. "How you doing?"

Frank smiled. He liked Susan. When he had seen her in Davies Valley this morning, and talking briefly, he thought she was the prettiest widow in town. With her long blond tresses and petite figure, there was a sparkle in her blue eyes that exuded a sexy aura.

"Oh I'm doing okay," he answered as she settled on her stool. "I was beat after the long hike. When I got home, I conked out in my chair."

Susan was reaching for a cigarette. "Me too," she said. "When I woke up, I had a terrible thirst, so I came down here for something wet and cold."

Frank had seen Susan a few times around town, and then at the archaeological meetings, but like other men, had never thought to ask her for a date because she was mourning for the loss of her husband in a mine cave-in. He knew that she lived in a doublewide mobile home up on Sierra Vista Avenue, and that she had a big flower garden in her front yard, but little else.

Frank watched as she lit her smoke. Her dainty hands held a Zippo lighter, a type he hadn't seen in a long time, and she arranged her drink, cigarette pack and lighter in front of her, more to keep her hands busy than for neatness, but he noticed that she still wore her wedding ring.

"That girl you were with," Susan began, "Nice looking girl. I understand that she's living with you."

Frank nodded. "Yeah, her and her mother. Name's Cindy. Her mom's that new waitress up at the café.

Susan nodded. "I know her," she said. "Well, I know who you mean." Susan sipped her drink and looked sideways at Frank, half-smiling. "It must be interesting to have two women living with you."

This surprised Frank. "No way!" He said. "If you're thinking what I think you're thinking, we're not sleeping together. She's not my girlfriend."

Susan was grinning now. "I'll bet."

"It's a long story," Frank retorted, "but she laid down some rules about our living together.

Susan was quizzical. "Is it your house?"

"Sure."

"And she laid down rules in your house?"

"That's right."

"Well, I'm just curious. What in the world could she make rules about in your house?"

"Sex. She said she would live with me until she got on her feet but not to expect sex."

"Oh boy," Susan started to laugh. "That's the best one I've ever heard. Why didn't you tell her to go to hell?"

Frank shrugged. "I don't know. I just felt sorry for her. Her car broke down in front of my place and I helped her."

"So she owes you something."

"Susan," Frank began, "If you broke down out in the boondocks, and some guy came along and helped you, would you sleep with him?"

"Of course not," she replied. "Not in the usual sense. But in a case like yours, where a good looking guy helped me and offered a long term solution...where I would be living with him, uh...where we'd be really close...I'd certainly expect to give him something in return. Give him what would keep him happy. But then again, it would depend on whether or not I was married." She got up suddenly and excused herself.

While she was in the ladies room, Tony came by, checking for empties. Frank ordered two more bottles, one for each of them and when she came back, he noticed she was dressed in Levis and a white short-sleeved tank top, which enhanced her lithe figure, a far cry from the camo pants and long sleeved shirt she wore this morning.

"Oh you ordered fresh ones," she said. "Thank you. But about Kathy...I don't think she should have said that. I think she should have just taken it one day at a time. Just left it open."

"Yeah, well she's leaving as soon as she gets enough money saved. She's headed for San Diego."

Sitting at the end of the bar in the dim light, Susan and Frank were in a cocoon-like world of their own, oblivious to the chatter of voices that filled the room, but as often happens, the alcohol was dulling their inhibitions.

Susan was twirling her bottle with idle abandon. "It's been a year and a half since my Greg died, and it gets pretty lonesome at times. I've just decided to go out more, hoping I'll meet someone. Matter-of-fact, I joined the archeology class mostly for that purpose, and then I thought of coming here. This is only the second time I've been here."

"I'm glad you came," Frank told her. "Glad we met."

They sat talking for hours and were on their fourth beer, when Frank visited the men's room. No sooner than he got there, Ralph Smith came in, and they began comparing notes.

"Looks like you've got a live one," Ralph smiled devilishly. "You stepping out on Kathy?"

"Hell no," Frank said. "Kathy's not my girlfriend. Looks like you're the one with the hot chick."

"Yeah, well pickin up women is an art," Ralph said gloatingly. "I've got her all primed for action. Y'know, Frank, this is a good place to find women. Get em drunk and take em to bed."

"Yeah," Frank jerked his head in agreement. "Well, picking up women is not my strong point. I sure as hell don't expect to make a game of it. I just like to have it happen naturally."

"Listen, Frank. Alcohol is the best aphrodisiac ever invented. Remember the old saying, 'candy is dandy, but liquor is quicker'? Get em drunk and they're hot to trot."

When Frank got back to Susan, she was lighting a cigarette. She laid her Zippo on the counter and pushed it away. Then in a cloud of smoke, she picked it up again and flicked it to life, gazing at the flame for a minute.

"Whatcha thinking?" Frank wondered aloud.

"Oh nothing," she answered.

Frank held out his hand. "Let me see that thing. I used to have one like it."

Looking at the lighter, he noticed that it was inscribed with the words, LOVE, GREG. "He was your husband?" She nodded. Frank could see that she was reminiscing. She was pensive and appeared to be on the verge of tears. "Oh Jese," he thought, "One thing I don't need right now is a weeping widow."

"Come on, Susan," he said cajolingly, "Let's drink a toast to Greg." He picked up his bottle and held it in mid-air in front of her. When she responded, he said, "Here's to Greg, a great guy." When their bottles clinked, she smiled.

"When he gave it to me, he said, don't ever let the flame go out."

Inches apart, Frank leaned into Susan and took her hand. "I'm sorry," he whispered, "but you've got to move on. He'd want you to enjoy life, wouldn't he?"

Susan put her head against Frank, nuzzling up to him and he brushed his face against hers, "Uh-huh," she answered.

Tony came in front of them testing the bottles. He smiled down on them, then left. The bar was half-empty now and the hour was late. Susan, with upturned face, kissed Frank on the lips. "I think I'd better go home. I feel so tired."

Frank agreed, but knowing she was drunk, vowed to follow her home, lest she have an accident, although he wasn't in much better shape then she was. Her Datsun weaved all the way home, and at her residence, he watched her almost fall on the front steps. Switching off the ignition, he hurried to help her up the steps and into her house, where he marched her to the bedroom.

"I'm awright," she said in a barely audible voice as she leaned toward the bed. He let her flop and looked down on her. She had passed out. Her hair disheveled, her body crumpled in a heap, he straightened her legs out and made certain she was breathing, then he bent over and kissed her on the cheek.

On the way home, he mulled over the evening's events. "Liquor may be quicker, but sometimes it can make you sicker."

CHAPTER EIGHT

"Frank. Are you awake?" He looked up to see Cindy standing in the doorway in her shorty nightgown. "I am now," he said. "What do you want?"

Cindy came closer. "Are you all right?" She asked demurely as Frank rolled over to face her.

"Of course I'm all right," he answered. "What's going on?"

Cindy said Kathy stayed up late last night worrying why he hadn't come home and wondered if something had happened to him.

"Well, I told her I was going down to the bar," he explained. But Cindy had also begun to worry this morning. She had gotten up, fed her little coyote and cuddled him, then had eaten some breakfast and looked in on Frank. Was something wrong? He had never slept this late.

"What time is it?" Frank blinked his eyes sleepily. Cindy said it was 9:30 and she wanted to go up to the dump and do some shooting, but Frank shook his head. He didn't want to go. She coaxed and wheedled to no avail. Finally, she came up to the bed and jerked the sheet down to his navel, pleading for him to get up.

"No, hon," he said as he pulled the sheet back up to his neck, "I don't feel like it." A tug-of-war ensued, with her trying to pull it down and him trying to pull it up. By now, she was giggling. She was having fun. Frank finally grabbed her hands while she fought back.

"Come on, Frank," she kept saying as they tussled, but by now, Frank was wide-awake. With their hands straining against each others, she toppled onto him and their faces were inches apart. Frank could smell her feminine odor and feel her warmth. Aroused, he pushed against her, telling her to get off. Finally, he gave in.

"Okay, okay," he said loudly. "Let me up and we'll go shooting."

Cindy, happily victorious, brushed her face against his, whispering. "I could kiss you for that," she intoned. Both panting, their chests heaving, she planted her wet lips on his, her tongue darting in and out quickly.

Frank was on fire. He wasn't aware of her kicking the sheet out of the way, or her lifting her nightgown. He grabbed her and rolled over roughly, lost in passion. They were transported into an ethereal world where reality ceased and nothing worldly existed. There were no inhibitions, no thought of consequences, no worry about the law or Kathy. Consumed in lust, there was only the burning hunger in their loins.

Hungry mouths seeking moist lips and tongues diving with pleasure, they lay locked in embrace, Cindy moaning, and he driving to a place he had often dreamed of. Here in the cool morning air was God and heaven, then Cindy screamed as a series of electric shock waves shook her body in a paroxysm of climactic convulsions.

As their sweaty bodies lay entwined, she began to cry. Weeping, she told Frank that she loved him and would love him forever. Frank began pushing away, telling her meekly what she wanted to hear at that moment. "I love you too," he said.

On the drive up Shell Canyon to the dump, Cindy broke the silence. "How come you're not talking," she wondered aloud. "Are you mad at me?"

Frank was looking straight ahead through the windshield, "No, I'm not mad," he said, "I'm just thinking."

Cindy was puzzled. "About what?"

Frank took a deep breath, glancing at the bare legs below her white shorts. Look hon," he said as he searched for the right words, "I don't think we should have done that, but it's done and we can't undo it. But I want you to know it was great, yet we must careful not to ever do it again."

"Oh? Uh, I guess it was my fault? Right?"

"Maybe, maybe not," he tried to be tactful, "It's what happens when a man and a woman get too close. It happened so quick we didn't have time to think. Ah… ah…I think you should stay out of my bedroom."

"Well, I'm sorry you feel that way about it," Cindy replied," but I can't see why you are so concerned about it."

"Look, hon, there's nothing I would like better than to have you as a lover. You are a beautiful and young, but you are not of legal age. If anyone found out about us, I could go to jail. See what I mean? I promised your mother I wouldn't touch you. If she found out about us she'd go to the authorities and they'd come looking for me. I wouldn't have a chance, because my word against yours wouldn't be worth a tinker's damn."

Cindy nodded. "I see where you're coming from. But not to worry. We'll just keep it a secret. If no one knows, you'll be safe. Am I correct?"

"Sorta. But if you get pregnant, the truth will come out."

The dump was a huge hole in the desert sand, bulldozed deeply by the county sanitation department, and when they arrived and parked close, they found a treasure trove of tin cans and bottles. As they surveyed the area, Frank said he was glad they had come today, because he hadn't done much shooting in a long while.

Cindy retrieved the .22 Marlin semi-automatic and started to fill the magazine with long rifle cartridges while Frank looked back over the valley. He pulled his cap down to block the sun, saying, "Be careful, Hon. Don't ever let the muzzle point towards a person."

"I know," she said.

Frank stepped over to the pickup, reached for his revolved and cartridges, took them up to the lowered tailgate where she was standing. "I'm shooting .44 specials. Less kick and less noise. My gun will take either magnums or these." He held a cartridge so she could see it.

When he started to load the cylinder, he mused aloud. "Y'know, Hon, I think you're the best buddy I've ever had. You like to shoot and hike, and we have the same interests. When the weather cools down in the fall – if you're still here – we'll go out and find Peg-Leg-Pete's nuggets. Okay?"

Cindy smiled exuberantly. "I'd love that. Wouldn't it be something if we found them? I know it's not likely, but supposing we got lucky."

"Yeah. Well, we can dream, can't we?"

Frank stepped closer to the deep hole and fired at a half-gallon jug, sending shards flying everywhere. Cindy clapped her hands over her ears. Frank chuckled, "I'd better hold off a while. You go ahead, kiddo." He stepped back to lay his gun on the tailgate.

Cindy walked to the hole and looked down at the rubbish, sizing up suitable targets as Frank came back beside her. "Take that green bottle over there by that big tire," he said. "See if you can hit it with one shot."

Cindy lifted the rifle and took a stance, holding her breath and firing. The bottle shattered. "Okay," Frank said. "See those bottles over to the left? See if you can hit them rapid fire."

She leveled the gun again, looked down the barrel and fired three times, smashing all of them. Frank grinned ear to ear. "Good shooting Hon. You're a natural."

Cindy was smiling proudly. "This is fun. I could shoot all day."

Frank picked up targets farther away and smaller. She only missed one. Once, while she was reloading, Frank emptied his pistol while she covered her ears, but as she got her rifle fully loaded, he suggested they go back home. It was getting too hot and they had had enough practice for today.

Cindy agreed. They could do this again someday. She had enjoyed herself immensely and felt good about her marksmanship. But as they drove towards town, they were to have an experience they would never forget.

As they drove down Shell Canyon Road and turned onto S-2, they saw a huge INS bus, parked near a salt-cedar tree. Painted on its side were words, Immigration & Naturalization Service. These oversize buses were conspicuous because of their barred windows, and were only used to pick up large numbers of illegals who had been rounded up, and Frank knew it.

"What the hell?" He said in surprise. "What's going on? He's parked, waiting for a signal."

Frank remembered when Ralph had told him the DEA and sheriff's department suspected the Mexican water trucks of bringing in wetbacks and drugs in the empty tankers, and then taking loads of water back to Mexico. And Kathy had said that Ralph told her about the proposed raid, yet Ralph hadn't mentioned it last night at the bar. Maybe he was too drunk or maybe he wanted to keep it a secret.

"We've got to go right past the well," Frank told Cindy. "We may see some excitement." As they drove up Manzanita Avenue, they saw the sheriff's car parked behind the DEA van, out of sight of the well. Frank slowed to a crawl as he approached the vehicles and Ralph gave him a nod.

Through the open windows, Frank yelled at Ralph. "What's going on?" Ralph said they had got word that a big load of drugs and illegals were headed to Ocotillo. Their spotter in Mexicali said that the target truck was a faded red diesel with a spare tire mounted in front of the radiator. "We've got another spotter up by the café," he explained.

Frank didn't want to miss the action. He decided to kill time by driving up Sierra Vista Avenue, not expecting to see Susan watering her flowers in her front yard. She looked up, recognizing his pickup, dropped her hose and came over to say hello.

"You're going to have a big water bill," Frank smiled. "What does it run a month this time of year?"

Both Susan and Frank wanted to comment on last night when Susan had passed out, but were hesitant because of Cindy's presence. Susan said 'Hi' to Cindy and seeing the rifle propped between her legs, asked if they were going hunting. Frank told her they had already been, then boasted about Cindy's marksmanship.

Susan glanced at Cindy, referring to their field trip. "You got a nice sun tan, Cindy. I always wear long sleeves when I expect to be out in the sun a long time," although at the moment, she wore a white tank top which showed a nice cleavage.

Frank told Susan that there was going to be a drug bust, and that he had just talked to the sheriff. "I'm just killing time right now. Later, I'm going to drive down by the well to watch." Then without thinking, he asked if she had had a hangover this morning.

"Did I?" She said emphatically. "I woke up at 6:00 and my head felt like it was splitting in two. I took an aspirin and lay back in bed. When I finally got up, it was 9:30 and I had some coffee and turned on the TV, and wouldn't you know it, I fell asleep in my chair."

Frank, smiling, chuckled. "You're not used to drinking, are you?"

When Frank and Cindy left, Cindy was curious. "Were you out with her last night?"

"No. I told you I was down at the bar. She was there and I talked to her once. When you're drinking, everyone is friendly. You talk to a lot of people."

Frank drove slowly from Susan's place to the post office when he realized that this would be a good spot to park. He could face the pickup east, out from the main parking area where he could watch for a tanker pulled by a red tractor with a spare tire mounted in front of the radiator.

He cut the ignition and told Cindy that he might as well pick up his mail while he was here, and he hopped out, she followed him inside where it was air-conditioned. As he walked toward the cluster of P.O. boxes, hearing a raspy voice, he glanced toward the Postmaster to see Libby Hatfield, the town's Bible Thumper.

When Frank took his mail from the box, he stood looking at it, sorting out the junk mail to discard in the wastebasket. Cindy was close to Frank. As Libby headed for the front door, she stopped short near them, looking them up and down.

"Oh, there you are," she sneered, "I've heard a lot about you two living together in sin. You ought to be ashamed of yourselves. No good girl would be caught dead living with a man twice her age. You'll go to hell, my dear, unless you accept Jesus Christ as your savior."

This infuriated Cindy. "Who said I was a good girl?" She snapped. "Mind your own fricken business, asshole."

Later, as they went back to the pickup, Frank was laughing. "Oh man, hon," he said. "You sure told that old witch off but good." But it was true that there had been some negative remarks made in regard to the girls living with Frank. Various locals had made disparaging comments from time to time, although no one really knew anything for certain. Even Ralph's joking had hinted at sexual improprieties, but now, after Libby's tirade, maybe Cindy was thinking introspectively, yet if she was, it didn't diminish her lust for Frank. This morning's romp in bed had blown her mind, for she had experienced something with him that she had dreamed of, something that would bind her to him forever, psychologically.

"I'm thirsty," Cindy said finally. "Could we go up to the café and get something to drink?"

"Sure. We can tell Kathy we went shooting, and we can see the road from there too.'

As always, the Roadrunner Restaurant was cool, but almost empty. Kathy was busy filling the sugar bowls and saltshakers. She smiled when she saw them come in and sit at the counter. She wondered what they had been doing all morning, but Cindy cut her short.

"Mom, I dying of thirst. Can you get me a Pepsi?"

Frank chimed in. "And I need a Bud Lite."

When Kathy returned with the drinks, Cindy started telling her that they had been shooting up at the dump, but Frank took his bottle and went to the window. Standing by a booth, he hoped to catch a glimpse of the truck with the spare tire in front.

Time passed. They had finished their drinks and Frank was impatient. He wanted to get closer to the well where he could see the action when the target semi arrived, if it did, since he knew there could be a snafu.

Driving down Imperial Avenue toward the well, a loaded water truck passed, groaning up the grade on its way to Calexico, water splashing out of the fill-hole. When they arrived within a block of the well. Frank pulled off the asphalt and parked near a large salt-cedar tree where he and Cindy could see the well property clearly.

"I hope we don't have to wait too long," Frank said as he cut the ignition and settled back on the seat. "It's going to be hot sitting here."

Cindy's rifle leaned against the seat. She lifted it over between her legs, the butt on the floor, the muzzle pointing up. She fiddled with the magazine tube. "I forgot to unload this."

"Just leave it," Frank said idly. "We'll do that when we get home."

He could see a white tractor with the cab thrown back and a man was working on the engine. Another man came around and they appeared to be talking. Another white tanker sat under the overhead spigot, filling with water. Everything seemed normal and quiet. A sleeping dog lay peacefully in the shade of a tree. The minutes ticked by.

Frank lit a smoke, his eyes glued on the Stouffer well. A sedan whizzed past, headed up S-2 Highway. He glanced at his rear-view mirror and saw another car coming, with a big 18 wheeler behind it in the distance. He glanced at his watch. The car passed them as the Mexican truck came closer. Frank's eyes grew wide. This truck had a spare tire mounted in front of the radiator.

Watching keenly as it made a wide turn off the asphalt, he saw it crawl slowly across the sand and park in front of the truck being worked on, obscuring the latter. After a few minutes, he saw two men walk around the truck, then a shiny Mercedes pulled in and parked back in the shade where a Mexican man got out and walked over to the others.

A white Ford sedan passed slowly, and Frank could see that the two occupants were looking to the right at the well. Then he noticed the car bore an "E" license plate, meaning that it was a California law enforcement, or state or county car. He saw it turn up Manzanita Avenue, where he had seen Ralph.

As Cindy and Frank sat in the sweltering heat waiting, they saw men on top of the tanker, then more coming out of the fill-hole. "Look," Frank exclaimed. "There's guys coming out of the truck."

"Are they wetbacks?" Cindy asked.

Frank nodded. "I suppose so. Three, four, five," Frank was counting the men. "Oh Jese!" When he stopped counting there were 11-suspected illegals climbing down a ladder. The Mexican dressed in a white shirt and slacks was talking to them and pointing. The men still on top were now being handed packages from inside the tanker.

Law enforcement was deployed all over the area, waiting for a signal to move in. Finally, it came, and there was a rush to apprehend the smugglers. The white unmarked sedan roared in a cloud of dust, two sheriff's car followed, and a white van brought up the rear. Seconds later, a plainly marked Border Patrol Blazer sped in off the asphalt.

His vision almost obscured by dust, Frank now saw a man running and he heard a shot. Then he heard three shots in quick succession. Adrenalin pumping, he became tense. The sights and sounds took him back to Vietnam. As the dust lifted, he could see some illegals breaking away, heading for the open desert to the east. There was another shot.

"Let's get out of here," Cindy cried out. "We're liable to catch a stray bullet."

"Look at that guy!" Frank shouted excitedly. "He's making a run for it."

The bigshot Mexican had jumped into his Mercedes and was kicking up dust as he accelerated from behind the trees. Heading for the road, he took a hail of fire from the police officers, but he kept on going. The big INS bus they had seen parked earlier came lumbering down S-2 and was about to turn onto the well property when the Mercedes sped toward the asphalt, but braked for the bus.

"Get your gun up here!" Frank screamed. "Shoot his tires! Shoot at his tires!"

Cindy, running on adrenalin, brought the rifle up over Frank, hunkering close to him and leveled it out the window. Frank told her to wait til the Mercedes got closer. Within seconds, she pulled the trigger, shooting at the front tire, and then at the rear. The car began to wobble. Then it swayed onto the road shoulder and stopped. It had been hit by the police fire and the tires on one side were flat.

As they sat watching, the sheriff's car roared down the road in hot pursuit. Right before their eyes Ralph jumped out, ran to the Mercedes and pulled the Mexican out. After a brief struggle, he had the man handcuffed.

Frank smiled with relief. It was like old times when he was in Vietnam. "Let's get out of here," he said to Cindy. "Let's go home."

When they arrived at Frank's place, Cindy headed straight to her little coyote. It appeared to be getting better. She picked him up and petted him, rocking in Frank's chair on the porch and talking baby talk to the little animal.

They hadn't been home over half an hour, when Kathy drove up. She got out of her car, looked up on the porch to see Cindy, and marched straight into the house where Frank sat at the kitchen table, drinking a beer.

"Did you and Cindy see the drug bust?" Kathy asked as she sat down opposite Frank.

Nodding, Frank answered in the affirmative. "Yeah, we did. It was the only excitement I've seen since I moved here. There was some shooting and we saw Ralph catch one of the smugglers."

Kathy took a deep breath, squirming on her chair to get comfortable. "There was a man who stopped in just before I left," she began. "And he said he was coming down S-2 past the well and he saw a big bus pull in there. He looked over that way and saw a lot of men and vehicles, and wondered what was going on."

"Yeah." Frank took a swig from his bottle. "Now, the people are really going to be mad at the Mexicans.

Cindy and I saw illegals coming out of the tank truck and the DEA was hauling out packages of something – probably drugs – but what will make the locals really mad, is that they have been taking our water and smuggling in illegals and drugs, and out law enforcement couldn't see what they were doing. No one suspected them. The water trucks came out of Mexicali, passed through Calexico, up Highway 98 to here, and they were never inspected or questioned."

"I hear a lot of gossip at the café," Kathy said. "People here on the border don't like the Mexicans. They say that they're taking jobs from Americans, but the biggest complaint is the smuggling and illegal entry."

"I know," Frank said. "They are brazen. Pregnant Mexican women wait until they are about to deliver, then cross over into Calexico and start yelling 'get me to the hospital. I'm going to have a baby.' The Calexico Hospital can't turn down people who need immediate help, so they take them in. At this point, that baby being born on American soil is automatically a U.S. citizen, and as such, is eligible to bring in relatives. It's the damndest thing I ever heard of."

Kathy was incredulous. "Is that a fact?" She said, "Do those Mexicans kids really become U.S. citizens if they're born on this side of the border?"

"Damn Right!" He said, reaching for a cigarette. "And you know who pays for it? U.S. Americans."

CHAPTER NINE

Jay Bradford's little red Jeep sat in front of the Community Hall and the student's cars were parked helter-skelter nearby in the large open space to the right. Everyone was inside waiting for Jay to open his usual discussion on archaeology.

There was a good turnout this morning. Most of the regulars. Frank and Cindy, Susan Rider, Pierre Miles, Geoff Weisse, Al and Juanita Hyer, Billie and Russ Dalton were present, and there were a few newcomers, Tom Goode and his wife Janet, and Bonnie Goldman a widow.

Jay, dressed in his usual laid-back fashion, stood leaning against the long table, smoking and looking out over the students. Glancing at his watch, he snuffed his cigarette out in an ashtray on the table, and stated in his usual words, "Well, I guess we're all here."

Frank and Cindy sat next to Susan in the first row of seats, with Pierre Miles and Juanita Hyer on either side of them. They were the closest to Jay. Pierre was somewhat hearing impaired, so he had chosen his seat accordingly.

"First, I want to tell you, we aren't going out today." Jay intoned. "We will view films here...ah...I don't have to tell you, it's going to be a scorcher." Everyone was nodding in agreement.

"I've got some good news about the cave," he continued. "But first, I want to ask, how many of you enjoyed the trip to Davies Valley last week?" Most of the students raised their hands. "Well, I've got anther field trip planned for a future date, a giant geoglyph. Geoff and I catalogued the pictographs up at Davies, but now want to record and map out a huge intaglio in the Yuha desert." He stopped and looked down as if thinking. "Oh yes," he began. "I want to mention it before I forget it. I see by the paper that they made a big drug bust here. Caught the kingpin of the Mexican Mafia. That really put Ocotillo in the big time news."

The people of Ocotillo were so fed up with the Mexican water trucks and so angry that the Mexicans were coming across the border that Jay's remarks changed the atmosphere from archaeology to rage.

"It's the kind of news we don't need in this town," Susan Rider spoke out angrily.

"That's right," Pierre Miles shouted, "Them damn Mexicans just ignore our laws, and the Border Patrol don't do anything about it."

Frank piped up. "We oughta shoot em," he bellowed, "That would stop em."

It seemed that everyone wanted to offer solutions, and they all were trying to talk at once. "Well, I'll tell you one thing," Juanita Hyer said, "We were talking about building a fence a few years ago, and I still think it would be a good idea."

Geoff Weisse was shaking his head. "What good would that do?" He said. "There's a fence between Mexcali and Calexico...been there for years, but you can walk legally through inspection without ever being stopped."

"Well, I'm with Frank," Tom Goode cut in, "You shoot a couple and that'll wake em up."

Frank flipped his hand in the air to draw attention. "I think we should form a vigilante committee; all volunteers. Patrol the border and turn em back. Be armed and threaten em. If you shoot and kill one or two, so what?"

Russ Dalton cut in. "You know how many men it would take? The border is over 2000 miles long. The problem isn't just here, it's from San Ysidro way over to Texas."

"That's right," Al Hyer agreed. "The hot spots are San Ysidro, the Calexico corridor, Yuma and Phoenix, way over to Brownsville, Texas. It would take thousands of men, and they'd have to work in shifts, night and day. Even if we could get enough men, we'd still have legal trouble with the INS."

"Okay! Okay!" Jay shouted over the others, seeing that the situation was getting out of hand. Waving his notebook, he began speaking in a normal voice as the students became suddenly quiet. "I told you I had some good news about the cave. Remember when I told you about Peter Williams, the curator of the Museum of Man? Well, he has been arranging an exploratory party to go in on the tenth of the month, a week and a half from now. This trip is not for most of you. It may be very grueling. There is some risk involved also. We don't know what is in there."

Susan flicked her hand in the air to get attention. "Can I go?"

Jay could see that she was young and slim, and therefore probably in fit condition. He nodded. "If you don't have any medical condition or physical limitations. Yes."

Frank spoke up. "Me too," he said. "I found it."

Jay nodded. "Of course, Frank."

Many of the older class shook their heads and Pierre fairly shouted. "Not me. I ain't going in no damn cave."

"We don't want too many," Jay explained. "Peter told me they would have a lot of equipment; food and water, cameras, bedding...ah...lights. There will be two porters to carry supplies, Peter, Geoff and me..."

Juanita spoke up. "How come so much junk? And beds? Do you mean to say they'll be sleeping underground?"

Jay reached for a smoke. "Peter has led expeditions all over the world, even in Egypt. He knows what he's doing. When you go into a new cave, you never know what you will run into. You can get lost, injured, sick... he's even bringing a spelunker or speleologist, a man trained in cave exploration."

Tom Goode spoke up. "I'd like to come along, Jay. I've been in a lot of caves. I'm no expert, but I just like caves."

Holding his lighter to his cigarette, Jay nodded. "Just you, not you wife. I'm afraid we'll have too many people." He blew a cloud of smoke, glancing at his watch. "All right. It's still along way off. I'll know more about it next week." He looked over at the projector and screen already set up. "Now, as I told you earlier,

I have some film I want to show you. I think we've got time for one, as it runs for an hour."

Cindy, who had sat patiently, yawned. She was tired of sitting. "Oh God," she whispered to Susan as Jay flipped the switched on the projector. "This is boring."

Frank leaned forward to look at the girls. "What did you say?"

Cindy grimaced, looking at him disdainfully. "My butt is tired." Her voice was barely audible, but she formed the worlds distinctly with her lips. Frank grinned, telling her to be patient.

The film was about archaeology of course, and it showed various digs, some geoglyphs and one of the pictures showed Jay beside a grave-shaped excavation where they had unearthed a skeleton. Jay had provided commentary throughout the showing, and though interesting, everyone seemed relieved when it was over.

While Jay packed up his paraphernalia, some students gathered around him, asking questions, but most headed outside for their cars. In the glaring sunlight, the heat struck them painfully. Frank said, "Oh Jese!" Susan alongside him and Cindy, said she was going home where it was cool and Cindy thought she'd like a cold shower. But as they walked toward their vehicles, a Mexican water truck lumbered by. Pierre looked up and shook his fist, shouting an expletive.

With no air-conditioning, Frank's pickup was as hot as the fires of hell, and when they got home, his house was almost as hot. When he looked at the thermometer on the porch, it was 120 degrees. He told Cindy he had never seen it so hot.

"Well, I'm going to take a shower," Cindy informed him. "My clothes are sopping wet." Frank told her he was going down to the saloon, where they had air-conditioning. She wanted to go along, but he told her minors weren't allowed where liquor was served.

"Well drop me off at the café where it's cool," she said. "I can stay there and ride home with mom."

At Frank's insistence, Cindy took a quick shower and put on fresh clothing, green shorts and a white tank top, but while he waited in the shade of the porch, he looked down at Cindy's little coyote. It looked up at him as if he was his mother, and Frank believed now, that the animal was going to live, despite the poison.

When Frank parked and was walking toward the door of the saloon, the sheriff's Blazer pulled up and Ralph got out. Side by side, heading for the entrance, Ralph asked Frank if he had made out the other night. "No," Frank answered. "She got sick and I took her home. Did you?"

Hand on the door, Ralph said, "I never miss. You gotta know how to pick em."

Once inside, Ralph said he had stopped to use the restrooms. Maybe he had time for a quick beer. As he headed for the restroom, Frank scanned the room, looking for a seat, but because of the extreme temperature today, the bar was full of hangers on, sots and some old men he had never seen before. Most of the patrons hung out in the saloon because it was air-conditioned, and few people in Ocotillo could afford that.

The only place to sit was at a table back in a corner some distance from the others, but it was stacked with ashtrays, napkins and miscellaneous junk, but Frank didn't have much choice. When Ralph returned from the head, he looked around, saw Frank and came over. As Frank took an ashtray and pushed some of the junk out of the way, a waitress came over to take their orders.

"Frank," Ralph began. "Did you see the big article in the paper?"

"No," Frank said with a shake of his head, "I don't take the paper, but I heard about it."

"The raid on the well was a smashing success. We broke the biggest smuggling ring in the history of law enforcement. The estimated value of the drugs was nearly a million bucks, and the illegals, at $500 a piece, $5000 at least, represented the highest dollar value of any DEA or INS raid so far."

Frank was lighting up. "That's great. But do you think this will stop Stouffer from shipping water?"

"Hell no," Ralph watched the waitress bringing their beers. "Selling water is legit. Stouffer didn't have anything to do with the drugs or wetbacks. That was the Mexican's idea and pretty damn clever. Unless they could prove Stouffer's collusion or his connection, he's clean."

They both took their drinks in hand. Frank took a long swig and looked questioningly at Ralph. "What was all the shooting about?"

"They were surprised but ready. When the DEA swooped in, they weren't going down without a fight, but we had a swat team with us and they didn't waste any time. They knocked off the guys with the guns. Yeah. Killed two, wounded a couple before they gave it up. The guy in the Mercedes was the kingpin of the Mexican Mafia, Enrique Careno, the big honcho. He was the most wanted drug runner in the country." Ralph took a deep breath. "Yeah, we've got him in custody."

"Yeah, but for how long?" Frank scoffed at Ralph. "A guy that powerful can put up a million bucks bail and if that doesn't work, the Mafia will likely break him out. The jail in El Centro is only a stone's throw from Mexicali, and the Mexicans virtually rule in that area."

Ralph tipped his beer to his lips and set the bottle on the table.

"We know that," he retorted. "Do you think we're fools? Careno is a high profile prisoner and the Mafia is just as powerful in Mexico as law enforcement. Years ago, when Careno was put in jail in Mexico City, they stormed the prison and got him out. So we are aware of that. We have transferred him to a prison hundreds of miles from here – its secret – under an alias and heavy guard."

Ralph picked up his drink and gulped it down. He consulted his watch and spoke up. "I've got to go in El Centro now. See you around, Frank."

Alone at the table, Frank finished his beer and ordered another. Oblivious to the hum of voices and lost in thought, his mind wandered. Sitting quietly in the corner, he thought of Cindy. She was probably at home now with Kathy. Probably in the shower.

He could visualize her naked, with the water streaming down her youthful body. He could see her on top of him and could feel her hot kisses. Sex with her had been mind-blowing. It had never been that good before at any time, and she was at the age where her hormones were raging, and he could probably have her any time he wanted to. Yet, the thought of getting caught haunted him.

Why was it that he didn't have a girlfriend? He was not bad looking; he came into contact with a lot of women, yet in the five years he had lived in the desert, he had never connected with a woman. The closest he had come to bedding a chick was recently when he followed Susan home. He could probably have scored that night if she hadn't passed out.

Come to think about it, Susan wasn't bad looking. Blond, there was a strong resemblance to Kathy; even to Cindy. She was widowed, available and friendly. Maybe he could pursue her and avoid Cindy, if that were at all possible.

As the hours passed, Frank had consumed 4 beers, but he was used to it. He might get a bit tipsy, more uninhibited, but never drunk. Most likely, he would become amorous when drinking. Now, as he glanced at his watch, he realized that the day was gone. It was evening and should be cooling off a bit.

He was getting hungry. The thought of going home turned him off. Kathy and Cindy were most likely there, watching television, but it would be boring. Maybe he could go up to the Roadrunner and get a good meal. Yes, he would have one more beer and then go up there.

As he sat smoking, he saw a woman come in. He looked again with disbelief. It was Susan, and she was looking around the room. When she saw him, she walked over to his table, "Frank," she smiled, "I saw your truck out front and thought I'd stop for a few minutes."

"Have a seat," he said. "I'll buy you a beer." He noticed she was wearing tight jeans and a frilly light blue blouse. She looked very neat, with her hair framing her face, and her disarming smile.

"No," she said, then changing her mind, "Well, just for a minute."

"Is it still hot outside?" Frank asked to make small talk. Smiling sardonically as she took her seat, she grimaced. "Are you kidding me?"

"Oh boy," Frank enthused. "When Cindy and I left the meeting this morning, we went home. The house was unbearably hot. My thermometer read 120."

"Don't you have air-conditioning?" Susan wondered aloud.

Frank shook his head. "No, but I just thought of something. There's an old water cooler…swamp cooler on my roof, never used. I think I'll hire someone to get it up and running."

"Well, after the meeting this morning," Susan began, "I went home for a while, decided to go into town and do some shopping and get a few groceries. They're in my car now, so I'd better get home."

"Well, you gotta do what you gotta do," he grinned and picked up his bottle.

"Have you had dinner?" Susan asked demurely. Frank told her he had just been thinking about going up to the café a few minutes ago, and she said she would like some company. "I'd like to barbeque, but it's too hot outside. I've got the makings for a nice salad and some pork chops. I drink a bit of wine with my meals. They say it's good for you. Will you come up Frank? You can help me carry in my purchases."

Frank was only too glad to go to her house. The meal was an incentive in itself, but the opportunity to spend some quality time with her was a big bonus. He liked her. They both smoked and she seemed like a very nice person. It could even lead to something more interesting.

When he followed her home and they had parked, she got out and opened the trunk of her black Datsun. As he approached, she was tugging at an ice chest where she had stashed her meat, milk, cheese and salad greens. Her other purchases were in Wal-Mart plastic bags, thrown in among gallon jugs of water which desert people always carried. As he tried to help her, she handed him some things from the ice chest and she reached for the Wal-Mart bags. But one bag spilled out on the ground. She had bought a set of colored panties and a bra. The panties were red, green, yellow, blue, white, beige and chartreuse, and imprinted with days of the week.

While Frank chuckled, he could see that she was embarrassed. He tried to cover the mishap. "That's okay. That's all right. I've seen the kind of stuff before. No problem. In fact, I find red panties are a real turn on."

Inside, Frank was quick to notice how tidy her place was. As she put things away, her back towards him, his gaze swept over the kitchen and ended up on her backside as she reached for the higher cabinet shelves. In her form fitting jeans, her little butt spoke volumes about her sensuality. As he thought about her pretty ass, she kept up a constant chatter.

"This morning when Jay was talking about the cave exploration, I thought it would be fun to go in it. I've never been in a cave, have you? But I was surprised at all the equipment he said they would be taking in. And sleeping bags. Gosh. I can't imagine a cave so big you'd spend days in it."

As she talked, she was sorting out the groceries, keeping out those needed for dinner, and those to be refrigerated. Then she asked if he'd like to set the table while she busied herself preparing the food. She told him where the dishes were, the silver, and the placemats. "I like to set an attractive table," she continued. "It's candy for the eyes, as food for the stomach." But when Frank saw her China and utensils, his eyes bugged out. Everything reeked of money. Her dishes were fine imported brands, her silverware was monogrammed and even the wooden table and four chairs in the dining alcove were of high quality he was unfamiliar with.

"You've got a nice place here, Susan," he said as he set the table. "I don't have anything expensive. When I moved to the desert, I just bought odds and ends of stuff. Nothing fancy."

"Well," Susan replied, "I'm not really an uppity person, but Greg came from a wealthy family and he had champagne tastes. He was making good money as a consultant when he bought this place, and he wanted good quality things. He was also a fanatic believer in insurance. He bought all kinds of insurance. He had mortgage cancellation insurance, all kinds of liability insurance and a $500,000 life insurance policy. Um... so when he was killed in a mine cave-in, this place was paid off in full and I started to get money."

As she talked, she had the salads ready and the meat was cooking. Two large potatoes were in the microwave. "So naturally, I don't have to work. But since he died, I haven't gotten around much. The people here weren't too friendly with us and I didn't go out much. But lately, I decided to get out and about, in the hopes I could make friends. That's the main reason I joined the archaeology class and why I started going to the local bar."

Later, as they sat at the table, she poured Chardonnay into her wine glass and asked if he would like some. He said he would take a small amount, but wine was not his favorite drink. Susan explained that she only drank it with meals, and didn't really drink much of anything excepting water or soft drinks.

"I can drink a little beer, but I have a limit. It makes me sick if I have too much."

"Yeah," Frank grinned. "Like the other night when I had to put you to bed."

"Oh that," she looked ashamed. "I guess I should apologize. When I woke up the next morning and found myself fully dressed on the bed, I didn't know what had happened, but when I came to my senses, I remembered you coming home with me."

"Yeah, and I'll bet you wondered if you'd been raped." Frank interjected.

"Of course," Susan smiled. "Under the circumstances, any woman would wonder."

Feeling capricious, Frank blurted out, "And I'll bet you said. Oh darn it."

Susan broke into a fit of giggling. "You must be a mind-reader," she joked as she poured more wine.

But Frank, feeling her mirth, sang out, "Red panties. Red panties." And she laughed uncontrollably.

When they pushed away from the table, she told Frank, "You're a lot of fun. I'm sure glad I met you."

"The feeling is mutual," Frank admitted, "I'd seen you around, but I never gave it much thought. But now we're getting to know each other."

Susan suggested that they take their wine and go sit on the sofa in the living room where it's more comfortable, but Frank wondered about the dishes on the table. Susan said she could clean up later. "Right now, we can talk." Frank said he'd help her wash dishes, not knowing she had a dishwasher.

Working together, they cleared the table, carried the dishes to the kitchen counter and while they scraped them clean, she arranged them in the dishwasher. Close together, they frequently bumped into each other and they'd laugh. Finally, Frank leaned into her, pinning her against the counter and silently looking into her eyes. Face to face, he stared, and she stared back wordlessly.

Breathing heavily, she began to tremble, their warm bodies pressed together. He could feel her breasts against him, and they hugged silently, then their lips came together and lingered long. The interlude was electric. Frank swept her up in his arms and was carrying her towards the bedroom when the phone rang. She stiffened.

"I wonder who that could be," she said as she struggled against him for release. Frank told her to ignore it, but when it kept ringing, it begged to be answered. The romantic moment was lost.

On her feet now, she hurried back to the kitchen and picked up the receiver, "Hello." There was a brief silence.

"Hi. Susan? This is Darlene."

Susan answered. "Oh, His sis. Long time no see."

"Whatcha doing?" Darlene asked to make small talk.

Susan thought a minute. "Oh, I was just getting ready for bed."

There was something ominous in Darlene's voice. "Are you standing or sitting," she wanted to know.

Susan said, "I'm standing." Susan sensed something wrong. "Darlene, is mother sick again?"

Darlene told Susan that their mother was in the hospital and not expected to live. She urged Susan to come home as quick as she could. Frank had come into the kitchen and when Susan hung up, she faced him sadly. "My mother is not expected to live." She said, "I'm leaving here in the morning. I don't know how long I'll be gone."

"Where does your mother live?" He wondered out of curiosity.

"Flagstaff."

"Are you going to drive?"

"Yes, it's a couple hundred miles."

Susan was downcast. Her grief was obvious. Frank put his arms around her, hugging her tight and uttering words of consolation. "Is there is anything I can do?" He said softly,

"No, I'm afraid not."

"Well, I'll wait for you," he said. "Have a good trip. Maybe I'll see you when you get back."

On the way home, Frank thought about Susan, comparing her to Kathy. After tonight, he could see that Susan was clean, decent woman who was only single because of her husbands death. Her home and the way she kept it, indicated stability, with purpose. What 's more, she was financially fixed for life.

Kathy, who he had dreamed of bedding when she came up to his house asking for help, was financially flat broke. She - by her own admission - had been shacked up with guys, had an illegitimate child, Cindy, and the spark he was expecting, never materialized. They had never been close. There hadn't even been any camaraderie between them. Not one bit.

Comparing Kathy to Susan was like comparing apples and oranges. Sure, they were both women, although Susan was closer to his age, but his experience with Susan left him wishing for more. The flame of desire that had swept over him tonight led him to believe that if he were to ever marry again, he would like to marry Susan. As he was almost home, he visualized him and her alone, and he had asked her to model those red panties. He could see, in his mind's eye, her pirouetting before him, and she was beckoning with one finger. But he was shaken from his reverie when he pulled into his yard.

Kathy's car was not there, but a light was still on in the house. Entering, he saw Cindy sitting in his chair with the .22 rifle on her lap. She was dressed in her nightgown and he could see that she had been crying.

"What in the hell is going on?" He bellowed. "Where's your mom and what are you doing with that gun?"

When she had seen him come in, she had her finger on the trigger, but recognized him, had quickly put the rifle on the floor as she sprinted toward him and threw her arms around him. "I'm scared," she sobbed. "This house is haunted." She was hysterical.

Frank hugged her protectively. "Calm down, hon." His voice was reassuring. "You've had a bad dream. Nothing is going to hurt you. Daddy's home now."

Cindy clung to Frank like a 2 year old who had seen a ghost. She had been spooked by something. No question about it, but in his haste, he assumed that she had had a bad dream, but as they stood entwined, a rattling sound sent shivers up Frank's spine. A loud banging followed, and then again, a rattling.

"Someone's out there," Cindy whimpered, clinging tighter.

Frank had noticed that a breeze had kicked up as he drove home and there were gusts of wind, yet Cindy's hysteria was contagious. He remembered boarding up the access hole under the house and had secured a large piece of tin over it. He reasoned that maybe the wind was rattling the tin.

"It's nothing to worry about," Frank told Cindy. "You go onto bed. I'm home now." But Cindy had never slept alone. She had always gone to bed with her mother. She wanted to sleep with Frank, but he wouldn't hear of it. He was tired, but wondered about Kathy.

"Where's your mom, hon?"

Cindy explained that when Kathy got off work, they came home, and Kathy freshened up and said she was going into town to do some shopping, but strangely, she didn't want Cindy to come along. Frank remembered Ralph saying he was going to El Centro this afternoon, also. Was it possible they were having an affair? It was almost midnight now, and Kathy wasn't home yet. She had never been out this late. Then Frank realized that tomorrow was Monday, her day off work.

"You go on to bed, hon," he told Cindy. "I'm tired. Don't worry about noises. It's just the wind. I'm going to hit the sack."

Cindy headed for her bedroom and Frank headed for his. The wind had cooled things down somewhat as he stripped off his clothes and fell onto his soft mattress, the 85-degree temperature being ideal for laying nude in the darkness.

As he squirmed to get comfortable, his thoughts were of Kathy. She had admitted that she liked Ralph, but then again, who didn't? Young and old, everyone was fond of that handsome man in uniform. Even Frank liked him. But Frank had seen him with a young chick down at the Eagle Talon, and he had heard Ralph boast of his prowess.

"Well, hell," he thought. "So what?" Even if she was having an affair, it was none of his business. If they were out there somewhere in a motel enjoying sex, he couldn't really blame them. Wasn't everyone obsessed with getting laid? Didn't everyone in the world hunger for a good romp between the sheets?

They say that wine makes you sleep well. In Frank's case, it was certainly true. He conked out and was unaware of the sand storm the wind was kicking up. The sand was driven against the metal housing of the defunct swamp cooler on the roof, making weird noises and waxing and waning with sporadic gusts. The rattling and banging, along with the shrieking wind, was unnerving, even spooky.

Cindy lay on her bed wide-awake, looking fearfully into the darkness, her imagination running wild. She could see hideous faces, grotesque figures. Something was coming after her. Hair standing on end, she considered running into Frank's bedroom, yet she feared if she put her feet on the floor, something under the bed would grab her legs.

Agonizing minutes passed and she was hysterical. She must get to Frank's bed where she would be safe. In a fit of desperation, she leaped from the bed and dashed into his bedroom. She carefully slipped onto the mattress beside him and lay quietly, making sure she wouldn't waken him, but when she heard him snore, she inched up to him and went to sleep.

When dawn broke, all was quiet. The sandstorm had abated and the sun was peeking over the horizon to the east. Cindy lay quietly, dreaming of the mind-blowing sex they had had. Unconsciously, she reached over to touch his manhood. Her heart was racing now.

Frank, lying on his back, was dreaming of Susan. She was dancing in front of him in her red panties. He grabbed her and they fell onto her bed. Sweet sensations coursed through his body.

Cindy felt the hardness, felt the throbbing. Wiggling down, she put her mouth on it, moving her head up and down. As Frank began to groan with pleasure, she leaped astride of him, impaling herself to the hilt.

They lay entwined on the soft mattress in the coolness of dawn, oblivious to the real world, when Cindy heard a coyote calling to its mate, and she knew what they wanted to do. Jumping out of bed, she headed for the bathroom, but later, she looked out of the kitchen window. Kathy's car was not there.

Still in her nightgown, she went out on the porch to feed her pet coyote, but when she came back in, Frank was sitting at the table drinking coffee. As she stood at the sink, washing her hands, he gazed at her backside, thinking erotic thoughts.

"Did you finally get to sleep last night, hon?"

"Yeah," she said, "but the wind kept me awake for a long time. Did you sleep good?"

"I must have." He replied, "I konked out, but I had the craziest dream."

CHAPTER TEN

July 5th, 1983

A galaxy of stars shone down on the little hamlet of Ocotillo, where a crescent shaped moon was sinking slowly below the horizon, over the Laguna Mountains. The town was asleep and deathly quiet, save for the occasional rumble of a big diesel on the nearby Interstate.

It was 3:30 am and a fighter squadron at the Naval Air Facility west of El Centro was readying for takeoff on a training flight over the desert, preparing for a covert operation in the Persian Gulf.

At a given signal, the planes – F-14's – roared down the runway and lifted swiftly into the nighttime sky, heading toward the open desert. At 3:45, as the flight passed over Ocotillo, a violent explosion shattered the still night air, jiggering the town awake with great alarm.

Lights blinked on and citizens ran into the streets in their nightclothes, looking frantically for the source of the blast. Though nothing could be seen, there wafted on the air the smell of gunpowder. Denny Hill, fire chief, had ran out also, but when he didn't see anything, he suspected that a live bomb had been accidentally dropped close to town. He dashed back inside and got on the phone to NAF headquarters, angrily accusing them of bombing the town.

On many occasions in the past, flights from the base had irritated residents of Ocotillo, resulting in angry calls to the Commander, but usually, the problem was a sonic boom, which was dismissed with an apology and a promise that it wouldn't happen again. And so it was this time.

"I'm sorry," the commandant said. "It's possible it was a live bomb, but unlikely. Are you sure it wasn't a sonic boom?"

Denny Hill responded, "I'm not sure of anything. It felt like a bomb exploded, but then again, I suppose it could have been a sonic boom. I'm going to call the Sheriff's Department and see what they think."

After NAF apologized again, Denny contracted the Sheriff's El Centro Headquarters. "Fire Chief Hill, Ocotillo," he said curtly. "We've just had an explosion out here. Or maybe it was a sonic boom, I can't tell which. I phoned NAF and they assumed it was a sonic boom. Did you feel anything over there?"

"Yes. We felt it and it was a good one. We haven't received any reports yet, but we'll be investigating."

"I'm going to look into it as soon as I get my pants on," Denny replied. "I'll get back to you if I get any information."

A few miles to the east, Frank Kelly had been jarred out of bed and he ran down the hall, yelling for Kathy and Cindy to wake up, but they were already in the living room.

"Something's going on," he said excitedly, "I heard planes going over and then this big explosion. There's no doubt that it was a bomb."

While the girls cringed in the darkness, Frank had ran naked into the living room where Cindy sobbed in fear as she clutched Kathy's nightgown. "Are we at war Frank?" Kathy wondered aloud, but Frank's mind was racing.

"I don't think so," he said. "But on second thought, maybe a plane crashed close by. I'm going to put on my slippers and go outside to have a look. If it was a plane down, there could be a fire, and you could see it for many miles around here."

After putting on his pants, he ran out onto the porch, with the girls following on his heels, but after a few minutes of gazing toward Ocotillo, they saw nothing in the breaking dawn's faint light. As they stood looking and wondering, the flight of F-14's flew over on their return to their base.

"Either a plane crashed or they dropped a bomb," he guessed. "I'm going around the back of the house and have a look."

Off to the northeast he saw a fire, but it was low level instead of angry flames shooting skyward. It was probably some farmer burning off his field, a common practice in Imperial County. Yet he knew of a bombing range over that way near the Chocolate Mountains.

Figuratively scratching his head, he pondered this. No, it couldn't be that. This explosion was too close. It was definitely close to Ocotillo, since the percussion had rocked the house, jarring him awake abruptly.

When he returned to the porch, Cindy was shivering. "I'm scared," she whimpered. "Could we be at war with the Iranians?"

"Oh no hon," he said, dismissing the idea completely, but Kathy suggested that the idea was not so far fetched at all.

It could be a terrorist bombing at the Naval Air Facility. "Yeah," he agreed. "I never thought of that." But after a moment of consideration, he ruled it out. "Too far away."

Streaks of light to the east were harbingers of a busy day. Kathy would have to leave for work soon, and Frank wanted to go into Ocotillo to solve the mystery. His experience in Viet Nam led him to believe that there was a violent explosion rather than a sonic boom. Either a downed plane or a bomb.

When he went into town, he questioned various people as to their opinion. Was it a bomb, a plane crash, or a sonic boom? Everyone had a different idea. But when he went into the Fire Station, volunteer radioman Harry Powell was arguing with Denny Hill. Reports of broken windows were surfacing by now and Denny said it had to be a blast, as a sonic boom couldn't possibly break windows. But Harry countered this argument, stating that Denny was wrong.

"Oh yes it can," he retorted. "A sonic boom can break windows the same as a blast. You better believe it!"

When Frank suggested a plane crash as a possibility, both Harry and Denny admitted they had never considered that, nor had any planes been reported missing. "Well, it's still too early," he explained.

"Anyway, I don't think the Navy would be broadcasting that kind of news."

As they discussed it, the phone rang, and Harry answered on the first ring. "Ocotillo Fire Department," he said crisply. "What? The Stouffer well? Are you sure? We'll be right down." He turned to Denny. "There's a hole in the ground where the well used to be," he said. "Somebody blew the well last night. That's where the explosion was."

They were out the door in seconds, with Frank close on their heels. Denny and Harry hopped into the Search and Rescue vehicle and Frank followed in his pickup. When they reached the well property, all that was visible was a huge crater and piles of twisted wreckage from the two tank trunks that had been left there after yesterday's raid. The closest salt cedar trees were denuded and a fender hung from a limb.

As they stood looking at the scene of disaster, Denny gloated. "Just as I thought," he said. "They dropped a bomb. Wait till I call NAF. Them bastards said it was a sonic boom. I told you so. I told you it was a bomb."

Harry glanced at Denny, frowning, then at Frank, trying hard not to laugh. "Well, they couldn't have hit a better target. The people of Ocotillo should give them a medal."

"Oh Jesus," Frank snickered, "Wait till Stouffer sees what's left of his well."

Denny grinned now, sensing the humor in it, and both Harry and Frank burst out laughing. "He wanted a deeper well and he got it," Harry snickered.

"Right on Target," Frank said in jest. "Them Iranians won't stand a chance against our fly-boys."

Harry was looking down into the twenty-foot deep hole. "If it had blown out a little more sand, they mighta struck oil."

This made them laugh even harder until the Sheriff's Blazer pulled up and Ralph got out. "What the hell happened?" He wanted to know. "I got an anonymous call to get down here. They said something about the well being bombed."

"That's right," Denny said. "There was a flight from the NAF this morning. They passed right over town. Them suckers dropped a bomb and accidentally hit here. No doubt about it. I'm lodging a protest just as soon as I can. It's just damn lucky it didn't hit someones house."

"You can say that again," Ralph enthused with a shake of his head. "Damn! What a hole. Look at what's left of those Mexican water trucks. Well, I'll file a report. That's all I Can do."

Frank was hungry. He hadn't had his morning coffee yet and it was almost noon. Deciding to drive up to the café, he visualized a plate of hotcakes and bacon, but he also wanted to talk with the locals. He wanted to hear the opinions of others; hear what kind of rumors were circulating around town.

The blast had been a wakeup call to the community, and as he entered the restaurant, he noticed Pierre Miles and Clanahan were sitting at the counter, as were Tom Goode and his wife, Janet. Juanita Hyer and Al were sitting at a table as many tourists were, but further down the counter he glimpsed Billie and Russ Dalton. It seemed the whole town was here.

Taking a seat between Clanahan and Pierre, he caught Kathy's eye, but she was already bringing the coffee pot. The room was a buzz with the hum of voices as Kathy took his order and he noticed a new waitress servicing the tables. When he wondered about her, Kathy told him, "That's Wanda. She's new here. I like her."

Frank lit a smoke as he waited for his order, and while he gulped coffee, he struck up a conversation with Pierre, but when Kathy brought him his order, she blurted out unexpectedly. "They found out what caused the explosion. It wasn't a plane crash like you thought. The Navy dropped a bomb on the Stouffer Well."

"Yeah," Frank said. "That's what I heard." He glanced sideways. Clanahan was eating silently with a sly grin.

Pierre spoke up. "That's true," he said. "They dropped a bomb on the well."

Kathy returned a few minutes later to fill the coffee cups. She wondered where Cindy was. "When I left this morning, she was playing with her little coyote," he said. "She's all wrapped up with the darn thing."

"Well," Kathy replied, "That's about the only interest she has, I guess. There's not much out there for a young girl."

Frank nodded. "I know. I know."

As he dug into his breakfast, he wondered about the Navy dropping a bomb on the well. Everyone seemed to believe that, yet Clanahan seemed a distinct suspect. He had the wherewithal, the motive, and he had made veiled threats, but in the real world, where truth is often stranger than fiction, you could never rely on a gut feeling, a cynical suspicion.

Frank was jarred out of his reverie when Denny Hill came in and sat down to the right of Pierre. Leaning around Pierre so he could see Frank, he said something that added to the confusion. "Say Frank," he began. "I called NAF and gave em hell, but they claim they don't carry any live ammo. I asked if it wasn't possible that one live round could have been aboard by accident and they hedged. They said anything is possible, but it was extremely unlikely."

"So they aren't' taking the blame?" Frank replied.

"No." Denny explained. "It's the old game of passing the buck. They said they will investigate the matter thoroughly."

"Oh, sure!" Frank said with disgust.

Frank noticed that Denny's attention was drawn behind him just as someone tapped him on the shoulder. Twisting around, he saw Libby Hatfield glaring. "Oh there you are," she said acidly. "I hope you are proud of yourself. Now you have brought another tragedy upon our town. First, the shooting and killing at the well, and now this terrible bombing. God is punishing us all for your sins."

Kathy stood in front of Frank now, and Clanahan was turning to face Libby, sneering. "The only sin in this town is you and your damn religion. Why don't you take a walk down to the well and jump into that nice big hole?"

Libby was looking into Kathy's eyes. "Come down to our church next Sunday," she said. "Give your life to Christ, for He died that we may live. We are all sinners, my child, but He will forgive us our trespasses if we give ourselves unto Him."

Kathy, staring into Libby's eyes wistfully – and much to Frank's surprise – said, "I think I will. You see, I have cancer and I am afraid."

"Well, my child, you come on down and we'll pray for you." Her voice was plaintive. "It's never too late when you accept Jesus Christ."

As Kathy stood in front of the men with downcast eyes, Denny sympathized with her. "I'm sorry to hear you have cancer," he said. "It seems like everyone's got it nowadays."

Pierre spoke up. "Yes Sir. It seems like everyone has it."

Though mystified by Kathy's statement, Frank added to the other's views. "Well, I've got it too," he informed them. "I got it from Agent Orange when I was in Viet Nam." Now, with introspection, his thoughts were regressive.

His cancer of the lymph nodes had remained quiescent over the last five years, the time he had lived in the desert, and it showed no sign of recurrence. But the doctors at the Veteran's Hospital had warned him it could reappear at any time.

Though his fears were mostly forgotten, he remembered the all-consuming horror of his dreams, when he would awaken after a nightmare, thinking he was dying. In a cold sweat, he would bolt upright in bed, his heart pounding and his mind filled with horrible visions of death. But his nightmares ceased when he moved to the desert. He all but forgot about his cancer.

Subliminally, his thoughts drifted to Kathy's remark. In front of strangers, she had revealed a dark secret. How come? He remembered when she and Cindy broke down and came to him for help. They had talked about cancer then. She had seen a book on the subject that Frank had, and she had mentioned that her father had cancer, but she never mentioned that she, herself, had it.

There was something about Kathy that puzzled Frank. She had never become warm and friendly with him. Living under the same roof as they did, she had remained somewhat aloof. In fact, he and Cindy enjoyed more camaraderie than Kathy and him. It seemed unnatural. The sexapades between him and Cindy were the expected culmination of male and female in close proximity, where intimacy develops from familiarity and common interests.

But not Kathy!

Oh, well...maybe Kathy's experience shacking up with Eric had soured her on romance. Whatever the case, burning with curiosity, Frank vowed to ask her – flat out- about her remark.

Clanahan had just left when Frank decided to go home, but when he reached his pickup, Clanahan, parked next to him, had the hood up on his car and was tinkering with the sparkplug wires. Frank caught his eye.

"Hey old timer," he said. "Do you believe that the Navy dropped a bomb on the well?"

Clanahan smiled wickedly. "It's possible."

"You don't think so?"

"Well, as Libby might say, God could have done it."

"You didn't have anything to do with it?"

"I'll never tell."

I won't either, Frank thought to himself. As long as everyone believed that a Navy plane had dropped a bomb; as long as the issue was in doubt, let it die there. Although he knew in his heart, the truth, it was better that no one actually knew for certain. And since truth brings heartbreak, lawsuits and incarceration, it's better to let it rest. Let it sleep.

On his way home, he thought about the explosion. Regardless of truth, without consideration for legality, sometimes force is the best answer. Sometimes an illegal action is beneficial to the masses. If blowing the well could put Stouffer out of business and bring peace to Ocotillo, it would also be a big step towards stopping illegal immigration and drug importation.

Maybe a Navy plane had dropped a bomb. Maybe Clanahan had blown the well, or maybe God did it. No one will ever know.

CHAPTER ELEVEN

It is late evening and with the sun low in the west, it has cooled off a few degrees. While Cindy is out on the porch playing with her little coyote, Frank and Kathy are sitting around the kitchen table, talking about things in general.

"You surprised me this morning," Frank said as he twirled his bottle of beer nervously. "You said you had cancer. What gives?"

"Well, I do have it," Kathy said demurely. "Why should it surprise you?"

Frank tried to explain. "Well, this is the first time I've heard anything about it. All this time you've been here, you go to work every day and now all of a sudden you say you've got it." He was puzzled and curious. "I just don't understand."

Kathy, looking downcast and sorrowful, her hair in disarray, fired back. "There's a lot you don't understand about a woman's body. Let's just say I found a lump. I don't want to talk about it."

"Okay, I assume it's on your chest," Frank said as he reached for a cigarette. "Today, we do talk about it. Everyone talks about cancer. Everyone knows a lot about the symptoms. Kathy, there's nothing to be ashamed of. I got mine from Agent Orange in Viet Nam, and I just live with it. I ignore it."

"Fine," Kathy said as she brushed her hair back, "But how can I ignore it? Women are taught to look for lumps and I found one. Because my mother died from it at my age, I have a right to be worried."

Frank lit his cigarette and blew a cloud of smoke towards the ceiling. "Jese, Kathy, I'm sorry," he said. "Y'know, I'm beginning to see where you're coming from, but as I said, your best bet is to ignore it. Get your mind off it. The lump may not be malignant anyway."

Kathy shook her head hopelessly. "My mother had a radical mastectomy. They took off her right breast, then a year later, they found that the cancer had spread to her left one. She went through hell with radiation and chemo...lost her hair...oh God, I can't face an ordeal like that."

Frank suddenly felt sick to his stomach just thinking about it. The idea of cutting off part of a woman's body seemed gross. "Well," he said. "You just have to take what life hands you. You've just got to live one day at a time. But if I were you, I'd go on as usual and not worry about it."

Kathy got up from her chair and walked to the refrigerator. She took a Pepsi and grabbed a bag of chips from the counter and sat down again. "Well, that's about all I can do right now. I don't have any health insurance...soooo!" Her voice trailed off and she stared down at the table when Cindy burst into the house, carrying her little coyote.

"Mom," she said excitedly, "I put him down on the floor and backed up and he followed me. He can walk good now."

Frank smiled at her. "He looks good and healthy, but listen, hon, I'd rather you didn't bring him in the house. Okay?"

"He's so cuddly," she said happily. "He's like a little teddy bear. I'm going to call him Wiley. That's his name now."

"That's cute," Kathy said as she popped a chip in her mouth. "You take him outside, now. Frank doesn't want him in the house."

Cindy backed toward the door. "You didn't think he would live, did you, mom?"

"Well, he looked pretty sad," Kathy reminded her. "Another thing. He's going to want a lot of meat as he grows up, and I'm not going to buy dog food. But I could bring table scraps from work. When I was your age, we had a dog, and that's all the food he ever got. In fact, he was healthy as could be."

As Cindy went outside, Kathy looked at Frank. The talk about Wiley had made her forget about her cancer. Half-smiling, she became nostalgic. "Gosh! The way Cindy is growing up. Things are so different now. When I was a child, we lived on a farm. We had cows and pigs, the works. We grew our own veggies and fruits and mother canned a lot of stuff. I remember winters, I remember the snow and cold. As I grew up and started dating, I was of course preoccupied with boys, but later as I watched television and saw pictures of sunny California, I dreamed of living there, and here I am."

"I think that Wiley might be good for Cindy in a way. He gives her something to keep her mind on, something to cuddle. You know, the maternal instinct…oh, I just happened to think. I'll have to start registering her for school." Kathy shook her head and glanced away momentarily. "She'll need new clothes. She doesn't have much in the way of a wardrobe, you know."

Frank sensed that Kathy had no intention of leaving Ocotillo any time soon. "Have you thought any more about going to San Diego?" He wondered aloud. "Have you saved enough money yet?"

Kathy reached for more chips and stared down at the table, deep in thought. "You know, Frank," she said demurely. "Those are good questions. I've asked myself the same many times. I've saved quite a lot, but still, the tips have fallen off somewhat. Buying the groceries and gas take a lot, so I don't have the nest egg I would need. But there is something else." She stopped to sip her Pepsi.

"Cindy seems happy here, for one thing, and I have grown to like it here also. I have made friends like Wanda and you; I've gotten to know a lot of people who come into the restaurant, I've even gotten to like the desert itself. The only bad thing about living here is that you don't have air-conditioning."

"Whoa!" Frank interjected. "I've been thinking about that. Cindy has also mentioned the unbearable heat…seems the summers are getting hotter now… You remember Cliff Brown, the old guy I asked to fix your car? Well, I've got an old swamp cooler on the roof and it hasn't been used for years. I'm going to ask Cliff if he will fix it for me."

"That would be nice," Kathy smiled. "Anyway, I'm not in any hurry to leave here in the foreseeable future."

Frank thought back, when Kathy had arrived here, she had been determined to get to San Diego. She had been unreasonable in dealing with the hard facts of life. When he had suggested that she take a waitress job, she had scoffed, but now, it seemed, she had learned a lesson.

He really didn't give a damn whether she left or not, since the romance he had dreamed of at first never blossomed. Not only that, but his growing camaraderie with Susan further blocked out any feelings for Kathy.

Still, he was rather happy that she had decided to stay. It was a pretty good partnership, with her buying most of the groceries and keeping Cindy in his house, for if Kathy left, Cindy would go with her. He wouldn't want that. Cindy was young and hot, she provided passionate sex, the kind he had always dreamed of. Aggressively pursuing him, she was uninhibited, and her body was tight. Worry about getting caught and going to jail for statutory rape was now gone. He had passed the Rubicon. There was no turning back now. After the first time, his innocence ceased to exist.

In Cindy, he had found a treasure greater than gold. A woman he could die for. He loved the way she came onto him, the way she thrusted, and the way her sweet lips kissed his body. For these reasons, he would be devastated if Kathy left, but today, after their conversation, he was assured of continuing his affair with this beautiful girl.

Frank took a swig from his bottle and reached for another cigarette. "Okay," he began. "I'm glad that you are beginning to enjoy it here and that you are making friends. When I get the cooler fixed, you will be more comfortable, I'm sure."

Kathy nodded. "Oh, without a doubt," she agreed. "Hmmm....a...oh yes. Do the school busses come out here from El Centro?"

"Yup. I see them every winter," he replied as he lit his smoke. "Say, Kathy, speaking of El Centro, Cindy and I were worried last night when you didn't come home. We figured you were caught in the sand storm."

Kathy became animated at the mention of it. "Oh that was terrible. I didn't go to El Centro because Wanda told me about Sam's Club in Calexico. She said I could save a lot on groceries there. When I came out of the store, the wind was kicking up and I could feel the sand hitting me. As I was getting in my car, a guy yelled at me. He said if I drove in the storm, my car would be sandblasted. He said to wait until the wind died down."

"Well, I waited and finally I went back into the store where everyone was taking shelter, and took a seat at the lunch counter. I ordered a hamburger and sat there as long as I could. I was frantic by then."

Frank could see her anguish as she spoke. She went on to tell of the hours passing, the crush of people in the store. She agonized over not being able to contact him, her worry for Cindy. She said that Cindy had no tolerance for storms. She would become hysterical. Cindy was in the habit of sleeping with Kathy, and what would she do if her mom wasn't there?

"I heard people saying that this was the worst storm they had ever seen," Kathy continued. "Then they announced over the P.A. system that the Highway

Patrol was warning motorists to stay put. Visibility was zero. Sand drifts were blocking roads."

Frank was shaking his head in amazement. "I agree that it was terrible," he said. "I've never seen a storm as bad as that one around Ocotillo, but what did you do next?"

Kathy said people in the store were cursing the weather. Some were peering out the front doors into the lighted parking lot, darkened by wind-blown sand, while others were stretched out on the floor, using their purchases as pillows, and she saw one enterprising woman resting her head on a package of toilet paper.

Frank smiled. "Yeah. Toilet paper. Makes a nice soft pillow."

"I didn't sleep much," Kathy said. "I dozed off a few times, but when the storm let up and it got light, I headed for home. When I got near Pinto Wash, they had machines clearing the road. There were drifts of sand like the snowdrifts I remember from childhood. Of course I had to sit and wait...and wait...and wait."

Frank was scratching his head. "Yeah, well...you're right about Cindy being scared. She was terrified by the storm. The old house rattled and banged so loud I thought it would blow away. It was kinda spooky. I had came home from the bar when the wind had started, and found her alone, sitting in the living room. She was petrified with fear. I went to bed and conked out, but this morning when I woke up, she was in bed with me. I got up and put the coffee on. Poor kid was so scared."

Kathy nodded with understanding. "It's a good thing you were here to keep her company. I guess I should never have left her alone."

CHAPTER TWELVE

July 10, 1983

A green Ford van pulled up in front of the Community Hall and Peter Williams stepped out into the early morning sun, followed by three other men. Peter, a tall, lanky Englishman, wore a brown Aussie hat, cocked to one side, brown casual slacks and a white military-looking short-sleeved shirt with two large pockets and epaulets. His mustachioed face and blue eyes engendered visions of Adolph Hitler or a Harvard professor as he walked jauntily past Jay Bradford's red Jeep and Frank's Dodge pickup.

As the three men followed Peter inside, Jay broke into a friendly smile, while Frank and Cindy gazed with curiosity at the newcomers. Geoff Weisse sat stoically, contemplating the new arrivals. Jay had told the archaeology class some time ago, that Williams was planning a trip to the cave, since the stories of the red-eyed skulls had piqued his curiosity.

One of the main reasons Peter was so interested in this particular cave was his research on Ancient Americans. For years, he had been compiling information on the Mayan Indians in Mexico, and the Egyptians, for he was known as an Egyptologist and could tell you more than you wanted to know about life on the Nile five thousand years ago.

Like Thor Hyerdahl, he was interested in the migration from Egypt to the Americas and beyond, since he believed that the Mexicans were derived from Egyptian ancestors who then interbred with Mexican native Indians. The basis for this belief was founded mainly on the pyramids that were found in both countries.

His theories didn't stop there, however. His hypothesis stated that ten thousand years ago, North American was, or could have been, populated by these Egyptian adventurers and not by wanderers over the Bering Sea land bridge.

Jay, standing in front of the seated early arrivals, cigarette in hand, greeted Peter with a handshake. "Did you have any trouble finding this place?"

Peter shook his head. "Not at all," he said, "but it's a long drive from San Diego."

Those scheduled to go in the cave were Frank and Cindy, Tom Goode, Geoff Weisse, Russ Dalton and Susan Rider, making a total of seven with Jay. But Susan was out of town, leaving six in Jay's party. Peter and his men numbered four, added to Jay's group, totaled up to ten, with Cindy being the only female in the entire group.

"These men," Peter gestured toward them, "will assist us and keep records. This is Andy Gifford, the photographer. This is Joe Holloway, the speleologist – cave expert to you – and this is Hank Lyman our porter. Hank volunteered his services to help us out."

The class acknowledged the men, whereupon Jay introduced his students to the strangers. "I guess I should introduce Peter Williams," he said, pointing to

Peter and nodding. "You've heard me talk about him before. He's the curator of the museum in San Diego and has a great interest in this desert." He went on to introduce his students by name.

"I'm Jay Bradford, head honcho of the Imperial Valley Desert Museum in El Centro. These people are my students, if you will." He swept his hand over his group, still seated. "I've been recording and cataloging the giant intaglios here and getting pictures which I intend to put in a book form for posterity when I get time. The cave we will examine today is an anomaly for this region. It is unusual in that human skulls have been found in it."

He stopped and smiled. He pointed to Frank in the first row. "This is Frank Kelly, the man who discovered the cave."

Frank removed his cap and waved it briefly over his head, smiling. "That's me."

Then Jay introduced the others. "That's Cindy, our little sweetheart. That's Tom Goode." He was pointing to each. "That's Geoff Weisse, my right hand man. That's Russ Dalton. We have many locals enrolled in our classes, but they're mostly older people who are unable to withstand the rigors of long walking and climbing."

Peter was getting antsy. "Well, we didn't want to have too many on this trip. Actually, today, we plan on making an exploratory first examination. See what's in there. See if it warrants further consideration. Are we ready?"

On the way up the grade, with Jay and Geoff leading in the Jeep and Frank and Cindy behind them, Frank was thinking about Peter's Aussie hat. It made him look macho. He glanced at Cindy. "What do you think of Peter's hat? Don't you think I would look good in one like that?"

But when the caravan parked up the grade, Peter donned a cap, saying the Aussie hat would be a hindrance in the tight quarters of the cave, and after they had lugged all their gear up the hill and Peter saw the small entrance, his first remark was that they should move some of the rocks and dig a larger opening, since that small hole made entrance too difficult. He ordered Hank to move some of the rocks, but when Hank started to enlarge the opening, Geoff pitched in, then Frank and Tom assisted.

They had brought headlights, cameras, some food and water, a ball of twine and miscellaneous gear and had piled it below the cave entrance and as Jay stood watching, he was lighting a smoke.

"We've got a good view of the Valley, here," he said thoughtfully. "It's the highest point at the 2000 foot level. Only In-ko-pah and the Smuggler's cave are higher. I'll bet the ancient natives had a ball looking out over the lake that used to be here."

"Yeah," Frank said, straightening up from his task. "I call it Pinnacle Point. I never would have discovered the cave if I hadn't climbed up the rocks."

Cindy, wearing tennis shoes, was wandering around, looking at the cactus, waiting for the men to clear the cave entrance. But she was watching where she stepped, remembering the first time she had been here with Frank and got a thorn stuck in her foot. As she gazed down at the agave, with its needle sharp spines, she wondered what it would be like if she tripped and fell on it. Would it pierce her heart? The thought was scary.

An hour passed and they were now ready to enter the cave. First, Peter equipped every other person with a miner's headlamp, fitted onto a helmet with adjustable headband. Joe Holloway, the cave expert, bearing a light, would lead the way. Peter would follow behind him without a light. Next would be Jay, with a headlight. Geoff would follow Jay. Then the others, in turn, would trail behind. Frank would bear a light, but Cindy behind him, would not. Hank Lyman would carry a backpack containing emergency equipment.

As they entered the catacomb, Joe, leading, was stringing a guideline of twine as a safety measure, should they need it. When sunlight gave way to darkness, lamps were lit, creating ghostly shadows on the smooth walls, and Cindy became apprehensive. She took hold of Frank's belt and clung to him fearfully as they moved along the smooth dirt floor.

"This path is well worn," Joe called out. "It looks like a good many people walked here sometime in the distant past."

No sooner had he said it, they came into a small room where their lights revealed the row of red-eyed skulls Frank had told about in the beginning. Five or six were immediately visible, glaringly white in the bright light of the lamps, and the light picked up a reddish glow in the empty eye-sockets.

While some of the party groaned, Tom Goode yelled out. "Wow! What the hell is this, a graveyard?" Frank felt Cindy's grip tighten.

Joe said with a chuckle, "Kinda spooky."

Peter commented, "I don't know what to think. It may be part of a ritual, maybe religious, but definitely Indian. We know for a fact that many early cultures practiced sacrificial rites. They would kill young girls to appease their gods. These skulls are small, indicating young females. I've seen skulls and skeletons all over the world, but not in American caves."

Andy Gifford, the photographer spoke up. "Peter. Have you noticed the burnt stuff on the floor?"

Peter looked down. "That's ocotillo, or what's left of it. Makes a good torch. I've never tested it, but they say it burns very well."

"Yeah," Jay said. "Torches were the only light they had in ancient times. They had a lot of nerve to come in here with something like that."

Andy snapped a picture of the skulls. "Not any more than ancient mariners. Them sailors risked their lives crossing uncharted oceans in frail boats, searching for new lands, new continents."

"That's right," Peter spoke up. "Like the rafts made of reeds. Thor Heyderdahl proved back in the fifties that it could be done, but I'd be reluctant to try it."

"Well, let's move on," Joe Holloway suggested. "Let's see what other surprises lay ahead. Those skulls, by themselves raise more questions than they answer."

Cindy released her grasp on Frank's belt. She had calmed down from her first fright, and Frank had squeezed her hand momentarily, assuring her that everything was all right.

The pathway sloped downward and there was a movement of air from below, which indicated that there must be an opening somewhere at a lower level. This did not go unnoticed by Joe, because he remembered Wind Cave in the Black Hills of South Dakota which was discovered by a cowboy who felt a strong updraft from a small opening in the ground.

"Peter," he said. "Can you feel the air moving past us?" Peter answered in the affirmative as Joe explained. "It has a dank odor, yet it isn't characteristic of most caves. I can smell fresh air, but it's mixed with earthy odors, so there must be an opening down below us. The chimney effect."

"I agree," Peter said. "Well, so far, we haven't found anything of much value. It appears to be just an ordinary cave that the Indians visited frequently for a reason unknown."

"A dud," Joe added. "I didn't expect much when you told me about it. But you never know. Looks like a drop-off ahead. You guys wait here a minute. I'll investigate; make sure it's safe to go on."

While the main group huddled behind, Joe walked ahead, examining the pathway, then yelled back. "It's a minor step-down. No loose rock. Just be careful." His light shone ahead. "Hey, Peter. It looks like the tunnel is widening. Wait. I can't see it clearly, but it looks like there may be a larger cavity ahead."

As the party advanced, with Joe ahead of the others, he exclaimed excitedly. "Wow! Hey guys, we've run into something." When the group stepped up their pace, they entered a large chamber where the walls sparkled like diamonds in the brilliance of the headlamps.

"Isn't that beautiful?" Jay mused aloud.

"Looks like my wife's Brooch," Andy Gifford joked.

But Peter was all business. "Record it and see if you can get a good picture," he said.

Frank spoke up. "Unbelievable. I've never seen anything like it."

Cindy agreed. "It's pretty. Are those real diamonds?"

Frank shook his head. "No, I don't think so."

Jay addressed Joe. As a speleologist, he would probably know something about minerals and gems. "They're not real diamonds, are they?"

Joe, his face close to the wall, was gazing intently at the shiny crystals. "We find stalactites and stalagmites in many caves – calcite, but this looks like crystals of quartz, probably barium and copper pyrites," he explained. "Most people call it chalcopyrite."

"Well, it sure is pretty Stuff," Jay admitted.

Peter glanced at the photographer. "Andy, make a note of this," he said. "We'll call this chamber the Devil's Jewel Box."

Cindy grinned and said to Frank, "That's a good name, isn't it?"

Pressing onward, the party moved lower into a larger chamber where they got the surprise of their lives. The floor was littered with burnt out torches and the smooth walls were virtually covered with pictographs. The surprise wasn't the hieroglyphics, but the nature of them. They were almost all related to sexual intercourse or they pertained to childbirth and fertility, but a couple were explicit in the extreme.

Crude as they were, a couple of them showed men and women copulating, others showed the sun and crops, but as Cindy stood gazing at the big fat caricature of a penis, Peter exclaimed in awe, "Joe, look at this!" He was pointing at a drawing of a flat-topped pyramid. The sloping outer walls were stepped, and a cupola-looking edifice sat on top.

Joe stared at the pyramid. "This is hard to believe," he said finally. "This may be the greatest discovery of all time."

"That's what I was thinking," Peter admitted. But Geoff spoke sarcastically. "What the hell is so great about it? I've seen pictures of pyramids before."

"It's the TYPE of pyramid that boggles my mind," Peter explained. "The Egyptian pyramids come to a point on top, but this one is flat. It is characteristic of those found on the Yucatan Peninsula. It signifies the Mayan culture. Nowhere else on earth do we find pyramids of this type."

"So??!!" Geoff sneered. "So what's your point?"

"Just this," Peter began. "Cave drawings like this tell us, with pictures, of the life and times of ancient people. I have often speculated that the Mayan Empire could have extended throughout Mexico, rather than being confined to the Yucatan Peninsula. This proves that the Mayans were here at some time, and my guess is that the Yumans were descendents of the Mayans." He took a deep breath. "Now Thor Heyerdahl proved that Egyptians probably migrated to the area around Yucatan, Honduras, Nicaragua, down to Panama and South America, and if so, this pictograph pretty well proves the connection to the Yumans. What I'm saying, is that I believe the North American Continent was populated by the Egyptians thousands of years ago, rather than by Asians crossing the land bridge over the Bering Sea."

Jay nodded. "I've often thought the same thing, Peter, but regardless, this simple drawing, as you and Joe believe, may be the greatest discovery of all time because it proves that the Mayans were here."

Cindy was barely listening to the men. Her eyes were on the copulating couples, and she wondered if there were penises that big in real life. She hadn't had a lot of experience with men, but she guessed that Frank's was about eight inches.

"Yes. They were here," Peter began. "My hunch was correct. But I've got another theory. I believe that the legend of the lost city of the Yumans could be true. This mythical city of gold could be in this desert or it could be in Mexico. Perhaps northern Mexico. But most likely within a radius of a hundred miles surrounding Yuma."

"There we go again," Geoff sniffed. "Legend of gold. Always gold. I don't believe in Santa Claus, I don't believe there's a man upstairs who created everything, and I don't believe in legends."

"What you want to believe is your prerogative," Peter fired back. "I base my belief on Egyptian antiquities. Their belief in an afterlife led them to bury many objects of gold with the pharaohs. And since about 1922, we have unearthed tons of stuff with gold inlay, or gold leaf, or solid gold...So I reason that this legend could be true. Look, Geoff, I first heard about the legend of a lost city years ago, and it intrigued me. Being a romantic, I fantasized about it, but this drawing of a flat-topped pyramid convinces me further...uh... well, it fortifies my belief. There could be thousands of things buried under the shifting sands out here."

"Oh. By-the-way, Peter," Jay cut in. "We had a hell of a sandstorm a few days ago. Drifts blocked the roads, sand stripped the paint from cars and pitted windows. I was lucky to be home at the time.'

Cindy, listening, recalled the storm. She had been terrorized by the sound of gale force winds whining through the eaves and rattling the house, and her imagination had run wild, but Joe Holloway, who had been in Yucatan, was staring at the pictograph as Peter and Geoff argued.

Reminiscing, he pointed to the pyramid drawing and said to Jay, "The first time I saw one like this was a couple years ago. I had joined a party to explore a 65 million year old cave about 100 miles from Tikal." All attention was diverted to him, now, as he spoke.

"Our group of scientists and archaeologists were to enter the forbidden cave, Naj Tunich, in search of artifacts, but also to ascertain it's depth, since it had never before been plumbed, never been explored. Our Mexican archaeologist was also our interpreter. He spoke fluent English and Mexican, but he also knew several other languages. Remarkable man."

Joe pointed a finger at the pictograph. "See how the pyramid sides are stepped? Carlos – his name was Carlos Sanchez – he told us an interesting story, although it was gruesome. He said that when they took children to the top to be sacrificed, the decapitated heads would roll and bounce down those steps." He grimaced in disgust.

"You may wonder what this was all about. Well, as Carlos told us, the river of blood running down the sides was symbolic of the sun going down." Joe was shaking his head. "Now isn't that stupid? For all their intelligence, the Mayans were nutty in their beliefs, especially their religious beliefs. What in the hell was killing and blood got to do with appeasing their gods? Maybe children were deemed extremely valuable and maybe the high priests wanted to offer something of value. I don't know."

"All religion is nutty," Geoff interjected. "How can modern man accept the idea of Jesus Christ? If he was alive today, we'd call him a hippie. They say he died for us. Well, how about our soldiers and policeman? Don't they die for us? I just can't understand the human psyche. People believe the damndest things."

"Well, I don't know about that," Jay replied, "but getting back to high priests, you know what I read years ago? Some article in a men's magazine told of religion in times of antiquity. The article stated that the high priests job was to deflower the young girls. Yeah, they broke their maiden heads, thus sparing the husband-to-be the nasty job of doing it." He was grinning at the thought of it.

Hank Lyman spoke up. "You mean they took the girl's virginity by natural means?"

Jay was nodding, "Yes! By intercourse."

Hank broke into a broad grin. "Yikes. How'd you like to have a job like that?"

"You know what I read one time?" Geoff offered another viewpoint. "I read a piece on religion years ago about Catholics. The article said that the Catholic religion was founded on sex. The priests wanted a steady source of young boys, so they made up this deal about their alter boys and using scare tactics about a vengeful god, they made their kids swear to secrecy. If they ever told anyone, they'd go to hell. I'll bet those priests are all pedophiles. They didn't want girls; they wanted boys."

"Brainwashed them," Hank added. "Yeah."

Frank was thinking about that. Men always wanted tightness. That was one reason he loved sex with Cindy. That was probably why so many men covet children. He glanced sideways at Cindy. He didn't see anything wrong with having sex with children, as long as they were teenage and the union was consensual. And if a well-developed teenager not only consented, but was EAGER to have sex with an older person, he couldn't see why it would be illegal.

Cindy was greatly amused by all this talk about sex. She nudged Frank and winked at him, grinning like the cat that got the canary. But she turned sober as Peter angrily defended Catholicism.

"Okay Guys," he said with authority, "I think we've had enough of Catholic bashing. It just so happens that I am Catholic, but the point is that this is supposed to be a scientific work of archeology, and it has turned into petty nitpicking. Let's keep ugly rumors and hearsay out of our discussions from here on. Okay? Now I think it's time to move on."

Jay was nodding in agreement, but Geoff was about to protest, when Jay shushed him. "Peter's right," he said to his class, "He made this exploration possible and I acknowledged his leadership. I don't want any hard feelings here, so let's get on with it."

As the group began to move forward, Peter said to Joe, "Now you got pictures, make a note of identification. We'll call this the Fertility Chamber."

Advancing downward through the enlarging tunnel, the party came upon a maze of branching passageways leading to multiple rooms. Neither Joe nor Peter could decide which way to go. Jay said it didn't make much difference which way they went, so long as they marked their trail with twine. The idea, after all, was to unlock the secrets of the grotto.

Moving along what seemed like the main route, the chambers became more expansive with higher roofs or ceilings, and the air seemed fresher the farther they went. Peter, musing aloud, was impressed by the size and magnitude of the chambers and of the maze as a whole.

"It looks like the entire mountain is hollowed out," he said. "It appears to be a natural cavity, and it must be the inside of an extinct volcano, it reminds me of the lava tubes up near Mount Lassen."

"Yeah," Jay agreed. "Man could never have excavated all this. But my guess is that the characters of the walls have changed...perhaps over eons of time, because they don't look like lava ever flowed through them."

"Peter!" Joe exclaimed. "Look at the dirt we're standing on. That doesn't look natural."

Everyone looked down. The floor of this section was a mixture of sand and gravel, with black soil mixed in, so the area viewed from a standing position appeared to have been a bog, or had been flooded and dried. Jay dropped to his knees and scooped up a handful of soil. Peter and Joe did the same.

"Desert clay and oil? Clay mixed with aggregate? Plain mud?" Jay offered his opinion. "Well it looks like sedimentary deposits mixed with oil. It had a distinct slippery feeling."

"Yes, it does," Peter replied. "It is odd." He looked down at the handful of gunk, deep in thought. "I don't know. In a way, it looks as if it could be just plain mud containing excessive minerals that has dried."

Joe spoke up. "That's what I think," he said, "This entire area appears to have been flooded, and this glop is silt. Doesn't that make sense?"

Jay rubbed the dirt between his fingers. "Yeah. That makes sense. What do you think, Peter?"

Peter agreed, but how could this cavern have been flooded? It was on the mountainside, high above the valley below. Jay came up with a plausible answer. "The only way, as I see it," he began, "would be if the ancient lake that covered Imperial Valley, was high enough to impact this grotto. Still, how would the water get in there?"

Cindy needed a bathroom and she wandered afar, looking for a place out of sight of the men. Suddenly, she started yelling, and her cries echoed through the passageways. "I see daylight," she screamed. "I can see the sun."

As the men rushed toward her voice, their lamps lit up the dim area she had chosen, and around a bend they too, saw a faint light. "That's where the air is coming in," Jay announced when he saw it. "That means there is an opening at the bottom of the cave."

"Right on," Peter replied gleefully. "It is probably the original entrance, closed by a rockslide."

While the main group passed Cindy, Frank brought up the rear, and abreast of her, she began wailing about her foot. She said she had stepped on a stone and twisted her ankle, but when Frank looked down his light illuminated the area. It wasn't a stone, but something was protruding from the soil. He kicked it with his heavy boot.

The object, about eight inches long, was dirty, but there was a bright reflection where the soil had been dislodged. Fascinated, he picked it up and rubbed the dirt off, revealing a penis shaped artifact in bronze.

"What the hell!" He exclaimed. "Cindy! Look at this." When he handed it to her, she turned it over several times, puzzling, then admiring it. She grinned.

"I'm going to keep it," she vowed. "Don't tell the guys about it, or they'll take it. I found it and finders are keepers."

"No, hon, it's an artifact. We've got to give it to Peter. The whole idea of us being here is to evaluate this cave. You were allowed in here because you were with me and I can't let you keep it."

As they talked, the main group was twenty yards away, nearing the hole where daylight streamed in. Their conclusion was unanimous; there must have been an opening here at some time, and it must have been covered by a rockslide.

When Joe suggested that they move enough rocks to escape without going back up through the labyrinth, Peter shook his head. There was no way they could move those tons of rocks, and furthermore, even if they could, they would be a mile or more away from their vehicles.

But something more ominous was in the air. Both Jay and Geoff had begun to complain about severe fatigue, and Jay had pain in his chest. It had been an arduous journey down through the cavern, and both Joe and Peter suspected heart attacks, although they kept silent out of fear of upsetting the two. Yet, they worried about getting them back to the top opening, and if they had known that Cindy had sprained her ankle, they would have been even more worried.

"We'll have to call it a day," Peter said knowingly. The rockslide would have to be blasted if they were to open the lower entrance. "I don't think there is enough interest here to warrant further exploration. It's unusual, but not earthshaking."

"Well, we learned one thing today," Jay advised the group. "If this was the main entrance to the labyrinth, it would be about on the level of the ancient lake Cahuilla, and right above Ocotillo. A period of exceptionally high water could have flooded this lower catacomb hundreds of years ago, thus explaining the silt here. In other words, there could be artifacts buried beneath our feet."

When the main group walked back where Frank and Cindy were, they saw Cindy bent over, rubbing her ankle and Frank was holding something in his hand. Peter wondered what was the matter with Cindy, and as Frank told him she may have sprained her ankle, he flashed the artifact.

"She tripped over this."

Eyes bugging out, the group stared in awe. "What?" Peter said, "What the heck...what...where did you get that?"

Frank jabbed his finger toward Cindy, "She stepped on it. It was sticking out of the soil right there." He pointed, then passed the artifact to Peter's outstretched hand.

As the group crowded closer to view it, questions flew freely. "What is it? Oh, it looks like a penis. Is it gold?"

Peter was incredulous as he exclaimed the piece. "Looks like bronze, but it may be gold with a patina. It's heavy enough to be gold."

"Yeah," Geoff smirked. "Could be lead too. Why would someone make a thing like that?"

"Oh," Peter said. "The ancient cultures were hung up on fertility rites. Depicting genitalia or copulating was common among all races around the world."

Geoff nodded, "Yeah, and present day societies are still hung up on the sex organs. Everything you read about is sex and more sex. It seems like sex is the most important thing in the world. I don't get it.'

Frank chuckled. "You don't get it? Maybe you aren't looking in the right places. Or maybe you're too old get it."

"Look, Geoff," Jay said. "Sex is the most important thing in the world. Without it, you and I wouldn't be here."

"Okay. Okay," Geoff agreed.

"Be that as it may," Peter said as he took the artifact from Jay, "This little item has changed my mind about further exploration. What I would like to do sometime in the future is to blast the rockslide and come in with a crew for a major dig."

Cindy, leaning on Frank for support, held out her hand toward Peter, "I found it and I'd like to keep it as a souvenir.

Peter shook his head, looking her in the eye. "I'm afraid not," he said. "It belongs to the museum. If we come back and find more specimens, they'll be catalogued and studied. Our job as archaeologists is to analyze, assemble facts and draw conclusions. That's how we read ancient history. Do you understand?"

Cindy shrugged. "I guess so."

Now, the long climb uphill faced them. With Cindy hobbling along, clinging to Frank, it took the group almost an hour to reach the 'Fertility Chamber', where the walls were inscribed with pictographs. With Jay and Geoff experiencing extreme fatigue, they had to stop and rest often.

By the time they had reached the 'Devil's Jewel Box', Jay was having chest pains again, and Peter worried about his heart. Jay, however, struggling to breathe, attributed the pain in his stomach to gas.

"I'm all right," he protested. "I've had this before and it goes away when I rest."

By the time the party had reached 'Pinnacle Point', the entrance, everyone was dragging. Cindy was hanging onto Frank and Frank was barely able to walk. Joe was helping Jay and Tom Goode was helping Geoff. Peter, carrying the artifact, was out of breath.

The trip down to the vehicles was a great relief from the strenuous climb up the cave, but the heat of the late afternoon was shocking, and when they reached their cars, Peter yelled at Jay, "I'd see a doctor if I were you. Better to be safe than sorry."

CHAPTER THIRTEEN

August 15, 1983

Frank Kelly lay sprawled out in his lounge chair, watching the evening news. The house was quiet, save for the sound of a reporter's voice telling of the cave discovery last month, which led to a heart attack of a local archaeologist.

"The mystery cave, recently in the news, has drawn the attention of people as far away as New York and was entered by a party led by the Museum of Man's Peter Williams. Two local men, Geoff Weisse and Jay Bradford, both of El Centro, suffered chest pains during the strenuous exploration, and both consulted their physicians the next day. Mr. Bradford was rushed into surgery where a six-way by-pass was successfully accomplished, while Mr. Weisse was treated with blood thinners and released."

"Doctors noted that Bradford was a heavy smoker, and blamed his coronary occlusion on cigarettes, but the story has a happy ending: Bradford, who lives only a few blocks from El Centro Regional Hospital on Imperial Avenue, is at home convalescing and will be back at work at Imperial Valley College soon."

Frank lit a cigarette and stared at the television screen, thinking. "Yeah, Jay smoked, but the reporter doesn't mention that Geoff is grossly overweight.

We were all tired, even Cindy, who is as healthy as a horse, but Geoff is the only non-smoker who got chest pains."

The sound of a car alerted Frank. He perked up his ears. Yep, it was Kathy and Cindy, home from a shopping trip to town to buy Cindy's school clothes. He knew the sound of her Pontiac and the sound of its doors slamming shut. Next thing he heard was footsteps on the porch. He snuffed his cigarette and glanced toward the door.

As the girls entered the living room, carrying their purchases, Kathy remarked on how nice and cool it was since Frank had gotten the swamp cooler fixed, but Cindy headed for the refrigerator for a cold soft drink the minute she dropped her packages on the carpeted floor.

"Oh boy," Kathy sighed, "The stores were wall to wall with shoppers. Everyone is getting ready for school. I got Cindy registered for high school. She's a sophomore. And I stopped at a body shop to get an estimate on painting my car. The poor old thing looks pretty sad since the sandstorm."

"How much did they want?" Frank asked out of curiosity.

Kathy grimaced. "Almost a thousand dollars. Well, at that price, I guess I'll just have to live with it. Can you imagine $987 dollars to paint a car?"

Frank got up and headed for the kitchen where Cindy had plopped down at the table with her Pepsi, while Kathy headed for the bathroom. As he took a beer from the refrigerator, he asked Cindy how she felt about going back to school after the long summer vacation.

"Well," she said thoughtfully, "I guess it will be okay. I'll have to make new friends...ah...it will be something to do..."

"You'll meet a lot of good looking boys," Frank grinned. "How does that grab you?"

"I dunno," she looked off into the distance. "I liked that boy that fixed mom's car. He was cute."

Frank was surprised that she remembered Don Shuger. What did she see in him? He wasn't especially handsome with his dirty blond hair and unkempt clothing, but maybe girls don't see with their eyes. Maybe they see with their hormones. Yet the fact that she remembered him at all was puzzling.

"Yeah," Frank agreed," He was kinda cute. He was smart too. I remember when we met him at the café, he said he could fix anything but a broken heart, and I think he could." Frank tipped his beer to his lips. "But he was way too old for you, hon. I think he said he was in his twenties. Maybe 26? Something like that."

"I don't care," she shrugged, "I like older boys. Boys my age are so immature. They don't even know how to kiss."

Frank knew where she was coming from. When he was her age, he was so naïve around girls that he didn't even know that a kiss was a knock on the front door for work in the basement, and he knew from his experience with her in the bedroom that a sixteen-year-old girl needed passionate, fulfilling sex as much as she needed food and drink.

"Yeah," he said. "They're too bashful."

Kathy came back into the living room and started to pick up the plastic bags. "Come on, honey," she said, "I want you to try on your new clothes. See what Frank thinks about them."

Cindy grinned at Frank as she got up. "I got lots of stuff. Wait till you see it."

Frank wasn't particularly interested in her clothes. He glanced at the television screen, got up to wait in his favorite chair, taking his beer with him, and was quickly absorbed in the story unfolding before his eyes. But his mind was far away.

As he watched the black and white movie, he thought of Kathy's car being sandblasted. He remembered Peter Williams talking about the possibility of a lost city buried under the sand. The recent sandstorm was violent, as witnessed by Kathy, and obviously, a lot of sand had shifted. He wondered if the storm had uncovered anything new.

Cindy would be in school in two weeks and he would be alone. All the time the girls had been here, he had neglected his hunt for treasure and that would be a good time to scout the outback. The one place he was interested in was the area around Pinto Wash, where the winds swept down from Davies Valley.

Kathy had said that the road had been blocked up by huge drifts, and he knew that the wind coming from the east would strike the mountain and deflect back like an undertow, creating a powerful sweeping action. Yes, he thought, I will drive out there when she is in school.

"Look, Frank," he heard Kathy's voice as the girls emerged from their bedroom. "What do you think of it?"

Cindy was wearing hip-hugging jeans with a blue tank top and a wide red belt. He looked her up and down as she wheeled around to show her figure from all angles. "It's nice," he muttered, "but she's been wearing those low-slung pants before."

Kathy nodded. "Oh yes, but she has to have a change. Don't you think the ensemble is cute?"

"Of course it's cute, but it seems to me kinda sexy."

The next time Cindy came out, she was wearing the same jeans with a white T-shirt and a black belt. Her midriff was exposed and there were letters on the belt buckle. Frank asked her what those letters said.

"Oh," Kathy explained. "It says THE GRATEFUL DEAD."

Frank shook his head in disbelief. "Oh my God."

Kathy put her hand on Cindy's shoulder, turning her around. "We saved the best for last," she said, steering Cindy back to the bedroom.

Frank took a swig from his bottle and lit a cigarette, waiting for them to return. When they came back, he was incredulous. He couldn't believe what he was seeing. As they stepped into view, Kathy was saying, "We'll see what daddy thinks of this outfit."

It was the first time they had referred to him as daddy, but the sight of Cindy all decked out was stunning. She was wearing tight jeans, a black short sleeved T-shirt emblazoned with the logo, THE GRATEFUL DEAD in dark red colors, high moccasin boots with fringes of buckskin, and the loose fitting shirt covering her midriff was also fringed at the bottom.

As she pirouetted in front of his chair, he noticed she was wearing a double bracelet on her right arm and a matching wristwatch on the other. He couldn't believe his eyes. "Jesus Christ!" He exclaimed with a roar. "Is she going to wear that to school?"

"That's what all the kids are wearing now," Kathy explained. "That's what she wanted."

Cindy's flesh-colored bra was conspicuously visible below the neckline, where her honey-blond hair hung loosely over the wide neck of the shirt, accenting her feminine charms. Cindy was not only beautiful, but her costume was so unique it was dazzling.

"You don't like it, do you?" She said demurely. "I told mom I didn't think you would."

"Well, I like it hon, but...ah...but it's so...so sexy. If you wear that outfit to school, you'll have all the boys groveling at your feet."

"You think so?" She wore a devilish grin, but Kathy spoke up.

"You know how kids are today," she said, looking directly at Frank. "They worship far-out clothes, rock bands and violent movies. It's the life in the fast lane, you know."

"Yeah, I know," he replied as Cindy headed back to the bedroom, "but if you're worried about her getting pregnant, those clothes sure as hell aren't going to help."

"Oh, I don't know what to do," Kathy spoke in a low voice. "I bought her some white pants and some blouses; I got her a rain coat…you know, Frank, raising a daughter is hell. Sometimes I just think I should let nature take its course. Girls are going to have sex sooner or later with some snot-faced boy, and a parent can't do anything to prevent it. It's a crap shoot."

Frank felt a twinge of guilt. Kathy was right, no doubt, but if only she knew that Cindy had already followed nature's course, and with him of all people, she would probably tear her hair out.

"Sometimes I think I should buy her a douche, and tell her to go at it. Get it over with."

CHAPTER FOURTEEN

September 15, 1983

The house was eerily quiet in the early dawn as the sun crept slowly over the hills to the east, and Cindy had arisen just after Kathy had left for work. She had fed Wiley, who was growing rapidly from the table scraps Kathy brought home daily, and she had dressed and combed her hair. Wearing blue jeans and a white tank top, she wore her new wristwatch on her left arm.

Frank had slipped into his pants and had came out to see her off, and proceeded to put the coffee on. As she gulped her cereal down, she would consult her watch occasionally, making sure she had time to walk down to the road where the big yellow school bus would pick her up.

Frank glanced at her as he stood at the counter. "How come you haven't worn your Grateful Dead outfit yet? You've been going to school for two weeks and I've never seen you wear it."

"I thought you didn't like it," she replied. "You made such a fuss when I modeled it, I felt ashamed of it.'

"Oh, I think it's great," he said apologetically, "but only for special occasions...uh...like Halloween."

"Yeah," she said in an almost audible voice.

"It's lonesome for me now that you're gone all day," Frank admitted. "I play with Wiley sometimes. He's sure growing fast."

"Yeah," she grunted.

When Frank asked her if she had made any friends in school yet, she pushed her empty bowl away and came alive. "Yes, I have. All the girls are friendly, but I like Clarisa best. She's a Mexican girl and we talk a lot."

"How about the boys?" Frank wondered out of curiosity.

Cindy said that she hadn't hardly spoken to any boys. There were only a couple of good looking ones and they were Mexican, but Clarisa had warned her not to get friendly with them, because they talked dirty and always propositioned the good looking girls.

"I see." Frank said as he turned to pour a cup of coffee. "Well, what do you girls talk about?"

"Sex and drugs, mostly." Cindy glanced at her watch. "Clarisa said the Mexican boys would try to get girls to try drugs, and once they got them hooked, they could control them; have sex with them."

"Oh sure." Frank nodded. "That figures."

There was a moment of silence as Frank sipped his coffee, then Cindy pushed away from the table and stood up. Glancing at her watch again, she looked him in the eye and spoke sadly. "Frank," she demurred. "I think I might be pregnant."

"Oh God, no." Frank moaned. "Say it isn't true."

Left alone as she hurried out the door, he agonized over the real possibility. If it turned out to be a fact, his whole world would crumble. He would be shamed

Ralph W. Harrington

in Ocotillo, harangued by Kathy and arrested for statutory rape. If he was convicted – God forbid – a prison sentence would be tantamount to death. It would be the end of his world.

His mind in turmoil, he must calm down. Pouring a fresh cup of coffee and sitting down to smoke, he tried to rationalize the perceived scenario. Maybe she wasn't pregnant. Having been married, he understood that a missed period wasn't definitely proof of a pregnancy, and maybe Cindy had miscalculated.

Staring down into his cup, deep in thought, he finally realized that his worry was premature. Why worry about something that existed only as a possibility? Now another thought crossed his mind. The cave exploration had been strenuous. Jay and Geoff had been overcome with fatigue, as were the others, and the extreme exercise could have affected Cindy's hormones. No, there was nothing to worry about. He would have to move on, think about something else.

Why not drive out to Pinto Wash? He had been wanting to go out there ever since the sandstorm. He was curious about the shifting sands. Looking up at the window, he saw that the sun was not up, and he had better leave soon, before it got too hot.

Hurriedly, he dressed and combed his hair and was soon out the door and into his pickup. As he drove into Ocotillo, he wondered if Susan was back yet. Maybe he could drive past her house to see if her car was there. But he soon found out that it wasn't.

Heading up towards the café, he suddenly realized that he was hungry. All he had so far was coffee. As he pulled into the parking lot, he saw the sheriff's car, a

Border Patrol Blazer and among tourist's vehicles, there was a black Datsun. It looked like Susan's car. When he parked, he got out and walked past it, checking the license plate. He remembered it vaguely from when he followed her home. The first three letters were AXE. It checked out. Susan must be having breakfast. She was home again.

When Frank stepped inside, his gaze swept the room. The counter seats were full, most of the tables were taken, but a lone woman was sitting in a booth on the far side. Kathy and Wanda were trying to accommodate the large breakfast mob, but as he sauntered toward Susan, the sheriff acknowledged him and he said, "Hi, Ralph."

As he drew close to Susan, Kathy saw him and stopped for a second to ask if Cindy had gotten off to school. Susan looked up and broke into a wide grin. "Well, look who's here," she said. "Have a seat, Frank."

Frank reached out and put his hand on her shoulder. "God, I missed you, Susan." She said she had missed him too.

As he took a seat opposite her, both extended their hands across the table and squeezed them together lovingly, but when he saw that she was eating a full plate of ham and eggs, his mouth watered.

"So how's your mother?" Frank asked politely. "Is she okay?"

Susan nodded. "She had some life threatening thing wrong with her, something about her pancreas, but they got her stabilized and said she might live another five years. We – my sister and I – put her in an assisted living facility because she's on six different medications and neither of us could possibly take care of her."

"Sorry to hear it," Frank said demurely.

Kathy finally came over to take Frank's order. He explained that Susan was in the archaeology class, and he told Susan that Kathy was the woman who lived with him. Both admitted they knew each other by sight, as Susan had came into the restaurant many times. And Susan knew about Kathy, because Frank had told her. So there were no pangs of jealousy in either woman.

"Cindy knows Susan," he said, "We all went up to Davies Valley together."

"That's right," Susan smiled at Kathy. "I understand you're her mother. Oh, that was the most interesting field trip I've ever been on. What a beautiful place."

When Kathy left the booth, Frank and Susan resumed their conversation. Frank lit a smoke as Susan resumed eating. Susan was cutting her ham. She wondered what Frank had been doing while she was in Flagstaff.

"Well, a lot has happened since you left," Frank began. "Did you know that Jay had a heart attack?"

Susan shook her head in disbelief. "No. I just got home last night. Jay had a heart attack?'

Frank began to explain the cave exploration in detail. He told of Peter Williams, the excitement of discovery, how Cindy had found an artifact and Jay's chest pains, all the while Susan was eating her meal. Finally, when Kathy brought his order, he sighed pensively. "Jese," he said, "You should have been there. It was really something."

As he dug into his breakfast, he took a bite, then reached for the salt and peppershakers, resuming his narrative. "We had a big sandstorm, too. It was one of the most violent storms to hit this area in a hundred years. Kathy had gone shopping in Calexico and was caught in it. It stripped the paint off her car."

Susan sipped her coffee and pushed her plate away. "That figures," she said. "When I got home last night, I noticed that sand had piled up in my flower bed. There was sand on the steps and porch, even in the house."

Kathy came with the coffee pot and held it over Susan's cup, pouring it slowly. Susan smiled up at Kathy. "Frank says your car got sandblasted."

"You better believe it," Kathy grimaced. "Mostly the front and the windshield is pitted so bad I can't hardly see out of it." She swung the pot towards Frank, but seeing his was still full, she withdrew. "It's in back of the building if you want to see it."

Frank was scooping up scrambled eggs. "Speaking of sandstorms, I'm on my way out to Pinto Wash," he said. "I'm curious about something."

Kathy looked away and left, but Susan wondered what he was curious about. Frank then launched into another story, explaining that while she was gone, the archaeology class, or at least part of it, had gone into the cave as he had already told her about, but Peter had been talking about ancient civilizations being buried under the desert sands – as in Egypt for example – and he had expressed his belief in an old Indian legend, the lost city of the Yumans.

"Well, I got to thinking about the sandstorm. If it was the worst in a hundred years, maybe it had uncovered something. You know, Susan, I've been looking for Peg-leg-Pete's black nuggets ever since I moved out here... oh, I don't expect to find them, but...ah...but I'm a dreamer...or maybe a nut, but in my mind I'm always searching. I'm driven by the thought of finding a pot of gold at the end of the rainbow." He looked down at his plate, wondering why he had spilled his guts to Susan. "Well, I just figured I'd drive out there and have a look."

Susan reached over and put her hand on his. "Frank," she said demurely, "can I go with you?"

Frank was overjoyed at her request. He liked Susan in a way he had never liked any other woman, and with Cindy in school, he had felt an emptiness he had never felt before. Susan at 36 was more his age, had been married as he had been, they were both into archaeology, and he wouldn't ever have to worry if she got pregnant.

"You bet!" He smiled across the table, "I'll be glad to have some company."

They could leave her car here and pick it up on the way back, as the Roadrunner Restaurant was only a stones throw from Highway 98. Susan's countenance was peaceful and serene. She looked happy. Her blue blouse accentuated the blue in her eyes, and the silver strands of hair embellished her matronly maturity.

On their way out, Frank yelled at Kathy. "Susan is going with me. I'll see you tonight."

Ralph was still talking to the Border Patrolmen about the illegals, and as they passed, he quipped. "You guys be good now."

As the big Dodge pickup hummed down the highway, they kept up a running conversation. Frank liked the way Susan expressed herself. She said what she thought, she was always rational, and she always had an opinion. She was, in other words, an interesting conversationalist.

When they arrived at the road leading to Davies Valley, they began to see sand dunes everywhere. This was where Kathy had met the big machines clearing the road. Huge piles had been bulldozed to one side, but beyond, the dunes had formed as far as they could see. The barren moonscape around Pinto Wash was punctuated by a few ocotillos, which had clung tenaciously rooted against the ravages of the storm.

Frank explained to Susan how the wind striking the mountain slope had created an undertow, a giant eddy current. The whirlpool effect had whipped the sand into the air and dropped it on the lee side, leaving great gouges in some places and mountainous piles in others.

As the wide tires rose over the blow-sand easily, Frank drove west where the road used to be, ever watchful for anything unusual, when Susan cried out. "Look, Frank," she pointed. "Over there. See that? There's something sticking up out of the sand."

"Oh yeah," he said. "I see it."

There was a deep gouge with blackened sticks jutting from the sand, but Frank knew he couldn't go in there. If he got into a steep depression, he would never get out again. They must stop here and walk in.

"Oh no!" Frank exclaimed as they stood looking down into the crater-like hole. "It looks like a ship. Or what was once a ship."

"It sure does," Susan agreed.

The blackened sticks they had noticed, were the ribs of a boat, no doubt, still attached to the rotted keel. There was no other explanation. As Frank gazed at the decaying hulk, he estimated that the boat had been about twenty feet long.

"Holy cow!" Susan said incredibly, "I'm glad I came along with you. I wouldn't have missed this for the world."

Frank stood thinking: He had heard rumors of a ship being spotted in this desert. As the story went, old-timers had claimed to have seen wreckage such as this, but when they went back to verify their sighting, they were unable to find it again. Why? The answer was simple. Sandstorms had covered these remains again. In fact, they had been covered and uncovered hundreds of times in the last thousand years, no doubt.

But there was another possibility. Since Imperial Valley had been under water eons ago, said to have been an inland sea at one time and a fresh water lake at another geological period, the Yuman Indians were known to have had boats on Lake Cahuilla, and this wreckage could just as well be of Yuman origin.

After searching the area further, Frank and Susan were tired and thirsty. They had enjoyed being out in the boondocks together and happy to have found the old relic, but now it was time to go back.

The wind in their faces through the open windows of the pickup was refreshing as the Dodge skimmed over the asphalt, past Nomirage, and when they arrived at the café, Frank suggested they have a beer before going home. Susan was more than willing. Not only was the idea enticing, but she enjoyed being with Frank, and as their bonding and camaraderie grew; they were rapidly cementing a partnership.

The café was almost empty when they went in. Kathy's shift had ended and she had gone home, but a new waitress took their order. Sitting at the counter, the hum of the air-conditioner was barely audible. Only two Border Patrolmen were present, and they were sitting at table near the big windows.

"Oh, it's nice in here," Susan said as the waitress set their drinks in front of them. "It's a relief to get in where it's cool."

Frank grabbed his bottle and gulped the cold liquid. "You can say that again."

Susan sipped her beer and reached for a smoke. "When are we going out on another field trip? I mean… is Jay going to be able to walk again?"

"Well, I don't know," Frank replied. "This cave thing, I think, is the top priority now. Whether or not Jay can resume his former health, only God knows, but Peter Williams is planning a major dig at the site, and we can't do anything until he has made arrangements. We've got to blast the rock slide first, we've got to bulldoze a road at the base of the mountain so we can get vehicles in close, and we'll need apprentices or college students to do the digging." Frank stopped to light a cigarette.

"Oh Susan," he smiled now, "I wish you could have been here when we went into the cave. This guy, Peter Williams is a funny lookin dude. He's tall and lanky. He's got a mustache. He looks like a college professor."

Susan smiled at the thought of him as Frank continued. "Once you see Peter, you'll never forget him. He isn't like the other guys. He would stand out in any crowd."

"I can't wait to see him," Susan said as she blew smoke over the counter. "He sounds interesting."

"When we met at the Community Hall, he was wearing an Aussie hat. Made him look even taller. But I liked that hat. I'd buy one if I knew where I could find it."

As they sat talking, old Clanahan came in, saw Frank and sat down beside him. "Ya find any more gold, boy?" He said jestingly, with sarcasm, "Ya know what P. Barnum said don't cha? You kin fool some of the people all the time, but you can't fool all of the people all of the time."

Frank chuckled. "And there ain't no fool like an old fool," he mimicked Clanahan. "When I get as old as you are maybe I'll be as smart as you are, sometime."

"He he," Clanahan chuckled. "It'll never happen, boy. You'll never get as smart as I am."

Frank began to like Clanahan. The old coot obviously just enjoyed idle banter, and maybe he was just an old prospector who was lonesome. Frank took a drink, looked sideways at Susan and winked. But after a minutes silence, Clanahan spoke seriously.

"I've been up at the dolomite mine, lookin it over," he said casually. "Can't make no money prospecting anymore. Thinkin of mining calcium. Thet mine ain't been worked fer a long time, but now they's a big demand fer calcium with dolomite in it. I've been reading a lot about it lately. The health food stores are selling tons of it."

Frank nodded. "Well, I'll take your word for it. I don't know."

Susan nudged Frank. "I gotta go," she said. "I've got a lot of cleaning up to do. I'll let you guys alone so you can argue about dolomite."

Frank patted her arm. "Okay, buddy. I'll see you around."

CHAPTER FIFTEEN

September 29, 1983

Frank watched Cindy board the big yellow school bus. It had rained during the night, but let up now. It seemed to be over. As he gazed from the window, it appeared to him, that it would be another hot day.

He turned back to the table and sipped his coffee, feeling a vague loneliness. Ever since she had started school, he felt an emptiness when he saw that bus pull away and disappear in the distance. As he drifted into reverie, he was startled by the sound of rain striking the window.

Jumping up from his chair, he looked out into the leaden skies to see black clouds moving rapidly north from Mexico, as the clatter of rain increased in intensity. He knew, now, that they were in for a good heavy rain.

Precipitation was rare in the desert. The Yuha basin's average rainfall was a mere 2 inches, but it came in small dribbles as a rule. A heavy or prolonged downpour spelled trouble. Because the sand couldn't absorb the water fast enough, it ran across the surface, cutting trenches as it flowed. The washes became swift moving rivers which could carry away anything in their paths; flashfloods.

Depressed by the gloomy outlook, Frank decided to drive to the café, where he could sit with a beer and talk to anyone who might be there, including Kathy. She would probably be worrying about Cindy. Later, he could pick up his mail.

Donning a yellow slicker with hood, he dashed out to his pickup and drove through the downpour towards Ocotillo, but when he crossed over a small highway bridge, which spanned a wash, he noticed that a river of dirty water was already running at near flood stage under the wooden trestle.

Sights like this always caused grave concern for desert residents, but Frank wasn't too worried about his own domicile, since it sat on high ground just below the Elsinore Fault and had withstood many floods over the years. If the rain continued as it was doing now, the water would come close to his house, but even a cataclysmic flood in a worse case scenario, would not reach the floor level because of the raised foundation.

Driving with limited vision through the downpour, windshield wipers slashing angrily, he finally arrived at the café, where numerous cars were present, clustered as close to the entrance as they could get. Making a dash for the door, he went inside where most of the patrons were lined up at the windows, looking at the downpour with trepidation, and hung his slicker on the back of a counter stool.

When Kathy saw him, she rushed over to ask if Cindy had got on the school bus and if she had worn her raincoat. He told her she had gotten on the bus, but she wasn't wearing her raincoat because it wasn't raining when she left. The skies had cleared and they thought the rain was over, but when the dark clouds moved in, the rain returned with a vengeance.

Pierre Miles saw Frank and walked over to him. "Looks bad," he said. "If this keeps up, we're in trouble. We're liable to have another flood like we had in 1976. I guess you weren't here then.'

Frank shook his head. "No, I moved here in 1978, but I heard about it."

"Hurricane Kathleen, they called it," Pierre said. "Dumped millions of gallons of water on the mountain and it formed a wall of water 11 feet high. That wall of water hit town and wiped out half of it."

Billie and Russ Dalton came over when they saw Pierre talking to Frank. "How's things out your way?" Russ asked Frank. "Did you notice any water in the wash out there?"

"Oh, jeese," Frank replied, "It's damn near running over its banks."

"Yeah," Billie said. "It's been raining all night. I heard the rain pounding on the roof and I got up and looked out. We've got a yard light and I could see it coming down by the bucketful and I told Russ it reminded me of Hurricane Kathleen, didn't I, Russ?"

"You bet!" Russ agreed.

At that moment, the rain hit the window with a clattering that drowned out the conversation. Moans went up from all quarters. "Oh my God!" Billie cried, "We've got to get home. Pid will be scared out of her wits."

"You ain't going out in this," Frank warned her. "I've never seen it rain this hard, even in Vietnam."

Billie and Russ lived in a trailer near Harry Powell, volunteer radioman for the fire department on the other end of Sierra Vista Avenue near the edge of the main wash that separated Unit 1 and 2, whose house was washed away in the 1976 flood. They had left their dog at home and had come to the café for breakfast.

People were gathering at the north windows now, for a panoramic view of the town below the restaurant. Many had left their food unfinished when the rain had started, but Kathy and Wanda had also got caught up in the excitement and were gawking with the others, looking down towards the little hamlet.

But there was little to see but the rain on the window. With visibility near zero, all they could see was water. While the downpour continued unabated for almost an hour, it finally tapered off to a drizzle, and by then, Ocotillo could be seen quite clearly. Water was pouring down the hillside, down the streets, and down the main wash between Unit 1 and 2.

No one paid any attention to Frank as he went behind the counter and poured himself a cup of coffee, and Kathy and others were gathered in little knots, talking wildly about the flooding but some had returned to their cold food and were again eating.

Frank wanted to get something to eat, but held off asking Kathy because of the confusion, when Brian came out of the kitchen, caught Frank's attention and asked him if he would circulate the coffee pot to those whose cups were cold.

Just as things became less hectic, four tourists straggled in, followed by Fire Chief Denny Hill, who took a few steps inside, stopped to gaze over the room, and bellowed out a warning.

"Attention!" He began in an authoritative voice, "Residents of Ocotillo; the town is being flooded. Go home and get your valuables while there's still time." He wiped his hand over his chin as water dripped from his slicker.

"We have reports of a log jam under the bridge on I-8, west-bound. Harry Powell is up there now, monitoring Meyer's Creek. He just radioed that debris is piling up against the piers, and a lake is forming upstream."

Moans went up in the room and people stared wide-eyed at Denny as he continued. "You are herby warned to be ready to evacuate on a minutes notice. I suggest that you go home now, collect your valuables and dogs...blankets etc., put them in your car and come back here where it's safe. Or go to the Community Hall."

The downpour had stopped suddenly as it had started, and the sun broke through. From the north window, the town was awash as water roared down from the mountainside.

"If you hear three consecutive blasts on the fire siren, run, don't walk if you're caught in town. Forget your dogs and valuables. Just get out as fast as you can."

"It looks like it's over," Pierre shouted. "The sun is shining."

"No, it's not over," Denny explained. "If the bridge goes out, a wall of water can bury Ocotillo. By the way, it might be a good idea to go to El Centro. No matter what happens today, Ocotillo may be unfit to live in for a few days. Our drinking water may be infected by the runoff, streets may be blocked by sand or trenches. If you go to El Centro, you've got nice motels and restaurants, and you'll be safe."

Denny said he was going down to the fire station, now. He would keep in touch with Harry Powell by radio, and man the siren if needed. AS he turned to leave, a babble of voices filled the café. People passing through would travel on to El Centro, but some of the locals decided to go there also. Billie and Russ Dalton, Pierre, and others thought it would be a good idea. Kathy came in front of Frank with apprehension, worrying about Cindy and wondering if they should go home, but Frank convinced her that Cindy was already in El Centro and therefore safe, and that she, herself was not in any danger here at the café.

Those who resided in Ocotillo rushed to go home and get their valuables. Billie and Russ hurried home to get their dog and suitcase. Because they lived on the edge of the main wash, they kept their important documents in an old Sampsonite, always ready to grab and run in an emergency.

When Frank decided to drive through town as a good Samaritan, he headed down Imperial Avenue over the sand and gravel strewn asphalt. He stopped before he came to Stouffer's old well, seeing a great river of brown water flowing flood stage between Unit 1 and Unit 2 and laden with debris. As he turned up Mesquite Avenue to Sierra Vista, he thought about Susan. Like many others, she must have decided to ride out the storm at home.

When he pulled up in front of her house, he saw that much of her yard was washed away. Her flower garden was gone; wiped out. Strong rivulets of water swirled around a metal-protected berm, but her house sat high and safe on a three-foot high concrete foundation. As he slogged through the liquefied sand and climbed the concrete steps, he wondered if she was all right, but she answered his knock in good spirits.

"Susan," he said with concern, "You okay?"

"Yeah," she said. "I'm okay."

"Are you aware that your whole yard is washed away?"

Susan explained that when they had bought this place, Greg had flood-proofed it by building the berm. They had heard about frequent flash floods and how sand washes away, so he had laid railroad ties around the foundation and faced them with corrugated sheet metal.

"I'm not worried about a little rain," she said. "I feel very safe here."

"Look," Frank warned her, "The fire chief says the bridge above town is threatened. It could go out any minute. Get in your car and go into El Centro now, before it's too late."

Susan protested. She wasn't interested in a bridge. What did it have to do with her house? But Frank was getting testy. "Susan," he said firmly. "I haven't got time to explain. This is an emergency. Just get yourself into El Centro NOW! I gotta go."

Highway I-8 is a divided highway. The eastbound lanes hug the Jacumba Mountains on solid rock, but the westbound lanes cross a void, which the concrete bridge spans. It rests on a tall cylindrical pilings that can cause a logjam when tree trunks and other debris collects when washed down the 6 percent grade at the head of Meyer's Creek. When floodwaters surge down Meyer's Creek, they explode over the flood plains below and the main current flows into the huge wash between the two units of Ocotillo.

When Denny reached the fire station, he sunk down on the chair in front of the switchboard when he heard Harry Powell's voice. Thirty-nine to thirty-seven, come in please. Thirty nine to thirty seven, do you read me?"

"Thirty seven to thirty nine, I read you," Denny answered.

"It looks bad up here," Harry was saying. "I don't know where all this water is coming from, but its rising fast above the pilings."

"Harry," Denny shot back, "I've driven around town warning everyone to be ready to leave for high ground on a minutes notice. You stay up there and keep me informed. Over and out."

At the café, people resumed eating, and the waitresses were busy as more patrons came in from the eastbound lanes, but Caltrans had closed the westbound lanes with barricades at the Ocotillo intersection. This meant that all westbound traffic would be shunted into Ocotillo where they would be stalled indefinitely or they would have the choice of going back to El Centro via the on-ramp under the overpass heading east.

Now, under sunny skies, cars and 18-wheelers were piling up in Ocotillo. Not knowing how long the road would be closed, most vehicles parked along Imperial Avenue, but as the number grew, they parked by the post office, up Agate Avenue and spread out along Brush and Seminole Avenues.

While tempers flared down there, Frank was driving out to Coyote Wells to check on his property. With his raincoat on the seat beside him, driving along the old Highway 80, he saw that water was running over the first small trestle over the wash, and when he arrived at the second trestle, it too was awash, but he drove over them with out any problems.

His house sat high and dry, but angry waters filled the wash behind it, and when he drove in to look around, he was greeted by Wiley, who seemed happy to see him. As he petted the little coyote, he spoke to him as Cindy always did. "There, there, lil guy," he said, "Your mom will be home in a lil while." Wiley seemed to smile, and he nipped playfully at Frank's hand.

Since everything was in good shape at his house, Frank drove back to the café, which was now filled to capacity by stalled motorists, but Billie and Russ and many other town folk had gone into El Centro. The large parking lot at the café was full of cars and motor homes, and when he parked and looked down, he could see that the town below was a sea of shiny vehicles.

At the Community Hall, locals were waiting patiently, but next door at the fire station, Denny was still getting reports from Harry Powell up near the bridge.

"We've got a lake a mile long," Harry radioed to Denny. "The pressure against the pilings must be at the breaking point."

After a short silence, Harry's voice crackled over the radio again. "Denny," he said in a voice bordering on hysteria, "I hear sharp cracking sounds, dull thuds. I think the bridge is cracking up."

Denny was stoic. "I read you. Are you standing clear?" Denny sat motionless, waiting for a reply. "Harry! Thirty-seven to thirty-nine. Do you read me?"

Minutes passed in silence. "Harry! Harry! Are you there?"

Ears attuned for the faintest sound, Denny heard a deep rumble, then a roar. Harry was screaming into his radio. "The bridge is cracking up. The center pillars are out. The roadway is sagging. It's falling in slow motions. THERE SHE GOES!"

Seconds passed. "The roadway is being swept away like a toothpick! Denny! God! A wall of wa…"

Denny hit the panic button and the siren's wailing sent shivers up the town's spine. Dogs howled, people huddled, and those in the café ran to the north windows.

A wall of water 30 feet high exploded from the bridge damn, spilling out over the valley below. Roaring as it burst free, it swept past Sugar-Loaf Mountain and Al Miller's old garage on the former Highway 80, now I-8, engulfing everything in its path and sweeping it all into the main wash, now a raging Amazon.

Washing out Harry Powell's house and a few others, the six-foot wall's fury was spent mainly along

Mesquite Avenue, the low end of Sierra Vista, but it had dispersed substantially further up, where Susan's house sat safely on its concrete foundation.

Denny, sitting by the radio was already calling for Search & Rescue units to respond, and by the time the main surge had dissipated, units from Jacumba and El Centro were arriving at the fire department, planning their mode of operation

With the bridge out, the danger was limited to deep mud and rocks on the streets, dead animals and contamination of the town's water supply. Search & Rescue's job was to comb the area for survivors trapped under downed trees, tipped mobile homes or in cars; and to search for the dead.

While the Community Hall, fire station and post office sat safely to the east, the river still ran high in the flood plain down past Stouffer's well, but things were chaotic everywhere.

Frank, still at the café, had seen the wall of water surge over the town, unaware of Search & Rescue's presence, decided to drive down to assess the damage, more out of curiosity than anything else. But when he saw what the flood had done, he was shocked.

At one point, he saw a dead dog lodged in a pile of debris. Further on, he saw a cat, wet and bedraggled. Tree branches washed down from the mountain, piles of sand, tires and lumber littered the streets. He saw a mobile home lying askew where the water had undermined it. On the lower end of Sagebrush Avenue, he saw an elderly woman surveying the damage to her yard. He called out to her.

"Are you all right? Is there anything I can do?"

"You can buy my place," she said bitterly. "This is the second time we've been flooded out in the last ten years. I've had it! I'm getting out of this damn town as fast as I can."

Frank saw a Search & Rescue vehicle coming down the street. He glanced at his watch. Surprised at how fast the time had flown by, he realized Cindy would be coming home soon and he'd better get home to greet her and tell her about the flood.

Heading out the old highway, to the left, he noticed that the lowlands were still under water and the wash was running strongly. As he crossed the first trestle, water was surging over the wooden planks, and when he crossed the second trestle, it was doing the same.

Accelerating, he sped across and was startled when the rear wheels dropped with a jolt, but his momentum carried him on. Once across safely, he stopped and got out to investigate. A jagged plank was sticking up and angry water swirled around it. But something more sinister shocked him.

The raging current had washed out part of the abutment, leaving the east end of the bridge vulnerable to collapse. If any vehicle were to come along now, they were in grave danger. If the school bus hit this weakened structure – heavy as it is – it could easily end up in the raging torrent and be swept downstream.

It was obvious that something must be done. He must intercept the bus. Continuing on towards Plaster City, he planned to turn on his headlights to signal a stop. He would wave and honk; maybe fire his pistol, which he carried under his seat.

He glanced at his watch. It was almost 4:30. The bus should be coming soon. He was five miles west of Plaster city when he saw the huge hulk coming toward him. He laid on his horn and waved, but the bus hurtled past him.

Maybe the woman driver had been afraid to stop, afraid it might be a set-up. There was only one hope now. He would have to turn around, race after the vehicle and attempt to cut in front of it. Time was of the essence.

With tires screeching and sliding on the wet asphalt, he made a tight turn and floor boarded it in a mad race to overtake the bus speeding toward its doom, but the driver had increased her speed, rather than slowing down.

Unbeknown to Frank, schools had been alerted to the possibility of hi-jackers. Two men had stopped a school bus, kicked the driver out and had taken the bus full of kids to a gravel pit near Livermore, and buried it. To law enforcement, the bus had seemingly disappeared from the earth. No trace of it existed, but for over a week the children lived in that gravel pit while the perpetrators sought ransom.

Roaring down the old highway, both vehicles tried to outdo the other, but finally, after several miles, the pickup was gaining on the bus. Minutes later Frank was passing it. At 70 miles per hour as they drew closer to the trestle, he worried that he was going too fast to stop, and that he might plunge into the raging torrent himself.

Inside the bus, Cindy and the other kids were hysterical. The high-pitched drone of the engine and the rocking motion instilled fear and awe. The bus had never gone this fast and they knew instinctively that something was wrong as it lurched from side to side at high speed.

The washout was a hundred yards ahead now as Frank cut in front of the speeding hulk and hit the brakes rapidly on and off, trying to slow the bus gradually. The bus driver had no choice but to do the same. As the vehicles neared the trestle, Frank locked his foot on the brake and the pickup skidded sideways to a stop, blocking the road completely.

The bus driver slammed on her brakes. The bus careened to a stop only a few feet from Frank, who had jumped out and stood facing it, but Cindy and the others were catapulted forward onto the floor.

As the bus's doors flew open, Cindy, up front, in panic mode, got to her feet and leaped from the door. The driver, seeing the swirling water ahead, exited also. Both in shock, Cindy saw Frank and ran to him, crying out. "Daddy, daddy." She sobbed incoherently as she fell into his arms.

The bus driver stared at the swirling water in disbelief, tearfully stoic, as Cindy found comfort in Frank's embrace. "There, there, hon," Frank said consolingly. "Everything is all right now. I love you, little girl."

CHAPTER SIXTEEN

October 30, 1983

A month had passed since the big flood, and restorative measures had been so rapid and efficient that life in Ocotillo was almost back to normal, yet some things had happened in their interim, which would change the face of the town forever. For example, Clanahan was drowned in the main wash when he attempted to cross the raging torrent to get home in Unit 1. His car was found a mile downstream, battered and full of sand, but his body was never found. Perhaps it was buried somewhere under tons of debris that littered the desert below the town.

Ralph Smith, too, was gone from the area. He had taken a better job in his native state of Washington, and a new deputy sheriff was assigned to western Imperial County. Harry Powell's house on the corner of Sierra Vista and Mesquite, which had been washed away, was replaced with a brand new doublewide manufactured home, but Billie and Russ's trailer, a few lots away, only suffered minor damage when the berm behind their place was breached and floodwaters inundated their property. When the water receded, it left their trailer full of sand and muck, but fortunately, it was covered by insurance, as Powell's was.

In the first week after the flood, the town's streets were cleaned, debris hauled to the dumpsite, and yards damaged, as Susan Rider's was, had been repaired. Caltrans had rushed to repair the two trestles out by Frank's place while work on the new I-8 bridge progressed rapidly. The swarms of workmen involved, brought a bustling business to the Roadrunner Restaurant, which in turn increased Kathy's tips and overtime, but by now, the workforce was mostly limited to construction workers on the big bridge.

Jay Bradford was in pretty good shape now, after his heart surgery, and he had bought a home in Ocotillo, where he had always wanted to live, where he would be closer to nature and the developing cave exploration. But what tickled his imagination was the rapid progress being made at the cave site. Working in conjunction with Peter Williams and environmentalists, they had gained permission to blast the rockslide and build a road to the lower entrance. The next step would be to arrange a major dig in the cavern.

Despite all the good things that had occurred, today was destined to be a sad one for Frank, since something unbelievable would happen that would tear his heart out.

Today was Sunday, one of Kathy's workdays. Frank had gone out with Susan to collect a few hedgehog cacti for her yard and a couple of fishhook cactus for a planter that was washed away, and she had made a picnic lunch to take a long. Cindy was home alone, but when Frank returned later in the day, he saw a nice looking older Chevrolet sitting in his yard up by the porch.

A strange car aroused suspicion. He had no idea of who it could be. He cut the engine and coasted up close, got out without slamming the door and tiptoed up the steps. Maybe Cindy was being assaulted. But when he threw the door open, he got the shock of his life. Cindy was sitting on Don Shuger's lap in Frank's lounge chair, and they were making out. Lip-locked, her blouse was open and Don had his hand on her breast.

"What the hell's going on here?" Frank bellowed, looking straight at Don. "I thought you were heading east, looking for work."

The kids straightened up when Frank came in, and Cindy was getting up. "Oh daddy," she pleaded mercifully. "He just came out to show me his new car. He's working in El Centro now."

"Quiet, Cindy," Frank spoke in a jealous rage. "Let him tell me." He threw his cap on the floor, his face reddened in anger. "I told you I didn't want you hanging around here," he said to Don. "Now get the hell out of here." He gestured with his thumb towards the door.

Don looked clean and wholesome, his hair combed neatly, a far cry from when he fixed Kathy's car months ago. He appeared to be frightened. "I got me a job at Tuttle Chevrolet, sir. I remembered Cindy, so being its Sunday, I thought I would drive out and show her my new car."

"Okay, she's seen it, so what are you waiting for?" Frank glowered. "Hit the road, bub."

Cindy tried to intervene, "Frank, you're embarrassing me," she cried, "This is the first time a boy has come to see me, and you're acting like mom always did."

"I don't care," Frank shot back. "This is my house and I'm the boss. I don't want no guys hanging around here. You understand?" He glared at Don, gesturing. "Get the hell outa my chair, boy, and get your ass outa my house."

As Don rose from the chair, Cindy put her hands on her hips defiantly. "Okay. If that's the way you're going to be, you can go to hell."

Frank's eyes shot daggers at Cindy. "Listen, kid, I ain't going to have no snot-nosed brat talking back to me. Not in my house."

"Oh. So I'm a snot-nosed brat, now," she said as tears rolled down her cheeks. "I thought we..."

As Don moved towards the door, he looked at Cindy wistfully, but when he put his hand on the doorknob, she tried to follow. "If that's the way you want it, I'm leaving with Don right now."

Don opened the door and stepped outside with Cindy right behind him, but Frank forbade her to leave. "You ain't goin nowhere," he said, as he grabbed the doorknob, cutting her off. "And I don't want you talking back to me. You are not to have boyfriends in my house, and I'm going to tell Kathy what you did when she comes home."

Cindy was wiping her tears and sulking, as they moved away from the door. "You better not," she said. "I didn't do anything."

"I told you I didn't want you talking back to me," Frank warned her, "and I don't want you screwing boys in my house. You got that?"

She had regained her composure by now. "Oh you got a dirty mind," she grimaced. "You're so jealous you're out of your cotton-pickin mind. I told you a thousand times I wanted a boyfriend and when a guy comes to see me, you rant and rave as if we're doing something terrible. Well, you just go right ahead and tell mom and see what happens. I'll tell her you molested me."

"Hey, listen, ya lil smart ass, you pull that kind of crap on me and I'll tell her you raped me. You did and you know it. Now you better think twice before you go telling people stuff like that. You're just going to get yourself deeper in trouble unless you forget it. I could have you sent to the reform school. Think it over, kid. Think it over good!"

"Oh you're impossible!" She spat as she went into her room and slammed the door.

The room was suddenly quiet, and Frank was alone with his thoughts. The silence was unnerving. He would grab a beer and go sit on the porch, but when he sat down and placed his beer on the small table, Wiley looked up at him, wistfully.

"Oh, you want some attention," he said empathetically, "Don't we all?" He reached down and stroked Wiley's back. "You're a good boy, Wiley. you don't have a care in the world, do you? But when you get older and start chasing girls, then you're going to have nothing but problems."

The feel of Wiley's fur was soothing and Frank had cooled off by now. He took a deep breath and closed his eyes as Wiley licked his hand. "There's a thin line between love and hate," he thought. "You can love someone one minute and hate them in the next. If that little sumbitch squealed to Kathy, this argument could develop into a full-blown, headline grabbing rape case. Or as bad, a molestation charge. Who would believe him versus her? Many in Ocotillo had cast suspicion his way, and several, including Libby Hatfield, had made snide remarks right out in public. If Cindy so much as hinted that he had even fondled her, much less rape, the whole town would turn again him.

As he thought about it, fear grew within him. If Cindy wanted to get even with him, there was no way out. Another thing that bothered him was that she might be pregnant. If she was, then that whole scandal would surface even if she didn't tell Kathy.

The thought crossed his mind that he could kill her. Pregnant or not, she would be out of the picture. It would easy enough to convince the court that it was an accident. Everyone knew that they often went out shooting. Yet, that idea didn't appeal to him.

Suddenly, an idea came to mind. He had made a big mistake, he realized now. If he'd kept his mouth shut, Cindy wouldn't have gotten mad at him, and if he hadn't interrupted them, they would probably have had sex. And if they had sex, and if she were really pregnant already as she might be now, then Don would have been named as the father.

So pervasive was this realization, that Frank vocalized his thoughts. Looking out past the well into the desert beyond, he said, "I made a big mistake! I was wrong!"

Wiley looked up at him, thinking he was speaking to him.

Drifting back into reverie, Frank realized Cindy's love of him had known no bounds, and his love for her was greater than he had ever known. They had hiked together, lived together, made love together and she had even said she loved him. So what if she had sex with Don? Wasn't he being unfaithful to her with Susan? Wasn't sex the downfall of all men? Wouldn't it be nice if we could erase our sins?

Out of the corner of his eye, he saw a car coming down the road and he knew it was Kathy. He began to worry again. When she went inside, Cindy would start blabbing. But Kathy didn't go into the house. She came over to Frank directly and without a hello, she blurted out a story that Wanda had told her.

"Wanda told me she heard on the radio this morning that a man raped a girl, and his neighbor shot him dead on the spot," she said with rising excitement, "Feelings are running high lately. People are getting sick and tired of these men who brutalize women sexually."

Frank felt his heart beating faster and he was breaking out in a sweat. He gulped, swallowing hard, but he couldn't say anything. He knew that in about two minutes he would be facing the wrath of both women. At this point, all he could do would be to tell Kathy first. Make it sound like he was innocent and Cindy was making up a story.

"It happened in a residential area near the high school," Kathy continued. "I'm worried about Cindy going into El Centro every day. There's so much crime there."

"Kathy," he began with trepidation, "Before you go in I want to tell you that Cindy and I had a fight. She's mad at me, so she'll probably make up a lot of lies to get even."

"Oh? What was the fight about?"

"Well, when I came home I found her screwing around with that boy who fixed your car. Remember him?"

Kathy frowned. "Yes, of course I remember him. his name was Don as I recall. But...but what...how...I don't understand. Are you saying that he was here at the house today?"

"Yes. He was here when I got home and he and Cindy were making out. I told him to get the hell outa here and he left."

"Oh my God," Kathy said as she started towards the door. "Well, I'll ask her about it."

Frank followed her inside so he could defend himself when Cindy started making accusations, but Cindy was still in her room with the door closed. Kathy laid her handbag on a chair and went back to the bathroom. When she came back, she knocked on their bedroom door, asking Cindy to come out.

With no response, she knocked again, then opened the door to see Cindy lying on the bed crying softly. Kathy asked her what the problem was, but Cindy told her to go away.

"Did you entertain a boy here today?" Kathy asked impatiently.

When Cindy refused to answer, Kathy raised her voice, "Well, did you?"

Barely audible, Cindy spoke through her silent sobs. "Don Shuger was here. The boy who fixed your car."

"What was he doing here?" Kathy wondered aloud.

"He just came out to see me."

"Did you sass Frank?"

Cindy denied it, but Frank snapped at her. "You did too!"

Cindy propped herself up to face them, dabbing at her eyes with a Kleenex. "Well, you started it," she said. "Mom, he came in and started screaming at us. We were just sitting in the chair talking, and he made a federal case out of it. He accused of us having sex and all kinds of things. Nobody wants me to have boyfriend or anything."

"Cindy," Kathy said, looking her in the eyes, "Were you having sex when Frank came in?"

"No, mom, we were just sitting talking."

"Well," Kathy sighed. "I don't know what started all this, but listen hon, this is Frank's house and you are not to sass him back. Am I making myself clear?"

Cindy swung her legs down to the floor, sitting upright and staring defiantly at her mother. "Oh sure. I know where you're coming from. The man is always right. Right? Whatever Frank says or does, I'm not supposed to make waves because this is his house. Well, mom, what would you say if I told you he's been molesting me ever since we've been here? What if I told you he raped me? Would you stick up for him then? Would you, mom?"

Kathy rocked back. "Well," she paused. "If you told me that, it would be different. But you're not going to tell me that...are you?"

Smirking, Cindy stood up. "Yes, mom, I'm going to tell you that! Frank raped me!"

"She's lying!" Frank shot back before it could sink in.

"No, I'm not," Cindy snapped before Kathy could comment. "Frank and I have been having sex all this time."

Kathy was more angry than startled. "Oh, I see now. You two had a little argument and you're trying to get back at Frank. This is another one of your wild fantasies. Listen, Cindy, I've had it with you. Here I am, trying to make a living, and you come up with some cheap shot meant to hurt me. Well, it don't hurt me, because I don't believe a word of it in the first place, and I haven't got time to worry about your sex life if I did. Now get out of my sight, get out of this house and get out of my life, or I'll blister you butt till its black and blue."

Frank was amazed at Kathy's diatribe.

Cindy, surprised but undaunted, sassed back. "You wouldn't dare. I'd tell my teacher on both of you. They'd get you for child abuse, and Frank for molestation."

Kathy was outraged. "Listen, smarty, you're not of age yet and your butt belongs to me. Now get out of my sight before I blister your behind."

Cindy, seething with anger and frustration, bolted out of the bedroom and ran outside. Frank sighed with relief that he was off the hook for now, and satisfied that his counter-arguments and nullified Cindy's accusations, as he and Kathy went towards the kitchen, but Kathy picked up her handbag and brought it to the table.

"Oh, that girl!" She said as she sat down. "I need a Pepsi. I'm all shook up."

"Me too," Frank said as he opened the refrigerator. "She's a spunky kid. That's for sure. But I'm glad that you didn't fall for all her lies."

Kathy pulled out a big wad of bills from her bag as Frank shoved her drink across the table. "Yeah, raising a girl is always hard. Every mother in the world worries about their daughter's virginity, and I'll bet that most of them have some kind of crisis like this before the child is mature enough to get married." Kathy was counting her tips.

When Frank started to speak, she shushed him. She couldn't count and listen at the same time. "Twenty-eight, twenty-nine, thirty." When she had finished, she had counted $39.00. "Not bad for one shift," she smiled as she stacked the bills on the table.

Kathy took a sip of Pepsi and glanced at Frank. "You know, getting back to Cindy, she has always been like this. When she was only ten years old, she used to carry on around my boyfriends, just to get attention. When she said those nasty things about you, I could tell she was lying. As I've said before, I know you wouldn't make passes at a girl so much younger than yourself, and I know that I can trust you."

Frank was nodding silently as he lit a smoke, but Kathy was still thinking out loud. "As far as Cindy goes," she said pensively, "I've got my own personal worries. You told me to just live with my cancer. To forget about it. And since I've been going to the evening prayer meetings, I have turned my life over to Christ, and I no longer think about dying. I'm going to live one day at a time and try to enjoy every minute I can."

"Atta girl," he said. "When I got my cancer from Agent Orange, I took it as a death sentence. I was afraid, too. But when I moved out here, I had so many new interests that I forgot about dying. I began thinking about living. I see so much beauty in this desert, the beautiful sunsets, the drifting sand and the vaulted mountains. Like you, I take it one day at a time. I enjoy every minute, and you know what? I don't have any sign of cancer anymore."

Kathy smile demurely. "You think that psychology has something to do with cancer?"

"Yes, I do. The book I have on cancer tells about people who live stressful lives. It listed case histories of patients who had cancer, and it showed how they had led stressful lives without even being aware of it."

"Wait," Kathy said. "Come to think about it, my youthful days were definitely stressful. I would call it anxieties. I knocked around from pillar to post, never feeling secure in my relationships. I was always on edge, nervous...and I got cancer when I was only 30 years old."

"Well, when I stop to think about it," Frank nodded, "My stint in Viet Nam was nothing but stressful. When guys are shooting at you all the time, when you're liable to get trapped or step on a booby trap, you don't have a minute of peace. You're always on edge. I tell you, Kathy, war is hell and don't let anyone tell you otherwise. Here, I feel at peace with the world. My fight with Cindy was the first time I've felt threatened. Maybe it wasn't Agent Orange that gave me cancer. Maybe it was burnout."

"Speaking of Cindy," Kathy said with alarm, "I wonder what she's doing out there?"

"Probably playing with Wiley," Frank guessed as he snuffed out his cigarette.

"Well, if she gives you any more trouble, I'll handle her. But if she tells her teacher, I don't know what I can do."

"Yeah," Frank agreed. "But whatever happens, we'll stick together. We won't let either Cindy or cancer ruin our lives."

Frank's words were soothing to Kathy. For the first time in her life, a man had expressed a loving, caring interest in her welfare. He had never once made a pass at her, but had given generously of his home and her subsistence, and now, she felt a deep respect and admiration for him.

She put her hand on his arm, reaching out in a physical manifestation of love, and said softly, "Oh, I like you, Frank. You've been so good to us. I don't know how I can ever repay you for all you've done."

At this moment, Cindy came in, glancing at them with hatred and defiance, her eyes focusing on Frank, her spiteful glare searing his conscience, conveying the message that she would get even.

With flaring nostrils, Kathy flew into a rage, "Don't you dare look at us like that," she bellowed. "You've been nothing but trouble since you were born. Now get in the bedroom and get out of my life."

When Cindy fled wordlessly, Frank looked at Kathy, shaking his head. "She's going to do something bad," he said. "We'd better keep our eyes on her."

CHAPTER SEVENTEEN

October 31, 1983

Frank is sitting at the kitchen table drinking coffee. Light from the early morning sun is streaming in the window. Cindy is in the bathroom, combing her hair and getting ready to catch the bus for school.

As Frank sits quietly, he is drowning in sorrow and self-incrimination. He had made a big mistake by reprimanding the kids. They weren't doing anything that any young couple wouldn't be doing, but god how it hurt to see Cindy in the arms of another guy.

Now, she avoided him. She made herself scarce. She wouldn't talk to him. She was giving him the silent treatment. And she was as mad as a hornet on a hot day in hell. But Frank's guilt was overshadowed by the fear that she would tell her teachers today, and if that happened, heaven help him.

When she came out of the bathroom, all primped up and smelling delicious from her hairspray, she headed for the door, silently. The air was charged with hostility.

"Cindy," he said, "Are you still made at me?"

"Shut up!" she snapped hatefully.

Frank jumped up and ran in front of her, blocking the door. "Are you going to tell your teachers?"

"Get out of my way!"

"Are you?"

"I said I was, didn't I?" She glared past him, avoiding eye contact. Reasoning seemed futile. She was adamant. There was only one ray of hope: bluff her. Scare her. He knew he couldn't stand in her way very long, for she might do battle. And if he were to grab her arms or strike back, she would bear bruises. Then she would really have a case against him.

"If you tell anybody on me and your mother, you'll go to jail."

"B.S." she spat. "You'll go to jail."

Frank let loose now. "No, dammit. You raped me! You started it all."

She glared at him derisively. "Who ever head of a girl raping a man? Do you think anyone would believe a shitty story like that?"

"You did! You know you did! The truth will come out. The person who initiates and carries through in the sex act is considered to be the aggressor. If I tell the cops you raped me, they won't wait for proof. They'll take you to jail and you'll have to sit there until the trial."

"You'll be taken away from Wiley and you'll be thrown in with a bunch druggies and homos. You know what they'll do to you? They'll tear your clothes off, they'll spit in your face. They'll burn you with cigarettes. They'll make you do dirty things."

Frank was now bent on frightening her. "I'm going to town the minute you get on the bus, and I'm going to tell the authorities before you can tell your teachers."

Cindy was visibly shaken. "Let me go. I wont' tell if you don't. I've got to hurry."

He stepped aside to let her pass. "Okay. I promise I won't tell."

Apparently his bluff had worked. As soon as he mentioned the treatment she would get in jail, the fire had died within her. But now as he watched her walk down to the road from the window, he was filled with remorse.

Poor kid. She must feel like everyone is against her, he thought, if she was a spunky kid, at least she stood up for the truth, and if she had sassed him and Kathy, it was not uncalled for.

Frank felt tears rolling down his cheeks. If only he could turn back the clock. If only he could ease her pain. If only he could take her in his arms and hold her tight. Let her know that she was loved. She must feel like an outcast. Her mother had told her to get out of her life. What a terrible blow to her ego.

In parting, she had promised not to tell her teachers, but would she keep that promise? If she didn't, someone would come out to investigate, and things would snowball. He dreaded the outcome.

He moved away from the window, looked down at his cold cup of coffee and decided to drive to the café. He had to get out of the house and away from his thoughts, and besides, he was hungry.

At this time of day, the restaurant was always full of early rises and Border Patrol officers, but today, there was construction workers from the new bridge, also. When he took a seat at the counter. Kathy and Wanda were scurrying about, trying to take care of the many patrons, but Kathy acknowledged him.

Most of the men sitting at the counter wore hard hats and were busily eating when Frank slipped onto the only empty stool available, but Brian saw Frank and brought him a cup of coffee. Frank removed his cap, ran his fingers through his hair and replaced it.

Glancing sideways, he struck up a conversation with a man next to him. "How's it going up there?" He said. "How long will it be before the bridge is finished?"

"Long time," the man said with his mouth full. "Several months, I'd say."

"You guys must be away from home a lot," Frank guessed. "You married?"

The man said his company had contracts all over the country and they were away from home most of the time. "It's hell being away from the wife and kids. That's the hard part, but the pay is good. Damn good."

"How many kids you got?"

"Two. A boy, three, and a girl, fourteen." He picked up his cup of coffee and sipped it, when Kathy came in front of Frank.

"Did Cindy get off to school?"

Frank nodded. "Yeah."

"She didn't sleep with me, last night. When I went in, she left. I suspect she slept in the bathroom or maybe in a chair."

"She was still mad when I tried to talk to her," Frank explained, "but she got on the bus all right."

"Well, I'm worried sick," Kathy said. "I'm afraid she'll do something foolish." Kathy broke off quickly. "I'll take your order while I'm here."

"Sounds like you've got trouble at home," the man said the minute Kathy turned away. "How old is your daughter?"

"She's sixteen," he said, not wanting to explain that Cindy wasn't his daughter.

"Well," the man said, "When they get to be my daughter's age, they start to get independent. My girl ran away one time. Couldn't find her. She was at a friend's house. That's why I'd like to be home more."

"Yeah," Frank said as he thought about Cindy.

The café was abuzz with the din of voices, and he lapsed into nostalgia, thinking how he had coveted her the day they broke down in front of his house. By now, many of the patrons were leaving the restaurant as Kathy brought him his breakfast, saying, "We'll have to give Cindy a good talking to when she comes home tonight."

As Kathy and Frank sat watching television, Kathy looked at her watch. "She should be home by now, don't you think?"

"Oh, she'll be along any minute now," Frank said nonchalantly.

Kathy settled back, but half an hour later, she expressed concern again. Wringing her hands, she worried that something must have happened to her, but Frank eased her fears, saying that maybe the bus had had a flat tire or something.

Kathy got up and went to the kitchen to get a Pepsi, and just happened to glance out of the window. "Frank!" She shouted, "The bus just went by and it didn't stop here."

"What?!!" He jumped up and ran to the window. "Why didn't it stop? Something is wrong."

"Something must have happened to Cindy," Kathy said. "We've got to drive back to the café and phone her school."

Kathy had been given the phone numbers of the high school and her teachers when she enrolled Cindy, but no one was answering the phones at El Centro High. She rummaged through her list and called Ms. Love at home. The teacher told Kathy that when she noticed Cindy missing, she had asked a girl who rode in with her if she had been on the bus, she said yes.

Kathy turned to Frank. "That little stinker cut class. She was on the bus. Should I call the police?"

Frank shook his head. "No, not yet," he said, "I've got an idea. Cindy spoke of a friend she had at school. Her name was Clarisa. Call the teacher back and ask her if she will contact the girl."

Kathy called, but the teacher declined, saying that Clarisa would probably talk more openly with Cindy's mother than someone from the school. She gave Kathy Clarisa's number. Kathy dialed and someone answered immediately.

"Hello. Is Clarisa there?"

"Who is this?"

"A friend. Will you call Clarisa to the phone, please?"

After a long silence, Clarisa came on the line. "Hi. Who is this?"

"Do you know Cindy Winters?"

"Ya. Who are you?"

"I'm Cindy's mother."

"What do you want?"

"Did you see Cindy today?"

"Ya. I saw her this morning before school started. Why?"

Kathy told Clarisa that Cindy was missing. She hadn't come home tonight and she was worried. Kathy continued interrogating the girl, who finally confessed. She had talked with Cindy outside the school grounds, and she was feeling bitter about her parents. She complained that they treated her like a child and her mother had told her to get out of her life. Cindy told her she wasn't going home again.

"She did? Well, did she say where she was going?"

"No."

"Did she mention a boyfriend?"

"She never had a boyfriend," Clarisa said, "but this morning she mentioned that she was going over to TUTTLE'S CHEVROLET. Said she knew a guy there."

"Don Shuger!" Frank exclaimed when Kathy told him. "We've got to find that boy."

Kathy favored contacting the police, but Frank had another idea. TUTTLE'S CHEVROLET would be closed now, but Frank knew where it was. He had driven past it a hundred times. He said they would go over there, check something out.

"What good will that do?" Kathy said.

Frank knew that all businesses posted telephone numbers on their front doors where their managers could be reached in emergencies. They would drive into El Centro, get the number and phone the manager.

It was 9:20 when they arrived in town, and Frank wanted to do the talking, since he planned on telling a few fibs to get the truth. "Hello. Are you the manager of TUTTLE'S CHEVROLET?"

"Yes, I am."

"Well, I'm trying to locate Don Shuger. I used to work with him in Los Angeles and I heard he is working for you, now."

"Yes. He's been with us for a few months, but he came to me this morning, saying he had to quit. Some big emergency. I don't know what it was, a death in the family or something. Anyway, he wanted to leave immediately and he wanted his pay in cash. The only way I could do that was to write a check and cash it for him. I don't know where he was going. He was pretty tight-lipped about everything."

Frank persisted. "It's important that I get in touch with him," he said. "Do you remember anything in his records where he listed a relative or anyone to contact in an emergency?"

"Not offhand," the manager replied. "But when he was gathering his tools, some of the other mechanics asked him where he was going and why he was quitting. He said that...I think he said his father was dying. I think he said he was going to Arizona or New Mexico. Anyway, it was some place east of here. That's about all..." He paused. "Oh yes, there was something unusual. When he was getting ready to go, he pulled his car up close to the shop, and the other employees noticed a girl sitting in the front seat. She was good looking, they said. They thought it was funny because he never mentioned a girlfriend, but it could have been his sister, I don't know."

"Okay," Frank said. "Thank you very much."

Frank turned to Kathy. "Cindy's with Don Shuger. They're heading east."

"Why that little snot," Kathy said sarcastically, "She's running away. I wonder if I should contact the police? Do you think I should list her as a missing person?"

"I don't know," Frank shrugged, "It would probably protect you legally if she files any charges against you, but I don't think it would bring her back." He paused, and as an afterthought, he said, "Ya'know, Kathy, it's kinda ironical. You told her to get out of the house and outa your life, last night, and now that she's gone, you are talking about bringing her back."

"Oh, I know," Kathy said. "In a way, I don't care. If she doesn't come back, I'm rid of her. I won't have to worry about her getting pregnant or anything like that, you know. But on the other hand, I am her mother, and that relationship forms a bond that lasts a lifetime."

On the way home, they continued to talk about Cindy, but Frank was thinking to himself: If Cindy don't come back, Kathy won't have to worry about her getting pregnant, and if the girl is already pregnant as she hinted she might be, then Don Shuger will be named as the father, and I will be in the clear.

Kathy broke into Frank's thoughts, "By the way," she said. "What was Cindy wearing this morning?"

Frank thought a minute. "Oh, it was that Grateful Dead Outift, with those high moccasin boots. Those clothes sure make her look older and if I might say so, quite sexy."

CHAPTER EIGHTEEN

December 31, 1983

The Eagle Talon Saloon was bustling with activity. Boisterous revelers besotted to the gills were singing along with the small band Tony had hired for the New Years Eve party, and Frank held Susan tightly as they danced the night away to the tune of Auld Lang Syne.

At one minute after midnight, amid the cacophony of music and voices, Susan wished Frank a Happy New Year and they kissed passionately in a long embrace as other revelers were doing. They had been coming down to the tavern often during the last two months since Cindy had ran away, and Kathy had been working with the church group and Libby, planning the Christmas program and yard sales.

Kathy had been bringing table scraps home from the café for Wiley, who was maturing rapidly, and she usually spent some time with him, petting and talking to him. She had never listed Cindy as a missing person for several reasons: She and Frank had decided that if Cindy was happy, let it be. If she got pregnant, at least they were rid of her, but Frank knew that if that happened, Don would be named the father, and this would free him of the stigma of rape. But Kathy also seemed to enjoy her newfound freedom from worry.

With Cindy gone, she no longer worried about her daughter's virginity nor the consequence of raising an out-of-wedlock child.

In fact, Kathy now could start the new life she had always hoped for, and her interest in religion helped to stabilize her position in the community. Putting down roots in Ocotillo was growing on her. With a steady job and a place to live, she had the security she needed, and with Frank and Wanda as friends, what more would she gain if she moved to San Diego?

Wanda, a widow, lived alone in a ramshackle two bedroom house in Unit 1, and her yard was overgrown with oleanders that needed pruning badly, and when Kathy mentioned that she would like to have a garden, Wanda offered her all the cuttings she could use. Kathy then asked Frank for permission. "Do you care if I plant some oleanders out in front?"

"No," he said. "I think maybe some flowers might be nice. A little color might be good."

She had taken the pieces and stuck them in the sand around the porch, the well, and some along the driveway, all within reach of the hose, and they were taking root rapidly. But there was something else that had happened in the last two months.

Jay, having moved to Ocotillo, completely recuperated from his heart surgery, had quit smoking and was put on a nutritious diet by his doctor, and was now seen around town often. Frank sometimes saw him in the post office when picking up his mail.

The regular meetings in the Community Hall had been suspended when he was felled by his heart attack, but the ongoing cave exploration had superseded everything else. In November, Peter William's crew and the able-bodied members of the class had begun a major dig at the cave site, and they had made some astounding discoveries.

With Jay, Frank and Susan, Geoff, Tom Goode and his wife Janet in the group with Peter's men, they had entered the lower chamber, the huge cavern with vaulted ceilings and a dozen connecting tunnels, and had begun excavating in the soft silt-like soil where Cindy had found the bronze phallus artifact.

Armed with shovels, picks, trowels and brushes, the large group of laymen, archaeologists and student laborers began to dig according to Peter William's plan. They would dig with shovels at first, with laborers carrying the soil outside the entrance, and hopefully, if they found artifacts, they would proceed more carefully.

Since the blasting of the rockslide had created a large opening, most of the lower chamber was well lit from the blazing sun outside, and there was no need for headlamps up front. But behind them, the tunnels were dark, and the farther back you went, the darker it became. That was where they went to relieve themselves.

Working in pairs and spread out about ten feet apart, they were shoveling the dirt into ordinary garden carts, which laborers wheeled to the outside and dumped. But as the work progressed, with nothing turning up, Peter believed that they might find something of value down deeper, based on Cindy's find.

He was right!

As the morning wore on, Tom Goode's shovel hit something that clinked like stone. He bent down and picked up an object about six inches long, rubbed off the dirt and yelled to the others. "I found something. Look?" He held it up and waved it, but no one could tell what it was from a distance.

"What is it?" Someone yelled, but Susan and Frank working nearest, were the first to get a good look and they burst out laughing. It was another bronze phallus.

When Peter saw it, he was excited. "Now we're getting somewhere," he said. "These were commonly found in the ruins of Mt. Vesuvius. There, it was the trade mark of prostitutes, but here, as I said, it probably represents fertility."

When Jay came alongside and looked at it closely, he remarked, "It's well done. Peter, I think we have hit pay dirt. This makes two artifacts we've found so far, so there must be more, don't you think?"

"Oh, absolutely," Peter nodded vigorously. "I'm getting excited, Jay. The deeper we dig, the more we may find."

As others came over to view the piece, Susan sunk her shovel into the soft soil and heard a clink. "I've hit a rock or something," she said to Frank, who told her to stop. He grabbed a trowel and dug around the object, finally pulling out a heavy piece encrusted with soil. When he rubbed the dirt off, he and Susan splashed water on it, washing it spotless and revealing a life-size human head artifact in bronze.

Since Frank was sweating, Susan offered her bottle of water to him, and he drank heartily, gazing down on the head. "I don't' believe this," he said, turning to Peter and shouting excitedly. "Peter. Look what Susan found."

Both Peter and Jay came over frowning in disbelief. "What the hell…"

When Frank handed the artifact to Peter, Peter exclaimed in a guttural voice, "Oh my God!" He hefted the piece and examined it from all angles while Jay looked on wide-eyed. "Now we're getting somewhere," he enthused. "Now, I feel vindicated for this exploration. This makes it all worthwhile."

"What do you make of it?" Jay wanted to know. "What is the significance?" Peter didn't know. He was as puzzled as the others as members of the search party gathered around him to view the head.

"It's an extremely valuable piece," Peter ventured, "Something like this is unheard of. It appears to be bronze, but I'm beginning to think all of these things we've found are made of gold with a patina, and not bronze. This piece alone could be worth millions."

As the group crowded around, Peter mused aloud. "We'll have to get some security on this and the other pieces. They're too valuable to have lying around where someone can filch them." He turned to Andy Gifford, the photographer. "Record this and get a good shot of it."

As questions flew, Tom Goode asked Peter: "It's a beautiful piece, but how would things like this end up in this cave in the dirt?"

Peter shook his head. "That's a good question, Tom. I've been asking myself the same. Tentatively, I think the ancient Mayans could have been this far north, and they themselves were ancestors of the Egyptians, who populated Central America. Obviously, some intelligent race of people, and they may have used these artifacts in religious rites. Something happened here, no doubt. Maybe floods, vandalism, warring tribes, I just don't know."

The floor of the cavern looked like a war zone, with holes dug everywhere and tools and carts lying at random. The sun streamed in through the large opening, illuminating most of the area.

"Yeah," Geoff said. "Something happened here, all right, but this is preposterous."

"Heh, heh," Jay chuckled. "I'm thinking about Robert Ripley. Believe it or not. There are many things in life that are unexplainable."

"I agree, Geoff," Peter said demurely. "Do you have any ideas?"

Janet spoke up. "I've got one. It's time to eat."

When Jay's voice boomed out, telling everyone it was lunchtime, students got to their feet and laborers dropped their shovels, and as they headed for their lunches, Susan told Frank that she had packed sandwiches and beer in her ice chest. With almost two dozen people present, they settled out in three distinct circles within the shade near the entrance, and as Frank carried the ice chest over, they settled with their backs against the wall with Geoff, Tom, Janet, Jay and Peter in the group nearest the opening.

Most of the young students had grouped together and were kidding around as they dug into their brown bag lunches, but those brought out from San Diego by Peter, sat with their feet in the deep holes they had dug, and were mostly enjoying a much-needed beverage and were wiping the sweat from their brows.

"Feels good to sit down," Frank said as Susan handed him a cold beer. "All this talk about how valuable these artifacts are, ya know, I can tell you right now that I wouldn't trade my beer for any of them."

"Me either," Geoff said. "I don't know why people are so interested in antiquities. So an intelligent race was here, so what? In the past thousands of years people migrated. They reproduced. They colonized new lands. Big deal! I couldn't care less. I enjoy going out and exploring like this, but I'm not really into the artifacts thing."

Frank removed his cap and tossed it to the ground. "We feel about the same," he said as he held the bottle in one hand. "Susan and I have become great buddies because we have so much in common. We both like to explore the outback, and we both like to smoke and drink beer." He grinned at Susan. "When I moved to the desert, I was determined to find lost treasure. I wanted to get rich, you know, but when she and I started going out in the boondocks, I felt the greatest satisfaction of my life. While I looked under every rock, she identified the plants. She's pretty good on plant names."

Everyone was eating in earnest now. Most had brought sandwiches, but Peter's wife had packed plastic containers with wet foods, such as coleslaw, baked beans and celery sticks. Jay, on the other hand, had a macaroni salad, a tuna sandwich, and an apple. Frank watched as he took his high blood pressure medicine and washed it down with water.

"Frank," Jay said, "Did you ever hear that anticipation is greater than realization? The seeking gives as much pleasure as reaching your goal. In archaeology, we try to unravel the secrets of the past, but in searching, we enjoy new discoveries we make, yet there is something deeper in the equation. It's the mystery. As Einstein once said, 'The greatest beauty in the world is the mystery of nature', or something like that. Growing up in Red Bluff, along the Sacramento River, I used to explore the hinterlands, and as you say, I looked under every rock. I don't know what I was looking for, I just had that insatiable curiosity to look. That's why I got interested in archaeology. In later years when I moved down here, I was intrigued by the geoglyphs, the pictographs, the legends. And I still am."

"Okay," Geoff cut in. "I can see all this as entertainment, or curiosity, but value, per se, I can't see. You take these artifacts and put them in a museum. People come and look. Where's the value?"

Peter was glaring at Geoff. "You miss the point," he said. "While archaeology solves mysteries of the past, it also provides entertainment. Yes, but I think you have dollars in mind. IF value means money to you, then you should know that many artifacts are worth millions on the black market. Others are priceless." He paused to look around at the others.

"The monetary value of anything is determined by demand. If no one wants it, it is worthless, but when demand is high, so are the prices. A good example is land. In the west, in early times, land could be bought for a dollar and a quarter per acre, but today when demand is high, it can be worth thousands."

"Wait a minute," Geoff interjected. "You said land could be bought for $1.25 an acre. Didn't you mean $125 dollars?"

"No, I meant what I said. In fact, most land could be bought for nothing. It was called homesteading. To encourage settlers to move out into Indian territory, a man could claim any number of acres just by filing the claim and then living on it and making $100 dollars worth of improvements."

"That's right, Geoff," Jay said in defense of Peter, "Long before your time, things were dirt cheap compared to today's prices. In my father's time, back during the depression, you could buy a brand new car for around $600 dollars. But we're getting off the subject. You mentioned that we put artifacts in museums, just so people can come and look at them. Well, that's true as far as it goes, but museums are kinda like history books. People can come and look to see what the past was like, what ancients did, what tools they used, on and on."

Peter's little circle had become quiet now, lulled by Jay's narrative. Jay got a far away look in his eyes. "Speaking of museums, they are dear to my heart. I dream of establishing one here. Ocotillo is halfway between San Diego and Yuma, about a hundred miles either way. I envision my museum here as a place where the weary travelers can stop to refresh themselves and get a glimpse of how the native Indians lived hundreds of years ago."

Peter was nodding silently, while Frank was lighting a cigarette, as Jay continued. "I've contacted the Department of the Interior about purchasing the

30 acres over by the Café, and if I can get it, I want to construct a building like the museum in Borrego Springs, with restrooms, cold drinks, free literature, and aerial pictures of the intaglios. I plan on having the grounds landscaped with native desert plants identified with signs along the pathways."

"Excuse me, Jay," Susan piped up, "But I can compile a list of all the major plants found here, with their botanical names if you'd like me to."

"Well, I appreciate that," Jay grinned, "But this is all a long way off. I haven't even got the land yet. But I'll surely keep you in mind, Susan."

With lunch break over, everyone was relaxing a bit. Janet stood up and headed for the darkness of the catacomb to relieve herself when Susan jumped up to follow her. Frank took another beer from the ice chest, while Peter sat picking his teeth.

"Ya know, Jay," he began, "I've been doing some thinking. As Geoff says, all of this doesn't make sense. For these treasures to end up here in the dirt just boggles my mind." In the eons of time, maybe this cavern was home to some tribe, maybe it was flooded, or looted. Maybe a war between two tribes. There are so many possibilities, but we'll have to wait until we can have these items radio-carbon dated."

Jay nodded. "Yeah. But that still won't tell us how these items found their way into this cave, or why they were buried in the dirt. There is one thing that I can understand though, the possible flooding. When Imperial Valley was an inland sea, or when it was Lake Cahuilla, the water level was about here at the entrance to this cavern. In high water times, when the

Colorado River was pouring into the lake, the water would be flooding this area. Standing for a hundred years or a thousand, silting would explain this soil." He took a handful of dirt and rubbed it between his fingers. "See this Peter? It's like sandy loam. Lots of organic material in it. It's definitely silt."

By now, most of the students and laborers had resumed digging, while Frank and Susan sat drinking beer and puffing away on their cigarettes. On the far side, near the opposite wall, a laborer had dug down six feet when his shovel hit something solid. He threw his shovel aside and grabbed a trowel, then squirming around in the narrow hole, began digging around the object.

When his partner stood looking down on him, asking how he could help, the man told him to lower a bucket and bail. Minutes later, he yelled up. "It looks like a big rock." His partner yelled over to Peter, "We've got a big rock over here. Andy is digging around it."

Peter looked at Jay. "Hear that? Let's go over."

When they stood looking down on Andy, he asked for a short handled shovel. Andy threw his trowel out of the hole and began to pry under the object. "For Christ sake," he said as the object popped out of the soil. "What the hell is this?"

Andy had gotten his hands around the object and was rubbing the dirt off. Jay yelled at Frank. "Bring that water bottle over here. We've got something and it looks pretty good."

When Andy stood up, carrying the artifact, he passed it to his helper as everyone gazed at the object in awe. Susan had come running with her water, and she splashed it on the piece while the helper washed it clean.

"It's a skull," Peter exclaimed. "It's shaped like a human head."

"Yeah," Jay agreed. "And it's a perfect rendition."

"God, yes," Susan said, reaching over to touch it.

But Frank just shook his head in disbelief. "Now, I've seen everything. Of all the screwy things we've dug up, this one takes the cake."

Peter took the skull from Andy's helper and hefted it. "Must be about five pounds," he said, "and it looks like it's made of bronze, like the other pieces we found. The quality of workmanship is equal to anything produced today."

"Another artifact, and another mystery," Jay said to Peter. "The way I see it, we're not finding answers, we're just discovering more enigmas."

Peter nodded. "But they were here," he said. "We have proof that the Egyptians established the Mayan civilization. Even if we never understand these things, at least my theory is verified; that North America was populated from Africa, and not from Asians crossing the land bridge over the Bering Sea."

"You may be right," Jay agreed, "but that gives me another idea. We know that this cavern has many branches. We haven't even explored one of the side shoots. If we could go way back into these tunnels, we might find the answers. There may be clues we can't imagine, clues that can be put together to form the whole picture."

Peter nodded approval. "I agree," he said. "We'll have to set up another expedition sometime soon."

CHAPTER NINETEEN

April 18, 1984

Kathy was cooking pork chops as Frank sat at the table drinking beer. Her day off, she had been into El Centro, shopping for groceries, while Frank had been with Susan all day, exploring the mud caves in the Anza-Borrego Desert.

"I wonder where Cindy is," Kathy said out of curiosity, "I wonder what she is doing?"

"Probably making babies," Frank said not entirely in jest, "Isn't that what young couples do?"

"Yeah," Kathy agreed. "She is so much like I was at her age. I was boy crazy, too. I wouldn't listen to my mother. I listened to mother nature instead. Oh well…"

"I know," Frank said, "I know. We all go through that stage in our teens. You want to listen to your parents, but your hormones speak louder than words."

AS the pork chops sizzled on the stove, Kathy became pensive. She took a seat opposite Frank's, looked blankly into space and said, "Well, I just hope she's happy."

"Yeah, I hope so," Frank agreed.

Kathy came back to reality. "Oh, by the way. Did I tell you that I'm moving in with Wanda?"

Frank shook his head. "No. You mean you're leaving? You're moving out?"

"Look, Frank. You've been good to me and Cindy. You got me a job. You've carried me all this time and never demanded anything from me, and I appreciate it a lot. But it's time for me to move on." She jumped up suddenly when she smelled the meat burning, turned the heat down and flipped the chops over.

"Our arrangement here is a dead end deal," she continued, "You are involved with Susan, and I'm involved with the church. Wanda is struggling to pay $500 a month rent, so we figured if we lived together and shared the rent, it would be a good deal for both of us. She's also interested in getting involved with the church."

Frank was lighting a smoke. "I see your point. I don't blame you. I think I'm falling in love with Susan. We want to be together all the time. I never thought I'd get married again, but now I'm not so sure. They say the second time around is the best, but of course, we haven't discussed marriage yet."

He blew a cloud of smoke over the table. "God! It's so ironic. You'll be leaving your oleanders and Wiley and..." His voice trailed off like the smoke through the open window.

"But I'll be gaining more oleanders over at Wanda's. And as for Wiley, I think he'll be leaving soon, too. I think he has a girlfriend. I saw him chasing a cute little female the other day."

A grin wrinkled Frank's face. "Jeeze," he said, shaking his head, "Everybody is out there fornicating.

The whole world is out there making babies. I guess Cindy and Wiley have that in common."

The day Kathy moved out of Frank's house and into Wanda's, she admonished him gently. "You take care of my flowers," she said, "I'll probably see you at the café occasionally. Right?"

Frank's world had changed profoundly in the past year. Ocotillo had gotten rid of the Stouffer Well and the water war; they had cracked down on the illegal aliens and druggies; Ralph Smith had moved away and Clanahan had drowned. Jay Bradford had been stricken with a heart attack, and Cindy ran away.

When Kathy left, his house seemed somehow empty, and he often thought about the day when the girls had came into his life when their Pontiac broke down in front of his place, but now he thought about Wiley.

In Jack London's CALL OF THE WILD, the big dog, once domesticated, had reverted to its wild state during the mating season. It had run away with a she-wolf, and started a family. Frank had read the book in his younger days and had never forgotten the story line. It was as if the world turned on sex; as if life was like a wheel and sex was the hub, from which the spokes all depended on the hub.

And wasn't human life similar to a salmon's? We grow from an egg, we fatten up and plant our seeds, then die. Our progeny repeats this scenario over and over. So sex must be the most important thing in the world. Our world.

Frank realized that he had not yet produced a child to carry on his name, but if Cindy was pregnant with his baby...if she was...then he had inadvertently done what all animals do: helped to carry on the species.

During the past 3 months, much had happened. Not only had Kathy moved out, but the cave exploration had run into a snag. In the first place, much to Peter and Jay's chagrin, the mysterious finds which they had tried to keep secret, was leaked to the press. While the news first appeared in the local newspaper, it was picked up shortly by the big city papers, The San Diego Union, then the San Francisco Chronicle, and from there it spread to the New York Tribune. From there it was carried by foreign papers, Jay learned.

"I wonder who leaked the story?' Jay said one day when he met Frank in the post office. "I wonder where they're getting all the details?"

"Beats me," Frank had said. "But with all those people digging, I'm not surprised."

The downside of all this publicity was that it attracted some foreign archaeologists to sojourn to Ocotillo, and a few unsavory characters, but it also attracted the environmentalists and the BLM. With the influx of vehicles and strangers, came the curiosity seekers. If all this activity was good for business, it was frustrating to Jay and Peter. While Kathy was making a fortune in tips, the little motel was doing a land-office turnover.

Some people came in motor homes and some in cars. Some had flown into San Diego and rented vehicles to drive the hundred miles east to this tiny hamlet, and the post office was swamped with names of those wishing to receive their mail here temporarily.

In short, Ocotillo was again a beehive of activity, as it had been when the bridge on I-8 was washed out.

Particularly galling was the BLM's stand. Never looking into the cave discovery at first, the sudden notoriety caused them to look into the legal aspects of the digging. The cave was on BLM land, they said, and no permits had been issued. In fact, they were now considering stiff fines for unauthorized bulldozing of the road to the lower entrance and blasting the rockslide.

A tribal chief of the Cahuilla Indians, Fred Lightfoot, had driven from Yuma, one day, and asked Jay to show him the cave. He was interested in the legend handed down from his elders, and when he had made his inspection and considered all the facts, he had told Jay in no uncertain words what he thought.

"This is the Lost City of the Yumans," he declared. "This is the place my people have heard about for a thousand years. This place is sacred Indian ground and you have desecrated it."

Like everyone else, he had heard about the artifacts the archaeologists had dug up and he claimed ownership for his tribe. But he was not the only one to make such a claim. The BLM was also demanding that the treasures be turned over to the government, although both claims were stalled in limbo. Peter had taken the skull and the icons of fertility back to San Diego, where they were locked away in a secret vault under the floor of the Museum of Man.

Peter and Jay just shook their heads in disgust. What was possibly the greatest discovery of all time, had turned into one of the biggest boondoggles in the annals of archaeology. But there was more bad news to come.

The environmentalists, especially the Sierra Club, had heard about the cave and the controversy, and had sent people out to investigate. Their scientists had discovered green strands of fiber in the soil in the cave, which they said was asbestos, and that word alone sent shock waves far and wide.

Both local and federal officials demanded that the dig be shut down and covered up, in addition to restoration of the new road back to its former natural condition. While the residents of Ocotillo complained about the influx of strangers the cave had engendered, Peter and Jay withdrew from the controversy, abandoning the project altogether. But Peter never returned the artifacts he had squirreled away, and the entire issue gradually faded from memory.

In the meantime, the Indians of the area threatened lawsuits. The bands of tribes inhabiting Imperial Valley fall into two broad spheres of ancestry, the Shoshonean and Yuman, but it was predominately the latter who complained the loudest.

Fred Lightfoot, who had declared the cave to be the lost city of his ancestors, warned that the spirits were unhappy, and they were growing restless. When finally instigating a lawsuit, it was aimed at the BLM, Imperial County, Jay Bradford and Peter Williams, but it was unclear who was actually responsible, and the suit generated as much controversy as the original discoveries had. However, it dragged along slowly and was finally forgotten.

If the spirits were unhappy, they surely made their displeasure known. An earthquake shook the valley shortly afterwards, causing another rockslide and closing the lower cave entrance again and forever.

CHAPTER TWENTY

May 15, 1984
   Susan Rider bent down to pull a wayward weed from her cactus planter as Frank Kelly looked on. "Isn't it beautiful?" She cooed with admiration. "To my way of thinking, these hedgehogs are the most stunning cactus of the desert. The botanical name is Echinocereus triglochidiatus. The Navajo Indians claimed the fruits were edible, but caused internal pains, hence the common name 'heart twister.'"

Frank, half-smiling, shrugged. "I don't see how you can remember all these scientific plant names. They're all 'tongue twisters' to me."

"Well, when Greg and I moved out here, I just needed a hobby. I loved flowers, and became interested in desert plants. Then I was curious to learn their names. It grew from there."

Susan's yard was nicer now than it had been before either the flood or the sand storm. After Kathy had gotten oleander cuttings from Wanda and planted them around Frank's place there had been a lot left over, and Frank had given them to Susan who stuck them in the ground around her place.

Now, with oleanders along her driveway and potted cactus on her doorstop, her yard looked better than ever. She had hung wind chimes near the front door, laid pieces of driftwood and a few rocks at the foot of the steps, creating a truly desert motif.

In the cool evening, they had gone inside where Susan fixed a light snack with a glass of wine, and they sat on the couch afterwards, talking. When Susan pulled out a cigarette, Frank reached for one also and he fondled the Zippo lighter she had given him last Christmas lovingly.

"You know," he said, holding it in front of them, "I appreciate this lighter more than anything else. I had one like it in Viet Nam years ago but somehow I lost it."

Susan had bought the Zippo in Flagstaff while she was there with her mother, and she had had it engraved with his name on it. Now as she smiled happily, her eyes radiated love. She was happy that he was happy.

"But how did you know I liked Zippos?" He wondered aloud as he held it up to her cigarette.

"You mentioned it that first night when I met you at the tavern," she said. "Don't you remember? You saw the one Greg gave me. Don't you remember he had mine inscribed with "Don't ever let the flame go out?"

"Oh yeah," he mumbled as he lit his fag.

"By the way," Susan began. "Have you heard anything from Cindy? Has she contacted Kathy at all?"

"Nope. Not a thing. It's been half a year or more, and she's never even dropped us a line. I think she may have been pregnant when she left. She may be too ashamed to contact us. But Kathy doesn't seem to mind that she's gone. I don't think she misses her at all."

Susan leaned over to the ashtray on the coffee table. "Do you ever see Kathy anymore?" She asked. "Do you ever go up to the café?"

"I stopped in the other day," he said as he reached for his wine. "She didn't mention Cindy, and I'm sure she would have if Cindy had contacted her. Oh, that kid was mad as hell when she ran away. I don't think she'll ever forgive her mother."

Susan was slipping off her shoes and letting them drop to the floor. "Take your boots off, honey," she intoned. "It feels so good."

As Frank bent down to unlace his clodhoppers, he brought up another subject. "Susan. What do you think of the big cave hullabaloo? They've closed it down and forbidden all further trespass. Isn't that ridiculous? I wonder what else we would have found if they hadn't stopped us?"

"Yeah," she said in lively banter, "We were having so much fun. I wonder what Peter did with all the artifacts?"

"I don't know," Frank replied. "Well, you know, Cindy wanted to keep that one she found, but he took it away from her."

"You know what I'd like to have? I'd like to have that bronze skull. It was neat," she said as she twisted around and put her head on his lap. "I'd put it on the front porch with my cactus and rock collection."

Frank wiggled to get comfortable, then massaged her neck tenderly as she spoke. "It was really something. I've been thinking about it, ya'know. We found human skulls at the top entrance to the cave, and then we found the one at the bottom. I can't imagine any connection between them, but there must be one."

"I don't know, honey," she sighed, "but we don't really need any answers as long as we have each other, do we?"

"You got that right," he murmured as his fingers played on her earlobes. "All we need is each other."

Susan cocked her head sideways. "Frank," she said pensively. "Do you think we should get married?"

Her words surprised him.

"Not a bad idea," he said tentatively, "I could see us living together forever." His hand now rested on her chest. "We have everything in common. Our likes and dislikes and our love of the outdoors..."

"Could you stand seeing me every morning without makeup and my hair all messed up?" She struggled to sit up and face him. "Could you honey?"

Face to face and eye to eye, they gazed hypnotically at each other. A dog barked in the distance. Susan's eyes were deep pools of azure blue. Her long eyelashes fluttered. They came together, arms clinging, and embraced in a passionate kiss. Frank attempted to push her down, his tongue hungrily probing her mouth. She was on fire.

Now she was struggling to break free. "Wait, honey," she whispered, "I've got a surprise for you." They broke apart and she headed for the bedroom. Thinking she was going to freshen up, he stripped to his skivvies and waited.

When he heard a feigned cough, he turned to see her coming toward him, wearing a beige housecoat, tied with a sash in front. As she sashayed toward the couch, the heady smell of perfume wafted over him, and his eyes grew large.

Coming in front of him, she pirouetted enticingly, her silken blonde hair swirling around her face and grinning mischievously. Holding his gaze hypnotically, she suddenly flung her housecoat open with great flare. "Ta-da!"

"Oh my god," he exclaimed. "Red panties. You remembered."

"Just for you, honey," she cooed.

Frank held out his hands. "Come hither, fair maiden, whilst I give you your reward."

As he grabbed her, they tumbled onto the carpet. The mantel clock struck 7. The house creaked. They heard a car drive by. Frank grasped her soft buttocks and she began to whimper as they writhed in unison. Susan was moaning and suddenly screaming with pleasure. "Oh God. Oh God." The clock struck 7:30.

CHAPTER TWENTY ONE

January 6, 1995

Cars were pulling up in front of the post office and groups of elderly people stood talking out front, since this was a favorite place to meet neighbors and discuss current events, and about the only place you would ever see more of them.

Because the desert nights were cold and the sun always came out about noon, the area in front of the whitewashed building was usually bright and warm, inviting locals to stop and chat. When Frank parked his pickup near the big ocotillo bush, he pulled his cap down to shield his eyes from the glare of the sun and walked in to get his mail.

Oblivious to the crush of patrons around him, he went to his box to gather his mail and turned to leave when he bumped into Jay Bradford who was also just leaving. Looking down at his mail, he didn't see Jay until he looked up to say, "Sorry," but then exclaimed, "Well, hi, Jay. Where you been keeping yourself?"

"Oh, I've been around," Jay replied as they moved to the door, "I've been keeping busy."

Outside, Frank told Jay he'd like to talk to him. It had been months since he had seen him. "You got time for a cup of coffee?" They decided to ride up to the café in Frank's truck, and they arrived about the same time as the noontime crowd.

"Jeese man," Frank said as they sat down at the counter, "I thought you'd died. Where you been?"

"I've been writing," Jay explained. "Been sitting at my typewriter for over a year now. Don't go out much except to my doctor in El Centro. He checks me over and reminds me to stay on my diet. I'm taking blood thinners, y'know."

Frank noticed two waitresses bustling about, women he'd never before seen. Assuming that this must be Kathy and Wanda's day off, he thought no more about it, but when Brian saw Frank, his face lit up. He brought two cups of coffee and smiled at Frank.

"Hi, stranger," he intoned. "Don't see much of you anymore. Have you been sick?"

"Oh I've been busy," Frank replied as he reached for a smoke. "Did you hear that Kathy moved out of my place?"

Brian looked puzzled. "That was a long time ago. I heard that her kid ran away too."

"Yeah," Frank stuck a cigarette between his lips. "This Kathy's day off?"

Brian frowned. "Didn't you hear? Kathy quit a couple months ago. Said she was moving to San Diego." He nodded for emphasis. "Yep."

"Well, I'll be damned!" Frank was taken completely by surprise. He remembered when she came to his place, begging for help, and how she had kept harping on getting to San Diego.

"Yeah," Brian continued, "She and Wanda quit at the same time. Left me in a bind. Course, they gave me notice, but still, getting waitresses out here ain't easy." Then as an afterthought, he said. "She told me she had cancer and wanted to be in the big city where she could get treatment. That's all I know." He turned away to man the cash register.

"Jeeze," Frank said to Jay, "I guess I don't get around much anymore. So many things have happened in the last year. Do you ever see Peter?"

"No. Not often," Jay answered. "As I told you, I've been sitting at home writing. Last time I saw Peter, me and Sherilee were in San Diego on business and I stopped to see him, but he was pissed."

Jay went on to explain how Peter had berated the BLM and the environmentalists for shutting down the cave exploration and said it was politically motivated.

"But you remember his theory that the North American continent was populated by the Egyptians and not Siberians crossing the Bering Straits? Well, I had also subscribed to that possibility. Now, I think we have some reliable research to prove it."

"I was reading about a skull they found in Africa in 1952 that dated back 36,000 years, that paleoanthropologists at Stony Brook University say closely resembles skulls found in Europe and Asia from the same period. Careful analysis of the skull and previous DNA studies showed that early humans living in Europe, Asia and Southern Africa were genetically quite similar and had common origins. The article pretty well proves that we all came from Africa about a million years ago."

Frank was sipping his coffee. "It's possible," he said. "Y'know, Jay, people have been migrating to and from so many places and interbreeding over thousand of years, it's possible that we did originate in Africa, specifically Egypt."

Jay nodded. "And those artifacts that we found tend to verify that they were here, as Peter said. We don't have to understand what happened in the cave, or why the icons were in the dirt. A lot can happen in a thousand or ten thousand years. Face it, we can't really grasp the significance of eons of time." He glanced at his watch.

Frank then looked down at his watch. "Yeah, I know. We gotta get outta here."

On the way back to the post office and Jay's car, Frank queried him on the museum. "Have you heard anything from the BLM?"

Jay was holding his hand up by the window, blocking the glaring sunlight. "Yeah, Things are looking good. Looks like maybe we'll get the land."

When Frank let Jay out at the post office, he drove straight up Agate Avenue to Sierra Vista and pulled in at Susan's place where he did often of late. He tapped on the door and walked right in as he was getting used to by now, and she was sitting at the kitchen table eating lunch.

"Hi honey," he called out as he walked towards her. "I was just talking to Jay. Met him at the post office."

"Wait," she interrupted. "Have you had lunch?"

Susan was holding a ham sandwich with a slice of cheese on it and mayonnaise. There were chips and dip in front of her. Half of the sandwich remained on her plate. "I can't eat it all," she said pushing the plate towards him. "Take it."

Frank pulled out a chair and sat down gingerly, reaching for the chips. "I just stopped by to see how my sweetheart was doing," he smiled. "You look great. You going someplace?"

Susan was wearing her regular tight blue jeans and a light blue long sleeved blouse. Her hair was neatly combed and she had put on her face. "I'm going into town," she said, "I'm going to Wal-Mart, the DMV and a couple other places. Wanna ride along?"

Frank was dipping a chip into the guacamole. "I don't think I'd better. My truck isn't running good and I was planning on going home to tinker on the engine."

"All right," she nodded. "You were saying you just saw Jay. What's the old boy been doing with himself?"

Frank reached for the half sandwich. "I haven't seen him for maybe close to a year, so we went up to the café for a cup of coffee. Well he looks pretty good, says he's writing a book on archaeology. Nothing earth shaking, but Brian came over and we talked a little. You know what he told me? I couldn't believe it."

"What? What did he tell you?"

"Kathy and Wanda quit and moved to San Diego. Kathy has cancer."

"Oh my gosh."

"Y'know what I think? Those gals were living together and they moved to the big city together. I'm thinking maybe they were lovers."

Susan was incredible. "Lesbians? Well, could be, I suppose."

Frank was consuming his food silently now. He liked the chips with his sandwich, but he needed a beverage. He could see that Susan was drinking water, and he was full of coffee, so rather than ask for a beer, he got up and helped himself at the sink. Susan apologized.

"Oh honey," she said. "I'm sorry. Can I get you Bud Lite?" There's a six pack in the fridge."

"No, this is fine," he said as he washed down his food. "I drink water at home sometimes. Our water is good, but I just prefer beer as a rule."

Lunch over, Susan glanced at her watch. Frank noticed. "Well, I guess I'd better go home so you can go to town," he said as he stood up.

"Okay, honey," she smiled, "I'll meet you down at the bar tonight."

As he started towards the door, Susan hurried after him, demanding a kiss. After they smooched, Frank smiled devilishly. "That oughta hold you till tonight. There's a lot more where that one came from."

When he arrived home, he parked up close to the porch, intending to check the engine. The Dodge had been running rough lately and he thought he would have a look under the hood. He got out, raised the hood, retrieved a small toolbox, which he set on the battery framework, and had just opened it when he saw a car coming slowly up his driveway.

Curious, wondering who it could be, he watched as it came closer. It appeared that there was a man and woman in the front seat, the man driving, but his vision was blurred by the glare of the windshield. He wondered what they could possibly want. Directions maybe?

As he stood transfixed, watching, the car drew closer and a woman got out and started towards him. He noticed she had blond hair and was wearing sunglasses. She was wearing faded blue jeans and a black long sleeved T-shirt under a tan vest.

She came closer. He stood motionless, waiting for her to speak. He was sizing her up. What did she want? Then he heard her voice. It sounded familiar. "Hello Frank," she spoke softly. "Remember me?"

"Cindy," he gasped, "Is that you?"

"Yes, it's me, Frank."

They came together and hugged tightly. "Oh my lil girl," he said tearfully, "Where have you been? I'm so sorry for what happened."

"That's all right," she replied. "I've had time to think it over, and I can understand how you felt at the time. I've forgiven you in my heart a thousand times. I've even forgiven mom for what she said. She's had a hard life and I guess I've given her a lot of trouble." She removed her sunglasses.

Frank held her at arms length, looking into her eyes. "You're still as beautiful as ever. How have you and Don been doing?"

"Fine," she said, "We get along very well. Don's a good guy. He treats me good and I've got a part time job."

"Gosh, you look so much older. I didn't recognize you until you spoke. Did you get married?"

"No," she said, "not yet, but we plan to. I dropped out of school, you know. We live in a small apartment and a neighbor woman takes care of the baby while I'm at work."

"Baby? You had a baby?"

Cindy turned to look back towards their car and called for Don to come over. He got out and reached back in to fetch the toddler. When he brought the baby over, Cindy took it and held it in front of Frank, pulling the blanket away from its face.

"Boy or girl?"

"Boy."

"Oh he's so cute. What's his name?"

"Junior," she said.

The baby seemed to smile, Cindy asked if Frank wanted to hold him and she passed Junior over to him. Frank cradled the kid in the crotch of his arm and wiggled his finger in front of Junior's face. The kid reached up and grasped it.

"Oh look at that," Frank smiled. "Such a cute little thing. He likes me."

Frank passed the baby back to Cindy and turned to Don, holding out his hand. As they shook hands, he apologized. "I'm sorry, Don. I was a fool. You're a great guy and you've got a great woman."

"Yessir," Don was just as polite as the day Frank told him to get out of the house. "Say, can I use your bathroom?"

Frank told him to go right ahead. "You know where it is." As he started away, Frank told Cindy, "Let's go sit on the porch. We've got a lot to talk about." She shifted Junior to the other arm as they stepped over to sit on the edge with their feet on the ground.

Cindy really opened up in Don's absence. "This is your baby, Frank," she began. "You fathered him. I wanted to name him Franklin, and Don wanted to name him Donald Jr., but we compromised on Franklin Donald Jr. But we started to refer to him as Junior and that's what his name is to us. That's what we call him."

"Does Don know that I'm..."

"No. I couldn't tell him. He thinks it's his."

Frank nodded silently, his gaze fixed on Junior. "My kid?"

"Your Kid!" She repeated. "He's your flesh and blood, Frank. Didn't you guess? I picked the name Franklin. Don't you see why?"

They were startled when a coyote cried out nearby and Cindy was reminded of her pet. "Frank. Could that be Wiley? Is it possible he hears my voice and recognizes it?"

"Yeooow yip yip yip." The coyote called out again.

"It sounds like him. I wonder if I call him, he'll come?"

"I don't know, Cindy. You can try it."

Cindy whistled, then talked as she used to. "Come here, Wiley. Come on, boy. Come over here, Wiley. Come on, boy."

Wiley came out of the bushes wagging his tail. He kept looking back as he advanced slowly and Frank saw another coyote half hidden in the foliage. Wiley came up to Cindy cautiously and she reached over to pet him, but he smelled the baby and bolted. She coaxed and begged but Wiley seemed afraid of Junior. He would come toward Cindy uncertainly as if he wanted to let her pet him, then he would point his nose at the baby and back away, looking over his shoulder at the coyote back in the bushes.

"I'll bet that other coyote is his girlfriend," Frank said to no one in particular, "and it looks like he's asking for her permission."

Don had come out and was standing above them. "Honey," he said, "does Junior need a change?"

Members of the Canines have an incredible sense of smell. They use their noses to read the area around them. They sniff out food, identify enemies and family by smell. Coyotes in the wild associate human excrement with man, their mortal enemy.

Cindy, checking the baby's diaper confirmed that he needed a change and said she was going over to their car where she had clean ones. Don had noticed Frank's truck with the hood up and asked him if he was having trouble. When Frank explained that the engine was not running smoothly, Don asked if he could take a look at it.

"Sure," Frank said. "You seem to be pretty handy with tools."

"Just remember," Don quipped. "I'm Mr. Goodwrench."

Frank said he was going in and get a beer and asked Don if he would like one too. When he came back out, Don was already tinkering with the spark plug wires.

Frank took a swig and set Don's bottle in the engine compartment. Don told Frank to start the engine. After a few minutes, Don had found trouble. There were two shorts, one at a spark plug and one at the distributor.

Cindy had walked back to sit on the edge of the porch again. Frank stepped over to sit near her. "What time does Mom get home?"

Frank shook his head sadly. "She doesn't live here anymore, hon. She moved out about six months ago. Moved in with that other waitress, Wanda."

"Really! I'm surprised. I'd like to see her before we go back home. We had two days free, so we thought we'd drive over and show you and her the baby. Do you know where Wanda lives?"

"Look, hon. I've been involved with Susan. Remember her? I've been eating up at her place a lot and I hadn't been up at the café for a long time. Well, this morning I was up there with Jay and I saw Brian. He told me that your mom and Wanda quit and moved to San Diego. She had said something about having cancer."

"Oh-my-gosh!" Cindy was bottle-feeding Junior, and she was shifting position to get comfortable. "That means I won't see her. We have to get back home."

"Yeah. Well, where do you live hon?"

When Cindy said they lived in Las Vegas, Frank pictured bright lights and ornate gambling casinos and wondered if they entertained themselves at the slots. Or does Don like to play Blackjack? Cindy said they didn't gamble. They couldn't afford to. She said they didn't even go near the casinos except occasionally to eat. She said they had great food and cheap prices, so they went there sometimes on Sundays.

Don had the engine running, but he stopped to drink his beer. He yelled over at Frank. "How does your engine sound now?"

Frank yelled back. "Sounds great."

Don looked down at the motor. "I'm going to adjust the carburetor. It's set a bit too lean."

Cindy resumed talking. "So you're involved with Susan. I liked her. Do you guys plan on getting married someday?"

"We've just barely talked about it," Frank replied. "I think we will." He reached for a cigarette. "She's a good woman in every sense. She's intelligent, clean and decent and she's very beautiful, at least in my opinion."

"Yeah, the first time I saw her, I thought she looked like mom," Cindy stated matter-of-factly. "A lot like her."

"I agree, hon," Frank nodded, "but I'd say more like you. Susan seems more upbeat, more full of life. She's older than Kathy, but she seems younger to me. Of course, you and your mom do look a lot alike, but Kathy looks tired. She lacks imagination. Susan and I go out in the boondocks several times a week. I'm still looking for Peg-Leg-Pete's black nuggets." He chuckled as he lit his smoke. "She's a good sport."

"I liked Don the first time I saw him. He's a real serious guy, but he does have a sense of humor. It's funny, though, we never talk about getting married. We just live together and enjoy each other, day after day. And we're happy."

Frank glanced over at Don. "Yeah. Maybe that's what Susan and I will end up doing. That marriage license is just a piece of paper. y'know."

Don cut the engine, set the toolbox on the porch and closed the hood. "I'm going to go in and wash my hands," he said.

Frank turned to face Cindy. "You haven't noticed all the plants in the yard. Doesn't it look different?"

"It does. I was going to mention it, but we got talking about something else. How come you planted them?"

"Your mom put them in. She started them all from cuttings. They are called oleanders."

Cindy stood up. "They look nice, Frank, but I've got to put Junior in the car. He's fast asleep. We've got to get going when Don comes out."

Frank looked down at the baby, knowing it was his very own and he felt a pang of sadness. "We've got a lot of memories here, hon, a lot of happy times. Those oleanders remind me of Kathy every day, and I think of you often. Now we've got a lasting relationship in Franklin. Thanks for naming him after me."

"And when I look into Junior's blue eyes, I see you, Frank. I'll always remember the things we did together."

Don came out looking at his watch. "Honey, we've got to hit the road. It's a long way home."

As they walked to the car, Frank followed, and when they were ready to leave, Frank and Don shook hands through the open window. Cindy called to Frank as the car moved away. "I hope you find the black nuggets, and tell Wiley I love him."

Frank watched the car move down the driveway in a cloud of dust and disappear on the horizon. His eyes got misty, and hot tears streamed down his cheeks.

"So long, Cindy. I'll never forget you, hon."

EPILOGUE

January 10, 2008

Ocotillo lies sleepily in the early morning sun. Few of the old timers remain, but the current residents still come and go at the little white post office. Nature has concealed the rockslide on the side of the mountain with blow-sand and vegetation. The cave is forgotten and will remain so, until someone eventually rediscovers it in the next millennium. Today's residents are unaware of its existence. Only Jay remembers.

In his eighties now, Jay is on the cusp of senility, but his dream of building a museum in Ocotillo has come to fruition. Not only is it built and landscaped, but it's ready to open.

Frank and Susan are gone, their whereabouts unknown, and his place in Coyote Wells lies in decay. Kathy's oleanders have long ago dried up and blown away, while native plants have taken over. The wind still rattles and moans around Frank's house as the coyotes howl in the outback.

Wiley's offspring are alive and well somewhere among the creosote bushes, but Cindy has dropped out of sight. Her and Frank's child, Franklin is a 23 year old security guard at a famous Casino in Las Vegas, but he is known by his middle name, Donald, after the man he thinks is his father.

Men come and go, but the mountains stand forever. When men come, they arrive full of dreams and anticipation, but fade away in disillusion. The museum that Jay built on a dream will live forever, and down through time will remind those who are passing through of those who peopled this desert long ago.